THE SCORPION'S CHASE

Also by Cap Daniels

The Chase Fulton Novels Series
Book One: *The Opening Chase*
Book Two: *The Broken Chase*
Book Three: *The Stronger Chase*
Book Four: *The Unending Chase*
Book Five: *The Distant Chase*
Book Six: *The Entangled Chase*
Book Seven: *The Devil's Chase*
Book Eight: *The Angel's Chase*
Book Nine: *The Forgotten Chase*
Book Ten: *The Emerald Chase*
Book Eleven: *The Polar Chase*
Book Twelve: *The Burning Chase*
Book Thirteen: *The Poison Chase*
Book Fourteen: *The Bitter Chase*
Book Fifteen: *The Blind Chase*
Book Sixteen: *The Smuggler's Chase*
Book Seventeen: *The Hollow Chase*
Book Eighteen: *The Sunken Chase*
Book Nineteen: *The Darker Chase*
Book Twenty: *The Abandoned Chase*
Book Twenty-One: *The Gambler's Chase*
Book Twenty-Two: *The Arctic Chase*
Book Twenty-Three: *The Diamond Chase*
Book Twenty-Four: *The Phantom Chase*
Book Twenty-Five: *The Crimson Chase*
Book Twenty-Six: *The Silent Chase*
Book Twenty-Seven: *The Shepherd's Chase*
Book Twenty-Eight: *The Scorpion's Chase*
Book Twenty-Nine: *The Creole Chase*

The Avenging Angel – Seven Deadly Sins Series
Book One: *The Russian's Pride*
Book Two: *The Russian's Greed*
Book Three: *The Russian's Gluttony*
Book Four: *The Russian's Lust*
Book Five: *The Russian's Sloth*
Book Six: *The Russian's Envy*
Book Seven: *The Russian's Wrath* (2025)

Stand-Alone Novels
We Were Brave
Singer – Memoir of a Christian Sniper

Novellas
The Chase is On
I Am Gypsy

THE SCORPION'S CHASE

CHASE FULTON NOVEL #28

CAP DANIELS

ANCHOR WATCH
PUBLISHING
** USA **

The Scorpion's Chase
Chase Fulton Novel #28
Cap Daniels

This is a work of fiction. Names, characters, places, historical events, and incidents are the product of the author's imagination or have been used fictitiously. Although many locations such as marinas, airports, hotels, restaurants, etc. used in this work actually exist, they are used fictitiously and may have been relocated, exaggerated, or otherwise modified by creative license for the purpose of this work. Although many characters are based on personalities, physical attributes, skills, or intellect of actual individuals, all the characters in this work are products of the author's imagination.

Published by:

** USA **

13 Digit ISBN: 978-1-951021-63-4
Library of Congress Control Number: 2024945892

Cover Design: German Creative

Printed in the United States of America

The Scorpion's Chase

CAP DANIELS

Chapter 1
No Fear

Spring 2013

I had long believed I feared no one except myself. I'd been beaten, stabbed, shot, dragged, and drowned, and though I'd been taken down, I had never failed to get back up. I believed I would never look into the eyes of another man and feel the terror of knowing I'd reached my end. But I was wrong.

My phone vibrated from somewhere deep in my pocket, so I mined it out and thumbed the button. "Hello, this is Chase."

"Is this Dr. Chase Fulton?"

Although I'd worked hard to earn the letters after my name, I'd never think of myself as anything other than just Chase.

"Who's calling, please?"

The voice said, "Dr. Fulton, this is Detective Carla Sensenich with the Hilton Head PD, and I need to confirm that you are the Dr. Fulton from St. Marys, Georgia, I'm looking for."

For the previous decade, I'd lived in St. Marys, on a beautiful piece of property called Bonaventure Plantation, that had been in my mother's family since the late eighteenth century.

"I am Chase Fulton, and I have a small clinical psychology practice. What can I do for you?"

"Do you have a patient named James Fairmont?"

"What's this about, Detective Sensenich?"

The tone of her voice made it more than clear that she was growing tired of the exchange. "Dr. Fulton, was Mr. Fairmont your patient or not?"

I scratched my beard. "You just spoke of Mr. Fairmont in the past tense. Did something happen to him?"

"Look, Dr. Fulton—"

I cut her off. "It's just Chase, okay? And yes, Jimmy Fairmont is, or was, my patient, but I'm afraid I can't tell you any more than that."

"Dr. . . . . Chase, your patient has been murdered, and I'd like for you to come identify the body."

"Murdered? How?"

She hesitated for a long moment. "I really think you should come see Mr. Fairmont's remains, Chase. I've been a cop a long time, but I've never seen anything like this."

"I'll be there in an hour, but how did you know to call me?"

"I'll explain all of that when you get here, but it's three hours to Hilton Head from St. Marys."

I checked my watch. "I'll be there in an hour. Have one of your officers pick me up at the airport. I'll be in an amphibious Cessna Two-Oh-Eight Caravan."

I ended the call and pulled up Sergeant First Class James Edward Fairmont's file on my cell phone. The medically retired Delta Force operator ended up in my office eight months before that day, with insomnia, clinical depression, and one of the worst cases of PTSD I'd ever seen. Through twice-a-week sessions, we'd worked through many of the horrors he'd endured while sacrificing his mind and body, a little more on every deployment, to protect and defend the interests and the people of what he believed to be the greatest nation ever established on the planet. Those had been his words, not mine, and even though I shared his belief, I never wore the uniform of the U.S. Army or any other branch of the uniformed service, but like Sergeant Fairmont, I'd seen far more combat than anyone should have to endure.

My wife, Penny, sat across from me in my favorite spot on Earth:

the gazebo on the back lawn of Bonaventure, overlooking the North River. The eighteenth-century naval cannon resting peacefully between us harbored the unspoken agonies of a life spent and lost at sea. I'd pulled the iron behemoth from the muddy bottom of Cumberland Sound less than five miles from where I sat, and I've longed since that day to have the old warhorse whisper her story, but she never will. For all the bellowing echoes of thunderous fire she'd belched, the gun would spend the rest of her days in utter silence.

In an uncharacteristic display of patience, Penny didn't ask about the call, or what I was so frantically doing on the screen of my phone, until I closed my eyes and sighed.

"What's going on? Are you all right?"

I laid my phone on the arm of the Adirondack chair in which I was cradled. "A patient of mine was murdered up in Hilton Head, and I need to go see him. Wanna come?"

She screwed up her face. "Of course I'm coming, but I've got a thousand questions. How was he murdered? Why would anybody murder one of your patients? Oh, and how did they know he *was* your patient?"

I pushed myself from the chair. "I don't have answers for any of those questions, and that's precisely why I want you to come with me."

She ran her fingers through her unruly, strawberry-blonde mane. "I can't go anywhere like this. I'm a mess. Give me half an hour."

I pulled off my University of Georgia Bulldogs hat and tossed it onto her lap. "Stick a ponytail through the back of the hat, and let's go."

I untied the airplane from our dock, and we climbed aboard. The turbine whistled to life the instant I introduced fuel, and we taxied away. The incoming tide against the slight breeze from New England made perfect conditions to take off to the north and climb out over coastal Georgia. The amphibious Caravan hauled her pontoons onto plane in seconds, and shortly thereafter, we were climbing away from Bonaventure and headed for the barrier islands of South Carolina.

When we touched down at Hilton Head Airport, the police car I'd expected to see on the ramp wasn't there, so I taxied to the parking apron and shut down the turbine. Even though the six-knot, northerly wind wasn't likely to blow the Caravan around, I tied her down just because that's what the Boy Scout in me demanded—to always "Be Prepared." Even though I'd never worn the little brown shirt or earned a merit badge for anything, I figured there had to be at least a hint of a Boy Scout somewhere in my skull.

As we approached the terminal, a tall, raven-haired woman pressed through the double glass doors and stuck out her hand. "You must be Dr. Fulton."

"It's just Chase, and this is my wife, Penny."

"Nice to meet you both. I'm Detective Sensenich. Thanks for coming. Nice plane, by the way. Which one of you is the pilot?"

I glanced back at the Caravan. "Thanks. Both of us. Do you fly?"

"I used to," she said. "I flew a chopper for Miami-Dade a long time ago before moving up here." She led us around the terminal building and through a chain-link gate. "I'm in the black SUV."

I opened the door for Penny, and she climbed onto the front passenger seat while I slid onto the seat behind her. A glance from the detective said she noticed our atypical seating arrangement, but she didn't mention it.

I wasn't surprised when Detective Sensenich wasn't the first person to start the inquisition.

Penny asked, "How did you know your victim was one of Chase's patients?"

The detective glanced up into the mirror—the primary reason I wanted to sit in the back seat—and took a long, deep breath. "We found your business card on Mr. Fairmont's body, and we spoke with the folks in the pro shop at Harbor Town."

Penny scowled. "Harbor Town? That's a golf resort, right? What does that have to do with Chase?"

Sensenich's eyes slowly made their way back to the mirror. "That's one of the things I'd like to clear up while you're here. Why did you pay Mr. Fairmont's greens fee?"

It was Penny's turn to shoot me a look I didn't like. "You paid for him to play golf? What's that about?"

I checked the traffic around us while I wrote the correct answer inside my head. "Doctor-patient confidentiality survives both parties, but I'll tell you what I can. I'm not a traditional psychotherapist. My methods are quite different than most. I treat mostly former and current military members suffering from post-traumatic stress disorder. One of my techniques is recommending a hobby or a pursuit that allows their mind to become involved in a learning process. I like to recommend activities such as golf, scuba diving, learning to fly, and other things that require a certain degree of dedication and learning. If the brain has something to do that it finds fascinating, often it'll begin the healing process all by itself, making my job easier and the patient's recovery faster and more effective."

The detective asked, "Do you routinely pay for these hobbies for your patients?"

"No, it isn't common practice, but I like Jimmy, and—"

"So, it's Jimmy, and not James or Mr. Fairmont? Did you have a personal relationship with your patient outside the office, Dr. Fulton?"

I pulled off my sunglasses. "It's Chase, and no, I did not have a relationship of any kind with my patient outside the office. Am I a suspect, Detective?"

She kept her eyes on the road. "I'm just trying to fill in some holes. We're in the first forty-eight, and I'm just doing my job."

Penny glanced between me and the detective. "Do we need an attorney for this?"

Detective Sensenich shrugged. "That's up to you, but I would like to know where you were today between noon and two p.m."

Penny pulled her notepad from her pocket, wrote several lines of something, and tore out the sheet. She laid it on the console between her and the detective. "That's a list of six people and their phone numbers. Both Chase and I were with all of those people from around eight this morning until half an hour before you called. Is that a suitable alibi for you?"

She pocketed the list and pulled into a parking spot labeled "Detective Parking Only." She said, "Let's go inside. I've got some things I want you to see."

We followed her inside the police department and down a corridor to her office. The space was small but neat, and nothing in the office hinted at a life outside of her work. There were no family pictures or personal items of any kind. It would be easy to believe Detective Carla Sensenich never took off her badge and gun.

"Have a seat. Can I get you anything to drink?"

Penny and I shook our heads, and the detective settled onto her chair behind a well-organized desk. She entered a combination of numbers into a keypad and opened a secure filing cabinet. A zipped pouch marked "EVIDENCE" in red letters landed on her desk, and she spun a computer monitor to face us. The first picture was a head-and-shoulders shot of a man lying on his back with his eyes closed and no expression on his face.

"Is that your patient, James Edward Fairmont?"

"Yes, that's him."

Penny covered her mouth but didn't speak.

Sensenich said, "This next photograph might be a little disturbing, so if you'd like to look away, Mrs. Fulton, this would be the time."

Penny shook her head. "I'm okay."

The screen filled with a new picture that was far less staged. It showed Jimmy lying in the shade beneath a massive oak. He was wearing a pair of cargo shorts and a Nine Line T-shirt with a crimson spot over his sternum. The outline of his pistol shone beneath the tail of his shirt on the right side of his abdomen.

I closed my eyes. "That's him. Where was he killed?"

The detective clicked her mouse. "We'll get to that, but first, I want you to see a close-up shot of the entry wounds."

Penny looked away as the screen filled with a detailed shot of the center of Jimmy's chest. The first bullet hole missed the center of his chest by three or four inches, but the second shot was perfectly centered through my business card and into his chest.

I swallowed hard and slumped back in my chair, then laid a hand on Penny's thigh. "You need to see this."

She turned and gasped. "My God, Chase! That's your business card. What's going on here?"

"I don't know," I said, "but somebody's sending a message."

The detective said, "Do you know anyone who wanted Mr. Fairmont dead and for you to know about it?"

"I don't," I said. "Do you have ballistics yet?"

She unzipped the pouch and produced two clear plastic evidence bags with a bullet in each. The first was mushroomed to more than four times its original size, but the second looked as if it had never struck anything.

I examined the bullets through the bags. "Caliber?"

"They're thirty-caliber, but we don't know anything about the casing."

"That doesn't help much," I said.

Penny asked, "Why not?"

The detective took that one. "There are so many thirty-caliber rounds on the market that it's impossible to know much about the rifle that fired it other than the inside diameter of the barrel."

I completed the explanation. "It's not specifically a military round."

"So, whoever did this probably isn't military?" Penny asked.

Sensenich said, "We can't make that assumption. The round is commercially available, so being in the military or not really doesn't have anything to do with the shooter having access to the round. The caliber isn't the most intriguing element, though. The difference between the two rounds is what has me scratching my head."

"Do you know how far away the shooter was?" I asked.

"Point blank for the second round, but we have no idea where he was when he fired the first round that killed Mr. Fairmont."

Penny furrowed her brow. "So, he shot and killed him from a long way away and then shot him through Chase's card after he was already dead. Is that right?"

"That's how it looks," the detective said. "The forensics team will come up with an estimate of the velocity based on the damage inside the victim's body. From that, we can work backward to determine how far the bullet flew before it slowed down enough to match the damage the coroner finds."

Penny asked, "Why didn't the second round expand like the first?"

"Three reasons. First, it was fired from only a few inches away, so it was traveling at maximum muzzle velocity when it entered the body. Second, the thoracic cavity had already been damaged so badly from the killing shot that there wasn't much mass for the second round to impact with."

"What's the third reason?" I asked.

She lifted the second bullet, still inside its evidence bag, and bounced it off the surface of the desk. "It's not a factory round. Someone custom-molded or machined it. I think it's steel, but we won't know until the metallurgist examines it at the state crime lab."

"May I see it?" I asked.

She slid it across her desk, and I pressed the plastic tightly against the bullet. I studied the projectile and tried to dig a fingernail into the metal through the bag.

"Don't tear the evidence bag," Sensenich ordered. "I can let you hold it out of the bag, but you can't do anything to damage it."

"That's okay," I said. "It wouldn't do any good for me to hold it, but what if I told you I could get it fast-tracked through the FBI crime lab in Virginia?"

She took the bag and leaned back. "How could you do that?"

"I do some contracting work for the feds, so I have a few contacts."

She studied me for a long moment until my phone chirped, and I glanced down at the device. Skipper's name flashed across the screen. She was not only practically family, but also one of the finest intelligence analysts in the business. I stood and said, "Excuse me. I have to take this."

I stepped through the door and back into the corridor. "Hey, Skipper. What's up?"

Her tear-filled voice cried out in agony. "Chase! Where are you? Somebody shot Tony."

Chapter 2
Fear

I stuck my head back through Detective Sensenich's door. "Come on, Penny. We have to go."

The two women rose in unison, and Sensenich said, "You can't leave yet. I've got more questions."

"They'll have to wait," I said. "We have an emergency at home."

"What kind of emergency?" Penny asked.

"I'll tell you on the flight. Let's go."

The detective frantically followed Penny through the door. "Dr. Fulton, we're far from finished."

"We're finished for now," I said. "I'll call you as soon as I resolve my situation at home, and we can continue. Until then, your questions will have to wait."

She huffed. "I guess you need a ride back to the airport, huh?"

"We do, and I'd appreciate lights and sirens."

She dropped us off only feet from the Caravan, and we were airborne before I had time to adequately work through the checklists like a good Boy Scout would do, but being home with Skipper in that moment was far more important than thirty items on a checklist I'd memorized long ago.

"What's going on?" Penny asked as we climbed away from Hilton Head.

"That was Skipper on the phone, and she said Tony's been shot."

"Is he okay? Where did they take him? Did they catch the shooter?"

"Once again, I don't have any of those answers, but we'll know soon."

We splashed down, taxied to the dock, and Penny said, "Go check on Skipper. I'll tie up the plane."

I sprinted up the back steps of the house three at a time and burst through the kitchen door. Mongo, our resident giant and former Green Beret, rose from a chair the same instant my boot hit the floor inside.

"Where's Skipper?"

In stature, the big man was a stalwart mountainside, but in that moment, the tear on his cheek gave him the look of a broken child. "She's at the hospital. He didn't make it, Chase."

I braced myself against the counter. "What happened?"

Mongo motioned toward a chair opposite his and ran the back of his hand across his eyes. "Have a seat, and I'll tell you what we know."

By the time I planted myself in the seat, Penny came through the door, and I held up a hand before she could unleash her barrage of questions. "Have a seat. Mongo's going to catch us up."

She slid onto a chair and leaned forward in anticipation as Mongo gathered himself.

"Here's what we know so far. Tony was riding with a patrol officer, as he does from time to time."

Tony Johnson, Skipper's husband and our handler's younger brother, had endured a traumatic brain injury on duty with the team overseas and found himself permanently sidelined. His skill and knowledge were too much of a goldmine to let go to waste, so he volunteered as a detective with the St. Marys PD.

"They had the closest thing to a high-speed chase this town has ever seen," Mongo said. "And they pitted the runner, sending him sliding into the ditch up on Charlie Smith Highway. There were three St. Marys PD cars involved, and Tony was second in line behind the PIT vehicle. He and the patrol officer, Benji Garrison, jumped from their car and engaged the runner. Shots were fired, and both Benji and Tony went down."

"Is he going to be all right?" Penny asked.

Mongo squeezed his eyelids closed. "I'm sorry. You missed what I told Chase before you came in. Tony didn't survive."

Penny covered her mouth with both hands and sobbed. "Oh my God. Where's Skipper?"

"She's at the hospital, as far as I know. I've not spoken with her in about thirty minutes. Singer's with her."

Singer, our Southern Baptist sniper—an ordained minister and one of the deadliest snipers on Earth—is exactly the person I'd want by Penny's side if I were the victim.

"What about the shooter?" I asked.

Mongo said, "Two through his skull and six in his torso is what I heard, but that's not confirmed yet."

"Why was he running?"

"He hit the liquor store for a few hundred bucks and took off."

"In broad daylight?" I asked. "That doesn't make any sense."

"Since when does robbing a liquor store and shooting it out with the cops ever make sense? Where have you been?"

I said, "We'll deal with my stuff later. Somebody killed one of my patients up in Hilton Head."

Mongo lowered his chin. "Tony and one of your patients getting shot and killed on the same day . . . You know how I feel about coincidences."

"I can't imagine them being related, but the thing up in Hilton Head is ugly. He was shot twice—once from a significant distance, and a second time from only inches away, right through the center of one of my business cards."

Mongo leaned back. "Oh, man. That's not good."

"No, nothing about it qualifies as good. Has anybody called Clark yet?"

"Yeah, Singer called him. Getting the call that your little brother's been shot and killed isn't something anyone should have to deal with, but he's on his way up from Miami."

"How about the rest of the team?" I asked. "Where are they?"

"I made a command decision since you weren't here. Even though I was ninety-nine percent sure Tony's murder wasn't related to the team, I ordered a perimeter around Bonaventure until you got back."

I considered his decision to place one of the most seasoned and battle-hardened tactical teams on Earth in a defensive perimeter around our home. "Good call. Who's running it?"

"Celeste is in the op center upstairs. I was waiting here for you, so it's all yours now."

I stood and laid a hand on his shoulder. "Nice work, my friend."

Penny stood beside me. "We're going to the hospital, right?"

"Not just yet," I said. "I need to check on Celeste."

Dr. Celeste Mankiller had been a DOJ Technical Services officer for ten years before we saved her from civil service and gave her a lab and a budget to create every gadget we could ever need in the covert operative business, and she had quickly proven to be an invaluable member of the team.

I climbed the stairs, entered my access code, and scanned my thumbprint to open the door to the operation center on the third floor of Bonaventure. The world-class war room gave us the ability to run an operation anywhere on the planet with unmatched communication and support.

When I walked in, Celeste looked up and stood. She wrapped me in a hug and fought back the tears. "This is terrible, Chase. It's just terrible."

I returned the hug. "Yes, it is. Thank you for running the perimeter defense. Do you have anything to tell me?"

She shook her head and pointed toward a monitor. "You can see the team's positions there, but we've not had any sign of an intruder or watcher."

I studied the screen and tried to calm my mind long enough to make a rational decision. Finally, I said, "Break it down. There's no need for those guys to sit out there. We're headed to the hospital to find Skipper."

She nodded and reclaimed her seat in front of the communication console.

* * *

We found Skipper holding Tony's hand in a trauma room at the local hospital. I stepped beside her and wrapped my arms around the woman I'd long considered to be my little sister. Seeing her so brokenhearted left me demolished, and for the first time that day, my tears came.

Words weren't necessary. In that moment, only love and concern mattered, but the warrior inside my chest beat his drum as my eyes took in the corpse of a man who'd been more than a friend. Tony Johnson had fought beside me in the mud and blood all over the world. He'd saved countless lives as a Coast Guard rescue swimmer before joining our team, but most of all, he was Skipper's husband and the only man she'd ever truly loved.

As I studied his body, a relentless question poured through my mind on an unending loop. I didn't mean for the words to escape my lips, but apparently, they did. "Why wasn't he wearing a vest?"

Skipper choked back her tears. "He was. It's over there in the corner." She pointed with one hand while keeping the other arm wrapped tightly around my waist.

Tony's bloody body armor lay on the brilliant white floor of the room, and I held Skipper for what could've been an eternity until a woman in green scrubs came through the curtain. "I'm sorry, ma'am, but we have to move your husband to the morgue."

Skipper bellowed, "No! You can't have him." She withdrew her arm from around my waist and gripped Tony's hand with both of hers.

I motioned for the lady to come closer. "Is there an officer sitting outside?" She nodded, and I said, "Could you have him come in for a moment, please?"

She turned and disappeared back through the curtain, and I led Penny to take my place beside Skipper.

I met the officer at the split in the curtain and whispered, "Will you please stay with Skipper and my wife and make sure that lady knows you're escorting them down to the morgue?"

"Yes, sir. Of course. Listen, I'm real sorry—"

I held up a hand. "Thank you, but it's not your fault. How are the other officers who were involved?"

"Benji probably ain't gonna make it. He's in pretty bad shape and lost a lot of blood. I think he's still in surgery."

"Thank you," I said. "Do you know if there are any forensic guys around?"

He shook his head and reached for the mic on his epaulet. "No, but I can get you one. What's up?"

I glanced at Tony's body armor and then back at the officer. "Why don't you do that? Give them a call, and have one of them meet me here while you escort Tony and the ladies to the morgue."

"Sure, no problem."

He stepped back through the curtain and made the call. Minutes later, the officer walked beside Tony's gurney as a pair of orderlies rolled him from the room. Skipper and Penny never left his side.

While waiting for the forensics tech, I took a knee beside Tony's vest and pulled out my pen. I gingerly lifted the Velcro shoulder strap and studied the Kevlar body armor. Without handling the vest, I saw three rounds caught in the layers of the front of his vest with no penetration through the interior surface. The blows would've felt like being hit by a truck, but they wouldn't have killed him. The front of the vest appeared to have done its job.

I slid to my left and tugged on the shoulder strap with my pen, but the weight of the vest was too much to relocate with just that tool. After scanning the room and finding three boxes of surgical gloves, I pulled a pair from the box marked XL and slid my hands inside. Before I could get back to the vest, a young man in a white lab coat and black-rimmed glasses stepped through the curtain.

He flinched as if surprised to see me. "Oh, hey. I'm Glenn from forensics. Officer Williams said somebody needed me up here. Are you that somebody?"

I stuck out a hand, and he stared down at the blue glove. "Uh, maybe we shouldn't shake since I'm not wearing gloves yet."

"Of course," I said. "I'm Chase Fulton, and I . . ."

He let out a chuckle. "Yeah, everybody knows who you are. Why did you need to see me?"

I motioned toward Tony's vest. "I think you might need to take a look at Tony Johnson's body armor."

"Why?"

"Just have a look and tell me if anything looks out of the ordinary to you."

He shrugged and pulled on a pair of gloves of his own. After draping a piece of plastic onto the floor, he carefully lifted the vest and placed it on the plastic. He examined every inch with the thoroughness one would expect of a forensic technician, and then, he turned it over.

Two perfectly round holes appeared in the center of the backplate, less than an inch apart. The tech pressed a metallic probe through each hole until the tip protruded through the inside of the backplate. His expression mirrored my own as he continued his examination.

He finally worked his way to the sides of the vest, where small plates should've been inserted to protect the wearer's ribs, but Tony's side plates were missing.

"Where are the plates?" I asked.

He looked up with an unreadable expression on his face. "Most cops remove the side plates to make the vest more comfortable. It's a gamble, but it's not rare. To tell you the truth, I'd be surprised if ten percent of the officers in the department wear their side plates, but even if Detective Johnson had been wearing his, it wouldn't have mattered."

"What do you mean?"

He said, "Take a look at this. The hole in the material where his side plate would've been is an exit path, not an entry."

"What are you saying?"

"It's simple. One of the rifle rounds in his back pierced the body armor but never left his body. The other round went through and through. My guess is, they'll find the first projectile in his chest, but the second one will never be found. It was probably still moving pretty fast when it left the body."

"How do you know they were rifle rounds?"

He furrowed his brow. "Because there's no pistol in the world that would've penetrated that backplate the way those two projectiles did. It had to be a rifle, and the holes are way too big to be from any of the five-five-sixes the patrol officers would've carried."

"Are you saying . . ."

"Yes, sir. Somebody other than the driver of that car shot Detective Johnson in the back during the gunfight, and those were the shots that killed him."

Chapter 3
More Fear

I found Singer on his knees in the hospital's small chapel, so I quietly took a seat in the back and joined my sniper and moral compass in silent prayer. The devout man of God rarely prayed out loud when anyone was around to hear him, and I often wondered what his private conversations with his God sounded like. I'd never known a more devoted believer, and I envied the faith he wore like a cloak to keep himself warm against life's relentless wind of icy assault.

Moments later, he stood, gave me a barely perceptible nod, and sat beside me. "Are you doing all right, Chase?"

I shook my head. "No, not at all."

I told him about Jimmy Fairmont's murder in Hilton Head and the discovery the forensic tech made concerning Tony's body armor.

As if he hadn't heard anything I'd said, he asked, "Have you spoken with Clark?"

"Not yet. But Mongo said he was on his way from Miami."

"He'll need a shoulder, and you're closer to him than anyone on Earth, except perhaps Maebelle. He won't come to me, but if he turns to anyone, it'll be you. Are you prepared for that?"

"No, no one is prepared to deal with a brother's grief after losing his only sibling, but I'll listen and let him cry."

"Listening and supporting are important, but he's not a psych patient. He's your friend, so pray with him, too . . . even if he doesn't want to." I nodded, and he said, "I'm on my way down to the morgue to try to get Skipper to come home. Any advice?"

I huffed. "Good luck. Do you want me to come with you?"

He glanced at his watch. "No, thanks, but you can pick up Clark. He should be landing anytime now. I'll let you know if I'm successful at talking Skipper out of the morgue."

* * *

The King Air carrying my friend and handler touched down at what had once been the St. Marys Municipal Airport, but after closing from budget constraints, Clark and I bought the property, turning it into a private airport solely for our use. The turbine engines whistled until falling silent when the propellers came to a stop. To my surprise, Clark climbed from the cockpit and bounded down the stairs.

I met him as his boot hit the tarmac. "You doing all right, brother?"

The look on his face said more than words ever could. Affection was never one of Clark's strong suits, but he dropped his head against my shoulder and wrapped his arms around me.

I'd wrestled with him, and we'd dragged each other in and out of foxholes all over the world, but I believe that was the first time we'd ever hugged each other.

He coughed back the coming tears and said, "I guess you're the only brother I've got left."

I drew a long, deep breath. "Brothers we choose aren't blood, but . . ."

He grabbed a handful of my shirt. "You and me have shed enough blood together to qualify as brothers by anybody's definition. How's Skipper?"

I took a step back. "She's not good, but who would be? Last I knew, Singer was trying to talk her out of the morgue."

On the ride back to the hospital, I filled him in on the murder in Hilton Head and the news on Tony's vest. When I told him what I knew about the ballistics, he yanked his phone from his pocket. His hearing was only slightly better than mine, so with his volume turned all the way up, I could hear every word of the conversation.

"NAT Lab, Kinsey."

"Mr. Kinsey, Clark Johnson, seven-six-niner-one-eight-echo-six."

"Stand by."

A moment later, the voice said, "Go ahead, Mr. Johnson."

Clark spent a lot of his life joking around and pretending to be far less intelligent than he was, but in that moment, he was all business.

"Thank you, Mr. Kinsey. I need authorization for expedited ballistics analysis on four projectiles from two cases. The first is Anthony Michael Johnson from St. Marys, Georgia, PD, and the second is . . ." He covered the phone with his hand and looked up. "What's your guy's full name?"

I gave it, and he said, "James Edward Fairmont from Hilton Head, South Carolina, PD, with a reservation for an unknown number to follow." He pinned the phone to his ear with his shoulder and said, "Give me something to write on."

I handed him a fast-food napkin and my pen, and he said, "Go ahead with the number." He scribbled on the napkin and ended the call. His thumbs went to work typing on his phone. "I'm texting you the expedited authorization number for the FBI ballistics lab. Pass it along to whoever's handling both cases. Whoever this guy is, I'm going to drive a dump truck through his skull."

Detective Sensenich answered on the first ring, and I gave her the code.

She said, "Hey, before you go, did your hasty retreat have anything to do with those cops who got shot down there in St. Marys?"

"You could say that. Give me twenty-four hours, and I'll brief you up."

She said, "I'm a police detective, Chase. You may have friends at the FBI crime lab, but I'm pretty sure I know more than you when it comes to cop killings on the coast."

"I'm sure you do, Detective. Nonetheless, I'll give you a call tomorrow."

"One more thing," she said. "Your victims down there . . . They didn't have your business cards on them, did they?"

"I'll call you tomorrow, Detective, but it's safe to say this thing is so far over both of our heads that we can't even see that high. We'll talk soon."

I thumbed the button before she could sneak in any more questions.

Clark asked, "Who's the detective on Tony's case?"

"I doubt if there is one yet. Until I examined his body armor with the forensics guy, everybody thought the shooter was the liquor store guy, and he ate way too much lead to tell us anything."

"I want to see him," Clark said.

"I thought you might say that. They were taking him to the morgue when I left to pick you up, so I'm sure he's down there."

"Drop me at the door, and get your butt over to the police station. Make sure your buddy, the chief, puts somebody on this thing who's got some sense. My choice would be Hunter."

Stone W. Hunter was a retired Air Force combat controller and former NCIS officer. He'd spent a little time on the disabled list from my team and found a temporary home with the local police department while he was convalescing.

I dialed Hunter's number, and he said, "Hey, Chase."

It took two minutes to bring him up to speed, and I closed the conversation by saying, "Meet me at the chief's office. I'll be there in less than ten minutes."

"I'm on my way."

I didn't have to talk my way past the desk sergeant. He buzzed me in as soon as I stepped through the front door of the St. Marys Police Department.

"Hey, Chase. I'm sorry to hear about Tony. He was a good man and a good cop."

"Yes, he was, Don. Yes, he was. Is the chief back there?"

Don nodded. "He's expecting you."

Chief Bobby Roberts's door was ajar, so I pushed it open and he waved me in. I took a seat and tried to stay quiet while he was on the phone. Hunter came in at the same instant the chief placed the receiver back in its cradle.

The top cop ran a hand through what remained of his hair. "Bad day, boys."

"Yes, it is, Chief. That's why we're here."

He nodded toward the phone. "That was Detective Carla Sensenich from Hilton Head. What's going on here, Chase?"

"I don't know yet, but we're going to find out."

The chief sucked air through his teeth. "There's no way to keep you out of this one, is there?"

"Not a chance. Somebody made this one personal, but I'll share everything we learn with you if the information doesn't turn out to be classified."

"That's all I can ask for, I guess."

"I can't promise you any more than that, and what I do share with you will be off the record, of course."

"Of course," he said. "How about an arrest? If it turns out we've got jurisdiction, will you throw us a bone? It'd mean a lot to the department if we got to cuff the bastard who killed at least one of our own . . . and probably two."

Hunter spoke up for the first time in the conversation. "Chief, I have to do this one with Chase, so I can't wear two hats. Whoever this guy is, he's not local, and he's likely not an American."

The chief cut in. "How can you assume he's not an American?"

Hunter continued. "I know you think you understand what we do when we disappear for days or weeks at a time and come back home licking our wounds, but the truth is, you can't know. What we do isn't police work. What we do is strike enough fear into the hearts of enemies of the United States that they choke on it. It's never pretty, and it's never clean. Nobody walks away unscathed. When we find this guy, it'll be in some hole we've chased him into, and there won't be enough of him left to handcuff. We're not in the business of collecting prisoners."

It appeared as if the chief was losing more hair as we spoke. "I get it, but that doesn't answer my question. Why do you think this guy isn't American?"

I said, "As Tony's brother, Clark, would put it, we pee in a lot of canteens, so we've got no shortage of enemies. Very few, if any of those canteens and enemies are American. Somebody's taking shots at me by killing people I care about. This guy is somebody we've hurt. It's likely we cut into his cash flow, or maybe it's personal. Maybe we killed somebody he loves. At this point, it's impossible to know, but we'll get answers, and we'll find this guy. It's what we do."

The chief finally abandoned running his fingers through his hair. "I have to call in the GBI. We're not equipped to run an investigation like this, so my hands are tied."

"Maybe not," Hunter said. "The Georgia Bureau of Investigation will stumble around and waste a lot of time chasing down leads that aren't leads. The whole thing will turn into a giant circus, and nobody wants that. How many people know the truth about Tony's death?"

The chief said, "Whoever you guys told, my forensics team, the ME, and the shooter."

"Can we keep it that way?" Hunter asked.

The chief leaned way back in his chair and squeezed his temples between the heels of his hands. "You're asking me to cover up—"

Hunter stopped him. "No. We're not asking you to cover up anything. We're asking you to keep critical details of a murder investigation classified, and limited to only those few essential people who need to know, until the moment these details absolutely have to come out. We do that all the time."

The chief said, "Yeah, we do that all the time, but there's a statute that says I have to call in the GBI. If I don't follow the law, I'll be un-employed and maybe even locked up."

I laid a hand on his desk. "How about this? Talk with the city attor-ney and get his opinion. If he agrees that you have to follow the statute and notify the GBI, then do it, but if he says there's some grey area, let us do what we do in that grey area because that's where we do our best work."

Chapter 4
How Dare You?

I assembled the team the next morning in the op center on the third floor of our house at Bonaventure, but unlike our typical meeting in that setting, everybody—including spouses, Tony's parents, and one temporary addition to the team—was there.

I opened the meeting by saying, "We've got a lot to talk about this morning, and I want to make sure everyone is up to speed on what's happening around us and to us."

Groans rose from the sea of troubled faces in front of me.

I continued. "Let's talk about Tony first."

To my surprise, Skipper said, "Let me brief this part."

I surrendered the floor, and she said, "First, please accept my deepest appreciation for the kindness and love every one of you has poured out to me in the last twenty-four hours. Without you guys, this would be impossible to bear."

She paused and gathered herself. "Okay, sorry about that. I don't know if I'll ever have a day when I don't cry when I think of Tony. He was the . . . Never mind. Now's not the time for that. Once the medical examiner releases him, we'll have a small, private memorial service, and then Tony wanted to be cremated and returned to the ocean, where he felt most at home." With that, the tears flooded her eyes, and she shook her head with her face in her hands.

I gritted my teeth and summoned the wherewithal to continue. "Okay, everybody in this room knows what we do, even if you don't know the full extent. The police will, of course, conduct their investigations, but they're not capable of dealing with this situation. Someone or some group is targeting us, and they want us to know. Do any of you have any early suspicions on who our attacker might be?"

Dominic Fontana, Clark and Tony's father and my former handler, cleared his throat. "At the risk of being out of line, I must assure you that every resource of the Board is at your disposal, and whoever these people are, we have not only the means to find them, but also the responsibility to make them pay."

"Forgive me," I said, "but do you speak definitively for the Board now that you're retired?"

He said, "I spoke with every current member of the Board this morning, and they assured me that I could make that announcement with certainty. They are waiting for our request, and they have their ears to the ground for anything that might hint at the responsible party in all of this."

I closed my eyes for a moment as I tried to formulate a plan—any plan—to start our search. With a long sigh, I said, "I have to confess that I don't know exactly what to ask the Board. The two bullets mean something, but until we get the analysis back from the lab, any significance we try to tie to them is just supposition. I'm wide open for ideas about where to start."

Clark lifted his mother's hand from his and said, "I talked with the Board minutes after Dad, and they made two suggestions—both of which are out of the question as far as I'm concerned, but I'm obligated to pass along the offers. The first thing they suggested was having another tactical team—or maybe two—come down and pull security for us. I dismissed that one because we don't need babysitters. We need resources to go hunting."

"I agree," I said. "I'm not interested in having another team in our way right now. What was their second suggestion?"

"They offered to fly us anywhere we wanted to go and put us under twenty-four-hour guard while another team investigates this thing."

That elicited a guttural sound from the crowd, and I said, "Yeah, that's not happening, but I won't stop any of you who want to take advantage of the Board's offer for protection. In fact, I think some distance and some bodyguards are a good idea for some of you."

My team of warriors sat in stoic silence, and I was certain each of their chests was full of the same fire that burned in me. But weighed against the burden of Tony's murder, that fire would be forced to endure the limitless volume of tears everyone in the room would shed in the coming days.

Reading the faces in the room, I felt myself buckle beneath the weight of the responsibility I bore for those around me. Eyes and hearts cried out for me to pilot our ship through the storm in which we lay foundering, and for the first time, I feared I lacked the strength to grasp the wheel and weather the storm.

When my eyes finally fell on Ginger, the analyst who'd turned Skipper into one of the world's finest intelligence analysts and mission directors in the business, I said, "We have one bit of housekeeping to take care of before we move ahead. As you can see, I invited Ginger to join us while we work our way through this thing. Skipper needs some time to overcome this overwhelming loss, so Ginger will fulfill the role of analyst on this one."

Skipper leapt to her feet. "Seriously? You've got to be kidding me! You don't get to shove me aside when my husband's killer is out there taking aim at the rest of us. You don't get to tell me what I need. I need to bring Tony's killer to justice beneath my boots. What I need is for you and the rest of this team to get out there and find him, drag him out of his hole, and put him on his knees at my feet. Nobody, not even Ginger, sits in my chair. I'm responsible for all you boys out there on the ground, and that's the one thing I've got left. How dare you try to take that away from me?"

The one move I'd made in confidence had just blown up in my face, and I felt like I'd been kicked in the chest. "I wasn't replacing you, Skipper. I'm merely augmenting you. Ginger is here to help. You have to sleep, and the op center has to be up and running around the clock. I'm not taking anything away from you. I'm making us stronger. That's all."

"I get it," she said, "but don't assume you know what's best for me right now, okay?"

I nodded while my heart broke for her over and over. A good psychologist wouldn't have made the mistake I did, but a good friend would do everything in his power to soften the blow she was feeling.

As I wallowed in self-pity over the decision to bring Ginger in the way I had, my wife said the last words I could've imagined coming from her mouth.

"Have you called Anya?"

Anya Burinkova, the former Russian assassin tasked with flipping me or killing me a lifetime ago, had turned against the Kremlin and defected to America. I once believed she loved me, and I undoubtedly loved her—or the person I believed her to be. Ultimately, the relationship I once wanted so desperately melted away, but the skill set she possessed surpassed that of any single team member in the op center, and, at times, that skill set was a required element in our operations. In our current op, however, I couldn't envision how the Russian could possibly bring anything to the table.

"Why would I have called Anya?"

Penny rolled her eyes. "Come on, Chase. You're smarter than that. You saw what they did to your patient and to Tony. What makes you think they won't hit Anya just to drive that stake through your heart?"

She was right, and I was left torn between continuing the briefing and pulling my phone from my pocket. Before I was forced to make that decision, the speaker in the center of the conference table lit up, and that unmistakable voice cut through the air.

"*Privet*, is Anya."

"Hello, Anya. It's Chase. Listen, I have some bad news, and you need—"

"Is not Penny, please! She is okay, yes?"

"Penny's fine, but someone murdered Tony Johnson and one of my patients yesterday."

"Why was Tony with one of your patients?"

"No. They weren't together. It was two separate incidents several hours apart."

"And you know this was done by same person, how?"

I spent five minutes laying out what we knew, and she said, "I will be there in five hours."

"No, Anya, I wasn't calling to ask for your help. I was calling to let you know that you may be a target."

"Target? Why would I be target?"

"If I'm right about the killer trying to get his revenge against me by killing people I care about, then you're logically on that list."

The line was silent for several seconds before she said, "This is compliment for me that you would be saddened by my death. Thank you for this, Chasechka. I will be there in five hours, and we will find this person together."

"No, Anya! We don't need your—"

The green light on the speaker turned red, and I was left talking to no one. "It looks like Anya's on her way to help."

Penny said, "Please don't take this as a shot against any of you guys, but I, for one, will sleep a little better knowing Anya is out there hunting this guy down."

I wasn't looking forward to the circus that never failed to follow Anya wherever she went, but I secretly agreed with Penny's assessment, and I liked having her working with the team again.

Pulling myself out of the temporary stupor, I said, "Let's hear some ideas on who this might be."

Mongo tapped his pencil against the table. "The obvious choice is the Russians. We've got a long track record of kicking them in the face at every opportunity. We all know it's just a matter of time before they kick back."

I said, "The Russians are a big group of people. Can you narrow it down a little?"

The big man shrugged. "I'd start at the top, but we can't rule out some of the small-time players."

Clark waved a finger. "What about that congresswoman's kid I told you to ignore, but you wouldn't listen?"

"Salvatore D'Angelo?" I asked.

"Yeah, that's him."

"I don't think he's got the tools for this, but I could be wrong."

Singer asked, "What about the guys from Ontrack Global Resources? They've got the tools, the talent, and the financials to put something like this together anywhere in the world. And don't forget, we slapped them around pretty good in Bulgaria."

Hearing the name OGR sent chills down my spine as the memory of the havoc they unleashed on our team poured through my head. In that instant, there was no doubt in my mind that Ontrack Global Resources was pulling the trigger on people I cared about in retribution for the damage my team and I had done to their operation. The task wouldn't be easy, but in the end, my team would find a way to drive OGR into the ground, and we'd have our pound of flesh, no matter the cost.

Chapter 5

Not Goodbye, but Farewell

I stood in front of the full-length dressing mirror and tried to remember the last time I'd tied a full Windsor. The black, silk tie felt foreign in my hands, and after two failed attempts, I tossed the ridiculous accoutrement across the mirror and pulled on my jacket.

Penny stepped behind me and took in my reflection. "You're not wearing the tie?"

"No, I don't think Tony would want us to pretend to be anything we're not, and I'm definitely not a tie guy."

She smiled up at me. "You're probably right. Are you doing okay?"

"Not yet, but you know what they say . . . Time heals all wounds."

"You don't believe that lie, do you?"

"No, of course not. Time only adds opportunities for other moments of grief and sorrow to claim the foremost spot in our minds. It'll get easier in time, but not because the wound has healed—only because another loss has taken its place. Have you spoken with Skipper this morning?"

She said, "Yeah. It's going to be a tough day for her. I'm going to stay close and catch as many of her tears as I can."

My phone chirped on the dresser, and Penny tossed it to me. I thumbed the button and stuck it to my ear. "Good morning, Hunter. How's it going?"

In the previous two days, I'd changed my mind about the offer from the Board to send us a team of security forces to watch our backs, and I was glad I did.

Hunter said, "Perimeter security is in place, and they're running drones as a second layer."

"Good. Is, uh . . ."

He said, "Yes, the hearse just left. I didn't want it sitting around during the service."

"Good thinking. We'll be there in fifteen minutes, and we'll have Skipper with us."

He said, "We're ready."

Hunter and the security team may have been ready, but when I walked into the church with Skipper's hand laced inside my elbow, I discovered I was not ready for the scene in front of me. The sight of my friend and teammate, Petty Officer Second Class Anthony Johnson, lying in a simple coffin and dressed in his U.S. Coast Guard full-dress uniform, sent my heart sinking into my stomach.

Skipper squeezed my arm as she quietly sobbed. Part of me thought she might falter, but she never missed a step as we walked down the aisle of the church toward her husband and my brother-in-arms.

As we approached, she slid her hand from my arm and gripped the edge of the coffin. I held my ground beside her in case she was over-come with emotion, but as the moments played out, my presence proved to be unnecessary.

She adjusted a strand of Tony's hair and stroked his cheek with the back of her fingers before laying her hand on his for the last time. She cried, but only softly as she shared an agonizing final moment with the body of the man she'd love until the day she drew her final breath.

After kissing his cheek, she turned back to me, and we took our seat beside Skipper's parents, Bobby and Laura Woodley.

Former Sergeant First Class Jimmy "Singer" Grossmann, also in his Army Class-A uniform, stepped into the pulpit. He opened his Bible and bowed his head. After a short prayer, he read several verses of scripture that most of us knew by heart and then closed the well-worn, leatherbound book.

He stepped from behind the lectern, his medals, ribbons, and decorations telling the story of a young man's sacrifice, bravery, and dedication to serving his fellow man. "As we say goodbye to a man who touched each of us in a way few people can, I ask you to remember one thing. This service and the spreading of Tony's ashes in a few days are ceremonies for the living in celebration of a beautiful life well and fully lived. These moments are not for Tony Johnson. They are for us so our hearts can once again remember and be full of the joy and love we felt from and for him while he stood beside us in the brief moment we are given on this Earth."

Singer stepped beside the coffin and said, "Those of us who fought beside him saw the heart of a compassionate warrior, a man of extremes, a man who fought with the ferocity of a lion, but also a man who loved with the heart of a child. We loved him while he walked beside us in this world, and we will love him eternally when we join him in the promised Heaven awaiting us and all believers. Let us pray."

Everyone bowed their heads, and Singer spoke to God in the confident voice of a devout believer and humble servant. "Almighty God, hear our prayer as we kneel before you as humbly as we know how. Thank you for your countless blessings, and especially for the priceless gift of our beloved brother-in-Christ, Tony Johnson. Thank you for allowing our lives to be touched by the heart and soul of such a man, even if only for an instant. We ask now for the healing touch of Your promised Holy Spirit for those of us left behind to await the glorious day when we'll be reunited with those who've stepped from this world and into Your loving arms. We ask for Your comfort, Your peace, and Your continued love to hold, shelter, and protect us as we soldier on, walking in faith and anticipation of eternal joy in Your presence, for it is in the holy name of Christ our Savior we ask these blessings and offer these thanks."

He paused, and the voices of everyone in the church joined his. "Amen."

Singer laid a hand on Tony's chest and whispered, "Not goodbye, my friend. Just farewell until we meet again."

With that, he closed the half lid that had been open for the ceremony and draped the waiting flag across the coffin. When Old Glory lay without a wrinkle, Singer turned to the Coast Guard detail commander, a chief petty officer, and gave him a nod.

The chief issued his orders in quiet but commanding reverence. "Detail . . . Post."

On his command, a pair of Coast Guard petty officers approached Tony's coffin with exceptional military bearing and grasped the corners of the American flag. They moved with robotic precision and snapped the flag aloft, stretching it taut above their fallen brother.

The sea of men and women in uniform rose as if yanked from their seats by some unseen hand. An instant later, in perfect unison, I watched as Air Force Colonel Blake "Disco" Riley, Army Master Sergeant Clark "Baby Face" Johnson, Air Force Staff Sergeant Stone W. Hunter, Army Master Sergeant Marvin "Mongo" Malloy, Army Master Sergeant Furgeson "Kodiak" Knox, and a dozen other uniformed men and women, snapped their right hands sharply to their foreheads in the salute Tony far more than earned and deserved.

The two Coast Guard petty officers folded the flag with measured precision until it became a perfectly formed triangle. The first petty officer held the flag in front of himself while the second saluted. He then passed the flag to the second petty officer and repeated the salute his teammate had offered. He then performed an about-face maneuver and placed the flag in the hands of a waiting Coast Guard captain, who'd been Tony's commanding officer in his last assignment as a rescue swimmer. The captain accepted the flag and marched silently, stopping and kneeling exactly eighteen inches in front of Skipper, who sat with tears streaming down her face.

The captain laid the flag in her hands. The instant she accepted the flag, a single teardrop left her cheek and landed precisely in the center of one of the bright white stars.

The captain spoke softly as if only to her. "Ma'am, on behalf of the president of the United States, the United States Coast Guard, and a grateful nation, please accept this flag as a token in remembrance of your loved one's true and faithful service, both in and out of uniform. May God bless and comfort you."

Skipper nodded in tearful appreciation but didn't speak. The captain rose to the position of attention and saluted as slowly and respectfully as possible. When he completed the salute, every uniformed man and woman inside the church dropped theirs as well.

Singer stood and faced the gathered crowd. "Thank you for sharing this time with us. Now, if you'll please allow the family some peaceful, quiet time with Tony, they would deeply appreciate your kindness."

Everyone except Tony's family filed out of the church in silent reverence, and when I turned to follow them out, Skipper grabbed my arm. "No. I need you and the team to stay with us. You're family, too."

Chapter 6
Monkey See

On the ride home from the memorial service, I wasn't surprised when Skipper said, "Get everybody in the op center."

Even though I expected her to plunge herself back into work, I said, "We've got some work to do with Gator on the firing range if you'd like to take the afternoon off."

Her expression never changed. "Nice try, but I need everyone in the op center ASAP. That made-up training can wait."

I pressed the accelerator. "As you wish."

Thirty minutes later, we were dressed in our everyday cargo pants, boots, and T-shirts, and Skipper was back in full analyst mode.

She wasted no time jumping in. "Now that everyone is *finally* here, we can get started. We don't need to talk about this morning. We did it, and I appreciate all of you being there, but it's time to go to work."

In her typical style, her fingers flew across the keyboard, and her mouse looked like it was ready to burst into flames. When she finished the keys and clicks, four monitors came to life above her head.

"Take a look at monitor number one," she said. "That's Courtney Kellum, physical security manager for Ontrack Global Resources, and he's missing."

"Missing?" I said. "What does that mean?"

"That means he hasn't been in his office for the past four days, his car hasn't left his home garage, and there's been no sign of financial activity on his personal or business credit cards."

"Is he alive?" Mongo asked.

Skipper said, "If he's not, there's been no reaction to his death. His wife is still shopping, and his son hasn't left Cambridge."

Anya spoke up. "Is common tactic. Someone who looks like him— I think this person is called body double—drove his car home pretending to be this man, Kellum, while real person was taken from office, hidden from sight. This person will have other identity including passport, credit cards, and plenty of cash. If I am right, this person is doing something . . . uh, I cannot remember word in English, but is *taynyy* in Russian."

"Covert," I said.

"Yes, this is word . . . covert. He is probably on mission, and maybe this mission is to kill all of us."

"I'm not buying it," I said. "This guy is an executive—a necktie guy. He's not a hitter. Maybe he was in his younger days, but he wouldn't come at us personally. We're not that easy to hit, so whoever's doing this has to be well supported by a solid team, not just one former action guy."

Skipper said, "Anya could be right. Maybe this is personal for Kellum. Maybe he's running the op and has a whole team of hitters under his command."

I chewed my lip for a moment. "It's possible. Let's move on and come back to Kellum later."

Skipper said, "Okay. Take a look at monitor number two."

I studied the screen, but nothing about it made any sense to me. It appeared to be a drawing of an atom. I barely passed chemistry, so I couldn't identify the element, but it looked like it had hundreds of electrons orbiting the nucleus.

Skipper said, "This is a piece of software developed in a joint effort between NASA and the National Reconnaissance Office. It was originally intended to track everything orbiting the Earth in almost real time, but when they developed the software, there weren't any computers powerful enough to run it because it's believed that over a hundred seventy million objects larger than one millimeter are currently in orbit around us."

"That sounds like a wasted effort," Kodiak said. "What harm can a one-millimeter object do?"

"Imagine getting hit by a thousand BBs at twenty-five thousand miles per hour."

"Oh," he said.

"Yeah. Oh is right. That's why we care about the small particles. Anyway, what you see on the monitor now is the software adapted for modern computing power and run by an entity called the U.S. Space Surveillance Network. Their most recent estimate is around twenty thousand significant artificial objects in orbit. About five thousand of these are operational satellites."

"Why are these estimates?" Mongo asked. "Don't we know exactly how many satellites are out there?"

Skipper said, "We estimate the numbers because space junk breaks apart all the time. A large satellite may strike a hammer or wrench that NASA lost while working on the robotic arm of the Space Shuttle. It doesn't matter what hits what. The fact is that debris is created almost constantly in space. Because of that, nobody, not even the software, knows exactly how many items are twirling around out there."

Mongo nodded, and Skipper continued. "So, with all of that useless knowledge now orbiting your brains, the image on monitor number two is the tracked manmade satellites in geosynchronous orbit. Those are the ones that are dangerous for us. Because they travel at the same speed the Earth rotates, they appear to constantly remain in one spot over the surface of the Earth. Couple that characteristic with an ultra-high-definition camera and coordinated GPS positioning, and you have the ultimate spying platform."

I leaned in and scoured the graphic. "What do the colors mean?"

Skipper said, "Thank you, Chase. I'm glad somebody's been paying attention. The yellow streaks indicate that a satellite in geosynchronous orbit has changed position relative to the surface of the

Earth, and the red indicates the new position of the satellite that moved."

Mongo said, "That's a lot of position data to track and crunch. Don't those things move all the time?"

Skipper said, "Yes, they do move, depending on the particular mission of the satellite. But, the problem happens when that movement directly involves us."

"Us?" I said. "We have the ability to move a satellite?"

"Not exactly. But I think Ontrack Global Resources has that ability. I wrote a program to use the U.S. Space Surveillance Network data to pluck out any satellite that appears to follow our movement."

"When?" I asked.

She frowned. "When what?"

"When did you write this piece of software?"

"I don't know . . . like two years ago or something. But that doesn't matter. What matters is that I got a hit the day before Tony was murdered. As you might imagine, I became preoccupied the next day, and I didn't have time to check on the notification from the U triple-S N. When I finally got around to it, this is what I found."

The monitor flashed, and the thousands of satellites on the screen were reduced to only three.

Skipper said, "These three satellites made a deliberate move. Look at satellite number one. It moved from a position over Havana, Cuba, to a position just offshore of Miami, Florida."

Clark cocked his head. "Is that my house? Why would a satellite be hanging out over my house?"

Skipper said, "Keep an eye on the screen."

The image zoomed in until the southeastern tip of Florida grew larger and larger until the buildings of Miami came into clear view.

"I'm still lost," Clark said.

"Keep watching."

When she stopped zooming in, Skipper said, "Take a look at that."

Clark shrugged. "It's a ship. So what?"

"It's not just *a* ship," I said. "It's *our* ship. That's the *Lori Danielle*."

Mongo asked, "Can you determine who owns that satellite?"

Skipper held up a finger. "Don't jump ahead. We'll get to that. Take a look at where satellite number two came to rest."

She didn't have to zoom in too close before Bonaventure Plantation came into sharp focus directly beneath the satellite. A collective sigh rose from the team, and my heart sank.

"Somebody's watching us and the *Lori Danielle*," Skipper said, "and I don't like it."

Mongo repeated his question. "Who owns those satellites?"

"A French company called Singe Voir."

I shook my head. "Why would a French company be spying on us?"

Skipper said, "I haven't had time to translate most of it, but so far, it appears that the Singe Voir—whatever that means—leases their satellites to anybody who can afford the ridiculous rate of a hundred thousand dollars an hour."

Mongo tapped on the table and spoke softly as if talking to himself. "Compared to the cost of building, launching, and maintaining a satellite, that sounds like a bargain."

"It is," Skipper said, "until you consider the daily rate of two point four million."

A low whistle emanated from around the table, and I said, "That means whoever's watching us thinks it's worth tens of millions of dollars to know our every move."

Kodiak said, "Forgive me and my simple mind, but isn't the answer obvious? We simply find out who's paying for the use of the satellites, and we've nailed our bad guys?"

Skipper said, "Ordinarily, you'd be correct, but there's a catch. Singe Voir—again, whatever that means—has an option to lease and operate their satellites through a double-blind arrangement, meaning that not even the company knows who their clients are. They simply receive blind payment from some entity with no way to track the payment routing."

Kodiak said, "So, does that mean they'll lease their satellites to any-body? Even North Korea, China, Russia, Iran, Syria, etcetera?"

Skipper nodded. "That's exactly what it means."

A hush fell over the room until I asked, "Can you do historical tracks of their satellites with your software?"

"I can. Where are you going with this?"

"You remember our little game of cat and mouse with OGR in the Black Sea?"

"Of course," she said. "How could I forget?"

"Can you rewind all the way back to that day and find out where those satellites were?"

"Probably, but it'll take some time."

I said, "Add that to the top of your to-do list. Oh, and find out what Singe Voir means."

Anya said, "Singe Voir means Monkey See."

I chuckled. "That's cute. Do the French have a company named Monkey Surrender? That seems to be what they're best at for the last thousand years or so."

"Be nice," Skipper said. "The French are our allies."

I scoffed. "No, the French are allies of the United States. If they leased their spy satellites to Ontrack Global Resources to keep an eye on us, they are most definitely *not* our allies."

Skipper rolled her eyes. "Let's move on. Monitor number three is an incident scene reconstruction sketch from Tony's murder."

Those words drove a dagger through my heart. I could only imag-ine how they must've felt for our analyst, but she soldiered on.

"As you can see, Tony was exposed and took three shots to the body armor by the driver of the car. The red X's indicate where we believe he was for each shot. He returned fire and continued advancing, which is in direct opposition to the SOP for the St. Marys PD. He learned that technique from you guys."

It wasn't meant to be a jab, but her words felt like those 9mm rounds must've felt as they were hitting Tony's vest. Advancing on aggressors in our world was simply how it was done. The police take a slightly different tack.

Skipper said, "So, as you can see in this graphic, the fatal round struck Tony in the back here. The impact spun him on his right foot, but he didn't immediately go down."

She paused, and I wanted her to be absolutely anywhere on Earth other than in the op center giving that briefing.

To my astonishment, she held it together. "Based on what we know from dashcam video and eyewitness testimony, Tony stood upright and fell backward just as the second rifle round struck him in the back at nearly the same point as the first round. The medical examiner believes he was dead and falling before the second bullet struck."

Singer sighed as if wrestling with his decision whether or not to add the wisdom of a sniper to the conversation, and I wasn't the only one who noticed.

Skipper swallowed hard. "What is it, Singer? What do you see?"

He hesitated before saying, "I've got two things. The first is a question. Can you draw a reciprocal line from the point of impact of the initial shot to get an approximate azimuth for the shooter?"

Skipper hit a key, and the graphic changed. "Yes, and that's exactly what this slide shows. I believe the shooter was somewhere on this line. The shaded area represents a fan of where the shot had to have originated to leave his body where it did. Is that what you wanted to see?"

Singer nodded. "I didn't want to see it, but if we're going to accurately recreate this thing, I needed to see it. I'll get out there today and find the sniper's hide."

"What was your second thing?"

He said, "I'm just thinking like a sniper here. We've all heard the old adage about one shot, one kill, and most civilians believe that nonsense. Sometimes, though, our first shot is so good that a second one isn't necessary. That was clearly the case here. The shooter—whoever he was—made the killing shot the first time he pulled the trigger, and he would've known that based on what he saw through his scope.

That can only mean one thing . . . The second shot was meant for some purpose other than eliminating the target."

I asked, "Did the police find the second rifle round?"

Skipper said, "Yes, they did, and here's a picture of it when they found it." She brought up another slide showing a close-up of a shiny silver bullet in nearly perfect condition, just like the second round from Hilton Head.

The dagger that was already in my heart just got twisted.

Skipper said, "All four of the bullets—two from here, and the two from Jimmy Fairmont's murder—are at the FBI ballistics lab in Virginia. We're hoping for some word from the lab in the next twenty-four hours."

Dominic and Clark reached for their phones simultaneously, but Skipper stopped them. "There's no need to call them. I've been on the phone with them every six hours since the Board gave me authorization to work directly with them. They'll have something for us soon."

Mongo pointed toward the screens. "I guess the fourth monitor is the same kind of re-creation graphic as Tony's."

Skipper nodded. "It is, but we've got a lot less data on that one. There was one eyewitness and one security camera that didn't have very good quality video. Everything else we have is forensic and inconclusive."

"Wait a minute," I said. "There was an eyewitness?"

Skipper flipped through a stack of notes. "Uh, yeah . . . One eyewitness, but he was the same guy who called nine-one-one. Just like most rational people, he ran *away* from the gunfire and wasn't there to see the second shot made from point-blank range."

Singer said, "If it's all right with Chase, I'd like to take Gator and walk both scenes. There's a lot we can learn from seeing the spots in person."

"Do it," I said. "We'll reconvene as soon as we get ballistics information from the lab." I turned to Skipper. "Are you staying in the op center?"

"No . . . I could use a little rest. I haven't slept much, and this was harder than I expected."

Ginger slid from her seat and planted herself on the custom chair she brought with her from Silver Spring, Maryland. "Don't you worry, girl. I've got this. You go get some sleep, and I'll wake you up as soon as we hear from the lab."

Skipper stood. "Thank you. I'll be back in a couple of hours."

Before she made it to the door, the phone rang, and Ginger hit the speaker button. "Op center."

A disembodied voice said, "This is Cam with the security detail. Somebody broke into the church and started a fire an hour after the hearse left. The cops and fire department are en route. I thought you should know."

Chapter 7

Fools Rush In

We slid into the church parking lot four minutes later, and Singer leapt from the front seat of the Suburban as if he'd been fired from a cannon. Black smoke billowed from orange flames as they danced like demons on the scorching air above the church.

A police officer shouted at Singer as he sprinted toward the front door of the church. "Stop! Hey, stop! You can't go in there!"

The sniper yanked his T-shirt over his mouth and nose and kicked open the ancient oak doors of the church he loved so dearly. The cop chased him but faltered before reaching the steps, forced back by the immense heat and blinding smoke.

The incident commander—the local fire chief—watched Singer run into the fully involved inferno and ordered two kitted-out firefighters into the raging blaze behind him. "Keep him wet!"

The helmeted pair grabbed a hose and gave chase. I had no doubt why Singer risked his life. He'd done the same thing when someone burned the original Bonaventure house to the ground. That day, he'd saved my family Bible that had passed through the hands of my mother's family for generations. When he emerged from that unearthly hell, he was burned so badly I couldn't recognize him, and I prayed he'd escape from the remains of his flaming church in better condition than he had last time.

I ran to the fire chief and yelled, "Give me an air pack!"

Everything inside me ached to follow the firefighters through those doors, but the fire chief clamped his hands around my arm. "No, Chase! My men might be able to keep one fool alive in there, but not two."

I paced back and forth, yelling like a madman into the blaze, beseeching my friend, my brother, to escape the torrent.

The chief put four more firefighters on the front door, pouring a wall of water into the orange and black gates that should've been where the faithful passed to see Heaven, but on that day, nothing lay beyond those doors other than a roaring hell that would likely consume any mortal flesh that dared trespass.

As I grew consumed by the thought of losing another brother on the same day we'd said goodbye to Tony, my soul wept, and my heart shattered inside my chest.

Just when I believed I'd never hear Singer's voice again, the water falling where the doors had once stood parted as if by the hand of some unseen force, and two firemen emerged, dragging what had to be a corpse behind them. They descended the stone steps that had been laid before the American Civil War could've been imagined. Singer's heels bounced down every step as the two men continued hauling their burden across the grass, finally depositing him beneath the shade of a massive oak dripping with Spanish moss.

I sprinted across the lawn as a paramedic landed on his knees beside the sniper an instant after his body hit the ground. He immediately went to work assessing Singer's injuries. The paramedic stretched an elastic band across Singer's head and situated an oxygen mask over his mouth and nose. That single act washed over me, allaying my horrible fears. Dead men don't need oxygen masks.

I slid to a stop and hit the ground like a sack of stones beside him and couldn't believe my eyes. Singer was clearly unconscious, but his chest was rising and falling in measured cycles, and wrapped in his arms was an airtight glass case, blackened and battered, but the container clearly had not lost its seal. It held fast and kept the smoke and flames at bay, not penetrating the interior and contaminating what could've been one of the oldest surviving copies of the King James Bible in existence.

Singer's eyelids fluttered and slowly opened. He stared up at me and then down at the case on his chest. With one hand, he lifted the oxygen mask from his face. "I guess I'm still alive because you sure ain't no angel."

I pulled the case from his chest and held it tightly on my lap. "You lied to me, you old scoundrel."

"Yeah, I know. I kept thinking about that the whole time I was in there. I know I said I wouldn't run into another fire to save another Bible, but I just couldn't let it burn. You'll forgive me, won't you?"

I took the mask from his hand and placed it back over his mouth and nose. "This time, but don't let it happen again."

Mongo stepped into the shade beside the paramedic who was still assessing Singer's injuries. "We've got it from here, Doc. Thanks."

The paramedic looked up at the giant looming above him. "We need to get this man to the hospital. He needs to be treated for smoke inhalation, at least."

Mongo reached down, took Singer's hand, and hauled him to his feet.

Singer shucked off the mask and patted the paramedic on the shoulder. "Thank you for checking on me, but it looks like I'm mostly fireproof. Who pulled me out of there?"

The medic pointed toward a pair of firemen pulling off their jackets beside the pump truck. "It was those two."

Singer's first several steps looked like those of a gentleman who may have imbibed a bit too long before staggering out of the tavern, but by the time he got to the truck, he gathered himself, and his confident gait returned.

Gator, the youngest and newest member of the family team, galloped up. "What was that all about? Why would he run inside a burning building? Please tell me it's not a sniper thing because I don't see myself ever taking that leap."

I held up the glass case. "No, it's not a sniper thing. It's a Singer thing. The first private contract we ever had paid far better than our typical work."

Gator scoffed. "Better than what we make now? You've got to be joking. You paid me over half a million bucks last year."

I gave him one of Clark's crooked smiles. "A half a million bucks wouldn't pay the taxes on the private gig we worked in the Gulf of Mexico. It turned into a human trafficking ring, but when we were hired, the CEO of the oil company believed it was ecoterrorists holding one of his oil rigs for ransom."

"That sounds like a job for the SEALs."

"They probably could've mopped it up faster and cleaner than we did, but unfortunately for the oil company, the SEALs aren't for hire. We were."

"How often does that kind of job come along?"

"Not often enough," I said. "Our daily rate isn't exactly negotiable." I held up the case again. "Anyway, when we got paid, Singer bought this."

Gator examined the filthy briefcase-sized container. "What is it?"

"It's a Kings James Bible."

He furrowed his brow. "Singer ran into a burning building to save a Bible?"

"Not just *a* Bible," I said. "*This* Bible. It was printed in sixteen twenty-nine, on the same press they used to print the very first copy in sixteen eleven."

He leaned toward the case, peering inside. "That thing's four hundred years old?"

"Indeed, it is."

Our history lesson came to an abrupt end when Hunter showed up. "It's got to be connected, right?"

I said, "Yeah, whoever's doing this is determined to hit us where it hurts the most. They thought they could shut us down by taking Skipper out of the game with Tony's murder."

Hunter said, "They probably thought the same when they dropped your patient."

"That's the one that doesn't make sense to me. Anybody who knows me would expect me to come out swinging. Killing my patient doesn't shut me down. It spools me up."

"Maybe that's what they want," he said. "Maybe they think getting you mad will make you sloppy and easier to kill."

Mongo said, "I think there's something we're missing. If whoever these guys are really want to get to us, they'll start taking shots at Penny, Irina, and Maebelle. I think we have to get them someplace safe, and I think we need to do it quickly."

Hunter nodded. "He's right."

"I agree," I said. "But first, have you guys heard anything about what started the fire?"

Hunter pointed toward the roof. "It's burning on both ends, but not in the middle. There's only one recipe that cooks that dish. It's the hallmark of a rookie fire starter."

"Not rookies," I said. "Somebody who wanted us to know it was arson as soon as we saw the fire. We're playing with pros on this one, and so far, we're losing every time they deal the cards."

Mongo said, "Maybe it's time for us to do a little dealing of our own."

I pointed toward a black sedan pulling into the parking lot of the church. "Isn't that the pastor?"

Hunter said, "Yeah, I think so."

I headed for the car. "Round everybody up and head back to Bonaventure. I'll be there in ten minutes."

I met Pastor Lincoln Talmage as he stepped from his car, wiping his brow with a perfectly pressed white handkerchief. He shook my outstretched hand, but he couldn't take his eyes off what had been his church for over sixty years. "My God, Chase. What happened?"

"It looks like arson, Pastor. Don't worry. Whatever it costs to rebuild, I'll write the check."

"Son, you can't make promises like that. We're looking at hundreds of thousands of dollars. Was anybody inside?"

"No, sir. The church was empty, but Singer ran in and saved the Bible."

Pastor Talmage wiped a tear from his eye. "Of course he did. Is he all right?"

I pointed my chin toward the firetruck. "He's fine. Just a little singed around the edges."

When Singer saw the pastor, he jogged to join us. "Lincoln, look what they've done to your church."

"I see it, son. I see it, but I don't believe it. Who would do something like this?"

Singer said, "We don't know yet, but we're going to find out. Don't you worry 'bout the church, though. We'll have it all cleaned up and rebuilt before you know it, and I'll take care of everything."

The elderly pastor fell into Singer's arms. "Your friend already made the same offer. I can't tell you what a blessing all of you have been to us, but this . . . this burning a black church in St. Marys . . . Nobody could've seen this coming."

Singer held his friend and spiritual mentor. "This isn't a racially motivated attack, Lincoln. It's something directed at Chase and me, but we'll get to the bottom of it, and everything will be all right."

Chapter 8
First Impressions

"Chasechka, I have maybe person who started fire at church."

Anya's unmistakable Russian-accented voice echoed through my head.

"You caught him? How? Where?"

"People who make fire usually want to watch it burn. You are psychology doctor. You should know this."

"Yeah, Anya, I know. Where are you?"

"I am between cemetery and water in what is maybe park, but not very good park. You know this place, yes?"

"Yeah, I know the place. Is the guy alive?"

"Do not be silly," she said. "Of course he is alive. I will wait until he tells us everything he knows before I kill him."

"We're on our way. Please tell me you're not out in the open."

"I am inside car with person who made fire. I have him handcuffed, tied, and gagged. This is what you would want, yes?"

"Bring him to the airport," I said. "We'll wait for you just inside the gate, and you can follow us to a hangar, where we can have some privacy."

She sounded muted, as if she'd moved the phone away from her mouth. "You hear this, yes? You are receiving very special treatment in private place so no one can hear you scream. You will like this place. Or maybe, on thinking second thinking, you maybe will not like it as much as I do." Her voice grew clearer and louder. "I will be there in seven or maybe six minutes. I do not want police to stop me for speeding. This would be difficult to explain."

I hung up and stomped the accelerator. Singer was in the passenger seat, and Gator was hanging on for dear life in the back. I thumbed the remote as we approached the gate, and the heavy metallic barricade retracted, allowing us entry into our private world, where only a select few were ever invited inside.

Anya pulled behind us as we rolled through the opening, and I gave her room to move inside the gate before closing it behind her. With the barricade back in place, things were on the verge of getting very uncomfortable for one firebug.

I made the sat-com call to the rest of the team, and they were there in minutes. I entered the access code to the hangar door, and the behemoth rose with a crescendo of cracks and pops as the framework endured the stress of movement. When the door was just high enough for the Suburban to pass beneath it, everyone pulled inside, and we closed the door behind us.

Mongo stepped from his vehicle. "Let me get him out. You know what they say—whoever *they* are—you never get a second chance to make a first impression."

Our jolly giant heaved open the back door of Anya's SUV and grabbed the trembling man by one foot. A massive yank brought the man sailing from the back seat and thudding to the concrete floor. Mongo leapt on top of his chest, pinning his arms to the cold floor.

I'd never had Mongo looming over me like that, but I could only imagine the first impression it must've made.

The big man drew his pistol from beneath his shirt and pressed the muzzle to the man's forehead. "If you move just one inch, the last fire you will ever see will be my muzzle flash. Run his prints!"

Hunter pulled out his phone and hit the floor. He pressed each of the man's fingers to his phone screen in quick succession and said, "It'll take ten minutes or so, but we'll know everything there is to know about this guy."

THE SCORPION'S CHASE · 61

Mongo grunted. "Ten minutes? This little piece of crap won't be alive in ten minutes if he doesn't talk." He ripped the gag from our prisoner's mouth. "Listen very closely. Lie once, and I pull the trigger. Hesitate once, and I pull the trigger. Try to escape just once . . ."

The guy mumbled. "Yeah, I get it. You'll pull the trigger."

Mongo smiled. "Oh, we've got ourselves a smart one here. But no, you're wrong. I love it when people try to escape. I get to holster my Glock and tear you apart with my hands. Sound like fun?"

"What do you want, man? I didn't start that fire. I was just watching."

"Oh my," Mongo said. "I think that might've been a lie. That means I pull the trigger."

"No! No! Please! I swear I didn't do it. I'm a fire starter, yeah. You'll see that on my record. I did nine years for it, but I didn't start that one."

"Imagine that," Mongo said. "A convicted arsonist who swears he's innocent. Who paid you to burn the church?"

"Nobody, I swear!"

"So you did it on your own? Is that it?"

"No, man. I told you I didn't start it. It was a rookie job, and I ain't no rookie. I would've started it where the electricity comes into the church from the pole. That's how you do it, man. I swear. The guys who did the church—"

"Guys?" Mongo said. "You saw them?"

"Yeah . . . Well, I mean, I seen 'em a little bit, but I didn't get no good look at 'em or nothing. I just know there was two of 'em."

"What's your name, Mr. Innocent?"

"Cal . . . Calvin Lynard. You'll see. That's what'll come back on my prints."

"All right, Calvin Lynard. Let's start from the beginning. What were you doing at the church?"

"I was just sittin' in the woods, you know? I like to look at the stained glass. I swear. That's all."

Mongo pulled the muzzle from Calvin's forehead and jerked him into the air. When he came down, he landed on the hard metal chair I'd placed beside him while the big guy was playing twenty questions.

When his body stopped moving, the man asked, "What kind of cops are you guys? I ain't seen no badges or blue lights or nothing. And that chick who arrested me wasn't speakin' American."

I took a knee in front of him. "You want to see our badges, Calvin? Do you think you have the right to remain silent and a lawyer and all that? Is that what you're thinking, Calvin Lynard?"

While Mongo's size was one of the world's greatest intimidation factors, I've learned that calm, persistent questioning can be even more frightening than the fear of being torn to pieces by the biggest human a person has ever seen. That's the tack I chose—at least for the introduction phase of our little chat.

"Yeah, I'd kinda like to maybe see a badge, and maybe, you know, get my rights."

"Rights?" I said. "You think you have rights? Interesting. Let me tell you about your rights, Mr. Lynard. You have the right to maybe walk out of here alive if you answer my questions. You have the right for that big guy to tear off your arms and beat you to death with them if you lie to me. You have the right to a Christian funeral. If you cannot afford a funeral, one will be provided for you about a hundred miles offshore, where you can play with the sharks before they turn you into chum. Do you understand these rights as I've explained them to you, Calvin Lynard?"

"Hey, man. I know you. You're that guy who lives in that big house on the water that used to be a plantation or something."

I spoke even more softly. "Right now, Calvin, I'm the guy who's keeping you out of Mongo's hands. If you don't want to talk to me, I'll be happy to step aside and let him ask the questions. It's up to you."

"I'm tellin' you the truth, man. I swear. I didn't start no fire."

"Let's back up a little," I said. "Where do you live, Cal?"

He dropped his head and stared at the hangar floor. "I ain't got no place to live. I stay down there in the black cemetery most nights. Sometimes, if there ain't nobody around, I'll sleep on one of them benches under the pavilion on the river, but the cops run us outta there most of the time. I guess they don't want nobody knowin' there's homeless people in this town."

"All right. So, tell me about the stained-glass window in the church. You said you like to look at it sometimes, so make me believe you."

"It's Jesus, man. Ain't you never seen it? It's Jesus and seven little children. You can't see the children's faces 'cause they're looking at Him. You can see His face and His hands. They ain't no scars in His hands yet 'cause that was supposed to be 'fore they crucified Him. It ain't got no words in it, but I always thought it should say that thing from the Bible. You know, suffering the little children to come to Me, or something like that."

I glanced up at Singer, and he nodded, so I said, "I believe you know the stained-glass scene, but I'm still not sure I'm buying your story about just watching."

"Why would I set that church on fire, man? And I told you already, it was them two other guys I ain't never seen. They started it at both ends. The cops knowed it was arson the second they laid eyes on it. I may be an ex-con who ain't got no bed to sleep in, but I ain't stupid enough to start no fire like that. Besides, that's a church, man. You don't go burnin' no churches. I ain't a good person, but I don't want to have to answer for nothin' like burnin' no church when I die."

I stared directly into his eyes. "If I uncuff your hands, are you going to do anything stupid?"

He looked around the hangar. "Are you kiddin' me? What kind of idiot would try to do anything? You people are crazy. Wait a minute. I didn't mean that no kinda way. I just meant that I ain't stupid enough to try nothing."

I pulled my key from a pocket and took off the cuffs. Anya caught them when I tossed them toward her, and Calvin rubbed his wrists as if he'd been bound for ages.

He looked up. "Thank you."

Glancing down at his ankles, he wordlessly asked for one more gesture of freedom, but I said, "We'll get to your feet if you keep talking and telling the truth. None of us wants to chase you if you decide to jump up and run."

"I ain't got no reason to lie to you. I didn't do nothing wrong. I'm telling you it was them two guys."

"Okay, let's pretend that I believe you. Tell me about the two guys. What were they driving?"

He sighed. "I didn't see no car. I just seen 'em walk up, but not together. One of 'em came from downtown. He was the one that broke out the window and throwed something in there. He run back the way he come, and that's when I seen the other one try to kick the doors open. Either he didn't know how to do it, or the doors was just too strong, but he ended up breaking out a window, just like his buddy. I seen what he throwed in there. It was one of them incendiary grenades like soldiers got. You know what I'm talking about?"

"Yes, Cal, I know what an incendiary grenade is. Do you think that's what the first guy used, too?"

"I don't know. I couldn't see him real good. It might've been one of them, but I can't say for sure. They wasn't no bang, though. I thought them things made a bang before they set somethin' on fire."

"So, this second guy who tried to kick in the doors . . . Where did he come from?"

"He come straight across the street like he'd been waitin' for his buddy to come up the road or something. They was definitely in cahoots. I mean, what would be the chances of two people trying to burn down the same church at the same time if they wasn't in cahoots?"

"Did you see them leave?"

"Yeah, I seen 'em. They run right back the same way they come.

They never said nothing to each other or even looked at each other. They just did it and run."

"And you stayed right there and watched the whole thing?"

He looked away. "I can't help it, man. There's something about a fire that just draws me in. You know how some people like to watch the sunset or whatever? It's the same thing for me. I know they's somethin' wrong with me, but I can't help it."

"I believe you, Cal, but I need to know one more thing. Why did you run? If watching a fire is so alluring to you, what made you run?"

"It wasn't no policemen or no firemen. All of them were too busy looking at the fire. None of 'em were looking for me or nobody else until you people showed up. I seen a bunch of you guys looking away from the fire, and it freaked me out, so I run."

"I get it," I said, "but why didn't you come forward and tell the police what you saw?"

He laughed as if he'd never heard anything funnier. "Are you crazy, man? Think about a homeless guy already been to prison once for settin' fires, comin' out of the woods and telling a story like I just told you. Man, I'd be back inside, and the case would be closed. They wouldn't even look for nobody else."

Every few seconds, he shot a quick glance at Anya and then looked back at me. When he discovered I'd noticed, he whispered. "Can I ask you somethin', man? Where'd she come from? She ain't no American. I know that much."

I glanced over my shoulder at the deadliest woman I've ever known and then back at Calvin. "Who?"

"That woman right there. The one who tied me up and brung me up here."

I looked back at the Russian again and said, "Calvin, you must be seeing things. There's no woman here. I picked you up by the cemetery and brought you here. What kind of drugs are you on?"

He recoiled and then squinted toward Anya, who stood perfectly still as if she were a statue. "Aww, man. You're messin' with me. She's right there."

"Those drugs, Calvin. What are they? What are you on?"

He couldn't take his eyes off Anya. "I ain't on no drugs right now. Sometimes, when I can get 'em, I might smoke some weed or something, but I ain't had nothin' in a long time."

I nodded and waited a long, uncomfortable moment before he said, "I'm tellin' the truth, man. I ain't had nothing in weeks. I'm clean, man."

"Describe the two men."

He shook his head. "I wish I could. I swear I'd tell you if I could, but I didn't get a good look at either one of 'em, and besides, my eyes ain't so good. I broke my glasses a long time back, and, well, I guess you can figure I ain't got no money for new ones."

As if they could read my mind, Hunter, Kodiak, and Gator stood side by side between Calvin and Anya.

I motioned toward them. "Maybe you can't describe the two men, but how tall were they? Think about the first man who came up the street, and point to the person who's closest to his size."

He pointed at Gator. "The first guy was about his height, but he wasn't skinny like him. He was maybe two hundred pounds. He had on long sleeves and a hat."

"That's good, Calvin. Now, what about the other guy?"

"He was shorter, like that one." He pointed at Hunter. "In fact, he was about his size altogether."

"I have just one more question, Calvin, and this one's important."

"I ain't lied to you yet, and I ain't gonna start now. Are you gonna kill me after this last question?"

"I'm not going to kill you, Calvin. I believe you, but I can't speak for these other guys or that make-believe woman you thought you saw."

"She's standin' right . . ." He pointed directly at the spot where Anya had been standing before my teammates blocked his view. "Wait a minute. Where'd she go?"

"You've gotta stay off the drugs, Calvin. Here's my last question, and all of this will be over."

He leaned in as if hanging on my every word, and I said, "Are you hungry?"

He screwed up his face and leaned back. "What?"

"I asked if you were hungry. It's a simple question, Calvin. Are you hungry or not?"

"Yeah, I'm hungry. To tell you the truth, I don't really remember last time I had anything to eat."

I leaned in closer. "That guy in the stained-glass window, He taught us that we're supposed to feed the hungry, so that's what I'm going to do. I'm going to check you into the hotel out on the highway. I'll bring you food and clean clothes. You can shower and sleep in a real bed. I might have more questions, so if you'll stay in the room I rent for you and don't leave, I'll keep bringing you food until I don't need you anymore. How does that sound?"

He cocked his head. "It sounds too good to be true. Why would you do that for me?"

"I'm not doing it for you. I'm doing it because I may need you again. That makes you important to me, Calvin, and I take care of people who are important to me. Do you understand?"

"No, man, I don't understand, but if you're gonna feed me and let me sleep in a real bed, I don't have to understand." He glanced at Hunter and grimaced. "I guess I gotta tell you something else. You're gonna find out when my prints come back anyway. I did twenty-two months for almost beatin' a guy to death. He was hurtin' little kids, and I seen him doin' it. You would've done it, too, if you'da seen it. That makes me a two-time con. If I go down again, I ain't never gettin' out, so I ain't gettin' in no more trouble. You can take that to the bank. That's the real reason I didn't run and tell the cops what I seen."

"Thank you for being honest, Calvin. Nobody's going to hurt you. Just make sure you stay in that hotel room. If I knock on the door, and you're not there, the deal's off, and I won't have any choice but to send the cops looking for you. Got it?"

"Yeah, I got it. I guess I should thank you for not lettin' that big guy kill me."

"You're welcome. Now, just keep your nose clean, and stay in that room."

I stood and turned to Gator and Kodiak. "Get him set up in the hotel and feed him. Get him some clean clothes, and pick up a couple over-the-counter drug tests. Let's see if we can get this guy off the streets. I get the feeling he just needs a break."

Chapter 9
Face-to-Face

Back in the op center, Anya pulled me aside and whispered, "My Chasechka, I am sorry I did not capture men who started fire. It was mistake to take this man, Calvin Lynard."

"No, don't apologize. Lynard was a great catch. I'm not certain how we're going to use his information yet, but I think he'll be an invaluable asset for local street knowledge. People who live like him are practically invisible in society, but they see everything. That kind of knowledge and information is priceless. You did the right thing, and you have no reason to apologize."

She softened her expression. "I am pleased you are not angry with me."

"Of course I'm not angry. You're an enormous asset to the team. When I first called you on this thing . . . Well, actually, it wasn't me who called. Skipper did the dialing, but it was Penny who insisted that I warn you about what's going on. I wasn't calling to ask for your help, but I'm glad you're here. Your training is unique compared to ours, and you have skills most of us will never have. So, like I said, I'm glad you're here."

She cocked her head and looked up at me the way she did aboard my boat an eternity before that moment. Something about the look in her eyes spoke a thousand volumes about what she wanted, and perhaps needed, from me. In that moment, though, I wouldn't—and couldn't —see her the way I'd seen her under the Caribbean sky so long ago.

The memory of that unforgettable moment washed over me, and the words she whispered that night would forever be a melody my mind couldn't erase. "We should kiss."

The night we met face-to-face for the first time, I'd never agreed with any statement more, but countless decisions and fifteen years later, I'd come to know that kissing was exactly the opposite of what we should do.

Without another word, I returned to the conference table and tried to wash the moment with Anya from my mind. The decisions we were about to make would change our lives forever, and allowing her to shape my judgment would be a costly mistake that I wouldn't allow myself to make.

I cleared my throat. "I know we usually start these things with updates from Skipper, but we're taking a different approach this time. She's still resting, but we've got Ginger. First, did you get Calvin tucked away?"

Kodiak said, "Yeah, me and Gator got him a first-floor room at the end, and we bugged the lamp and door so we'll know when he comes and goes. You're not really expecting him to stay in that room twenty-four seven, are you?"

"No, he'll sneak out and try to score some dope, but if we can keep him clean and fed, I think he'll prove to be an asset. Thanks for taking care of that."

I turned my attention to Ginger. "How about updates from the ballistics lab?"

She said, "Nothing yet, but I'll rattle their cage as soon as we finish here."

I closed my eyes and drummed my fingertips on the table for a moment as I formulated the words to express my plan. When I opened my eyes, every face in the room was staring back at me in anticipation of what was to come.

I said, "We're playing defense, and I don't like it. That has to stop. Does anybody disagree?"

Although my team would never be a democracy, knowing what was going on in the heads of my warriors was paramount in my decision-making.

It was Hunter who spoke up first. "I disagree. I don't think we're playing anything. We're just watching bad stuff happen to us. But I agree that it has to stop."

Heads nodded, and Mongo said, "Hunter's right. We've got to do something. Otherwise, we're sitting ducks waiting to be hit again."

I looked across the room to Ginger sitting at the analyst's console. "Who's the CEO of Ontrack Global Resources?"

Ginger's fingers didn't possess the speed of Skipper's, but she had the large monitor glowing in seconds. "This is the guy. His name is Roger Dean. His pedigree isn't bad. Rutgers undergrad in geopolitical studies, master's degree in communication technology from MIT, and Harvard Law, so he's no dummy. He worked his way through middle and upper management in European telecommunication companies." She paused, frowned, and seemed to disappear into her computer.

"What is it?" I asked.

She grumbled and said, "There's a strange outlier in his professional career. Before going to work for OGR, he did almost four years with Switzerland's second-largest bank, Credit Suisse, as vice president of international security."

"What does that mean?" Mongo asked.

Ginger said, "I don't know, but it sounds impressive. Apparently, Ontrack Global Resources snagged him up with a salary he couldn't resist, but his résumé isn't impressive enough to qualify him for the top seat at OGR."

Mongo leaned back and scratched his chin. "Do you have a way to find out who provided operational financing for OGR?"

Ginger shrugged. "Maybe. Give me a minute."

Precisely one minute later, she sighed. "Wouldn't you know it? Ontrack Global Resources has on open line of credit for two point five billion—that's billion with a B—from none other than Credit Suisse."

"Where's his office?" I asked.

"It's in Zurich at OGR headquarters," Ginger said.

I twirled a pen between my fingers. "It's time to find out if Skipper really learned everything she knows from you. Can you find Roger Dean's calendar for the week?"

Ginger let out a low whistle. "That's a tough one. Give me a little time, but I'm sure I can find it."

She dived into her keyboard at the same instant Clark's phone made a noise I'd never heard. He pulled it from his pocket and had a moment of private celebration with a hearty "Oh yeah!" and a fist pump.

"What's that about?" I asked.

"There's a nasty storm building in the Gulf, and it's headed straight up the Keys."

"And you're celebrating?"

"You bet I am, College Boy. What always comes with storms?"

I ran through the list in my head, but thunder, lightning, wind, and rain didn't give me any reason to celebrate.

"Got it yet?" he asked. I shook my head, and he said, "Cloud cover. Satellites can't see through cloud cover."

I joined him in celebration and snagged my sat-phone. A few seconds later, Captain Barry Sprayberry aboard our ship, the Research Vessel *Lori Danielle,* answered the line. "Bridge, Captain."

"Barry, it's Chase. Are you tracking the coming storm?"

"The literal storm charging up the Keys or the crap storm you're about to unleash on somebody?"

I chuckled. "Both, I suppose."

He asked, "Where do you want me?"

I said, "I want you to get lost as soon as you have adequate cloud cover to run."

"Any particular direction?"

"Open ocean would be my preference," I said. "I don't want you trapped against a coastline."

He said, "There's another low-pressure system churning near Bermuda. If this storm will ask that one to dance, I could put a thousand miles in our wake without anybody knowing where we went."

"That sounds perfect to me, plus it gives us a rendezvous point if we need to come aboard."

"We'll make ready and pour on the coal as soon as the satellite goes blind."

When he said the word *satellite*, I felt like I'd been hit by an electric cattle prod. "Ginger. Stop what you're doing, and tell me where the third French satellite is parked."

Her fingers froze above the keyboard, and she spun around to face me. "What?"

"The third satellite," I said. "Skipper told us there were three satellites that had repositioned. She told us about the one over us and the one over the ship off the coast of Miami, but she didn't say where the third one went."

Ginger grabbed the mouse and scrolled through several pages of electronic notes. "I'm looking . . . I'm looking . . ."

Clark palmed his forehead. "Why didn't we ask that question during the briefing?"

I said, "I don't know. I can't believe none of us thought about it, especially Skipper."

Ginger looked up. "Give the girl a break. She's had a tough week."

"I wasn't blaming her," I said. "It just proves the point that we're all a little off our game. Losing Tony and Singer's church is enough to send all of us down the tubes, so let's make a conscious effort to keep our heads in the game and hold everybody accountable."

Ginger shouted. "Got it!"

I asked, "Dean's calendar or the third satellite's position?"

"Both," she said. "Which one do you want first?"

"The satellite."

"The first two satellites are still in geosynchronous orbit over St.

Marys and forty-five miles offshore of Miami. The third one returned to its original position before the reassignment. That probably means it was a contingency bird in case either of the other two satellites failed to position themselves correctly. Nothing holds still in space. Everything orbits something, so it's not always possible to position a satellite exactly where you want it."

"That's good news," I said.

Pressing the phone back to my ear, I asked, "Are you still there, Barry?"

"Yeah, I'm here. What's going on up there? It sounds like a circus."

"That's a pretty good word for it. I don't have time to brief you fully, but we're getting hit from every angle, and it's time to strike back. It may become necessary for you to get involved at some point, but for now, try to stay out of sight."

"Wilco," he said. "Keep your head down and your powder dry. I'm here if you need me."

I ended the call and said, "Let's see Dean's calendar."

Ginger sent a list of bullet points to the large monitor. "Technically, it's not his calendar, but it's a list of travel dates. That's really what you were looking for, right?"

"That's exactly what I wanted."

She said, "It looks like he returned to Zurich from Rome two days ago, and he doesn't leave Switzerland again for six more days when he's headed to St. Petersburg."

"Russia or Florida?"

Ginger tapped her fingernails against the console. "It doesn't say, but it's a quick turn either way. He's scheduled to hit Paris the next day and back to Zurich that night."

"When was the last time he was in the U.S.?"

She worked for a moment and then said, "Hmm. His passport records aren't synching with his prior travel itinerary."

"Neither do mine," I said. "That probably means he's got more than one passport."

"I'm sure you're right. I'm running a cross-referencing program to try and piece together who he's pretending to be."

"I'm not sure that matters to us right now. What I want to know for certain is where he'll be for the next forty-eight hours."

"According to the itinerary, he'll be at home in Zurich for the next several days."

Disco and I locked eyes, and he gave me a confident nod.

I knocked twice on the table. "Gentlemen . . . and lady . . . it's time for a face-to-face with Mr. Roger Dean."

Mongo's eyes seemed to be the only ones not focused on me.

I said, "What's on your mind, big man?"

"I don't like the idea of the whole team running off and leaving Penny, Irina, and Maebelle here under the protection of a bunch of guys we don't know. I'd feel a lot better if we could get them tucked away somewhere nice and quiet before we head off to kick in Dean's door."

"I'm already on it," I said. "I've got a plan."

Chapter 10
The Shell Game

General Patton is credited with saying, "A good plan executed violently now is better than a perfect plan executed next week."

My plan was far from perfect, but I was determined to execute it as aggressively as possible. If it went well, violence would not be required. Much like General Patton, though, should violence become a necessity, I possessed not only the willingness, but also the capability of delivering that violence with extreme prejudice, leaving scorched earth in my wake.

No one, be it a Zurich-based, Harvard-educated billionaire, or a homeless firebug in a rented motel room, was going to put my wife in harm's way without feeling my blade pierce his flesh.

When night fell, four identical black Chevrolet Suburbans pulled beneath the portico covering the front door at Bonaventure. They proceeded one after the other, each driven by one of the team members sent to provide physical security for us. When the third Suburban came to a stop, Penny, Irina, and Maebelle slid into the back, and the fourth SUV took its place. Vehicles one, two, and four each carried one of the women's cell phones. If our foe possessed the wherewithal to summon satellites at will, tracking a cell phone would be child's play for him, but taking every caution to safeguard the people we loved was absolutely essential.

When the Suburbans left the long, tree-lined drive of Bonaventure, and the small, Southern town of St. Marys, Georgia, they scattered to the four winds as they played the ultimate high-stakes shell game with the lives of three of the most important people on Earth in the minds of Clark, Mongo, and me. If the ruse worked, they would be practically untouchable.

With the plan in motion, I called the remainder of the security team into the op center after collecting each of their cell phones and depositing them in the lead-lined container outside the entry doors.

"Gentlemen, first, let me tell you how much it means to every one of us that you'd sacrifice precious time with your families to come down here to keep us alive while we work through the chaos of whatever this is."

"We're not volunteers," someone said. "You're paying us well."

I chuckled. "Probably not well enough, but maybe next time you'll negotiate a little better." That got a chortle, and I said, "Seriously, though, we thank you. If we pull off the crazy plan with the SUVs, the drivers will be back in a couple of days to rejoin your team. Meanwhile, the tactical team and I will be flying to Mexico City to follow up on a lead that gives us reason to believe the true origin of the threat resides in that country. We'll be back in a few days, but while we're gone, I'm leaving two world-class intelligence analysts and a former foreign national, who's now part of our organization, in your capable hands. These three women are now your charges. Don't fail them, and don't fail yourselves."

"Don't worry, Chase. You're leaving them in good hands." The voice came from the back of the room, but it carried the weight of experience, confidence, and competence.

I continued. "If there's a piece of equipment you need to make your job easier or our teammates safer, ask for it. You've all met Skipper. She has full access to our arsenal of equipment, and she can put anything you need in your hands in minutes, if not seconds. If you need it and don't have it, it's because you haven't asked for it." Heads nodded, and I said, "I heard a rumor you guys have a squid in your midst. Is that true?"

A guy about Hunter's height, but who looked like he could bench press a school bus, leaned around the man in front of him and made eye contact with me. He didn't have to speak. The quiet confidence in his gaze said everything I needed to hear.

I said, "Special Boat Team, right?" He nodded once, and I said, "We've got a Mark V Patrol Boat in the boathouse, and Skipper has the keys. If you ask nicely, she'll probably let you take it for a spin."

Surprising a SEAL is a rare accomplishment, but I had done it, and in doing so, I'd earned a modicum of respect in the warrior's eyes.

On our way down the stairs, Gator elbowed me. "Mexico City?"

I pulled him into the library and closed the door behind us. "Have you ever heard the saying 'trust but verify'?"

He said, "Sure. Reagan said it, right?"

"That's right. I trust the guys pulling security for us, but there's no reason to tempt them with information that might have a high monetary value for the people who are after us. If they think we're going to Mexico, and they sell that information to somebody, then we're not in any danger. A little misdirection goes a long way in a global game of hide and seek."

* * *

Six hours later, still in the predawn darkness, we reconvened at the airport, where Disco had the Gulfstream IV *Grey Ghost* fueled, pre-flighted, and ready to soar. I took my seat on the right side of the cockpit, where the inferior pilot belongs. To my left sat a man with a lifetime of aviation experience, and from whom I'd learned more about flying everything with wings and rotors than any other flight instructor in my life. He was a combat pilot with no equal during his days in uniform as an Air Force A-10 driver, and in his time as the chief pilot for my team of covert operatives, I'd seen him coax aircraft of every flavor into doing things they were never designed to do and accomplishing what lesser pilots would declare impossible. I had the same confidence in the cockpit with Disco as I had in Singer when a two-thousand-yard shot had to be made, in Clark when a building full of killers had to be cleared, in Mongo when a tree had to be ripped from the earth, and in Skipper when buried information had to be excavated. I was surrounded in every direction by professionals of unrivaled skill, character, and devotion to duty. With my team, I would demolish any foe and vanquish any opposition, and in that moment, Ontrack Global Resources and Roger Dean were squarely in my sights and destined for defeat.

Our plan was simple, but execution of that plan was not. Getting lost in the U.S. National Airspace System should've been impossible. The core purpose of the system is to keep track of thousands upon thousands of military, civil, and commercial aircraft simultaneously. It worked well, but like any massive system orchestrated by the federal government, the NAS has its weaknesses and loopholes. If we could pull it off, Disco and I would fly our seventy-thousand-pound jet right through one of those holes.

The two Rolls-Royce Mk 610-8 engines forcing us through the black morning sky burned over twenty gallons every minute as we rocketed across the Georgia flatland, barely high enough to clear the television and cellular antennae dotting the landscape. The terrain rose as we continued north until the rolling hills of North Georgia gave way to the peaks of the Great Smoky Mountains dividing the Carolinas from East Tennessee.

Racing across the sky just a thousand feet above the mountaintops of Southern Appalachia, Disco said, "There's no place like home."

"What do you mean?" I asked as I watched the forested landscape roar beneath us at two hundred fifty knots.

"This is where I grew up," he said as he pointed across the panel. "In fact, I learned to fly right over there in Sevierville. Man, that feels like a thousand years ago."

"I guess I always thought the Air Force taught you to fly."

He adjusted his sunglasses against the rising ball of orange consuming the eastern sky. "The boys in blue taught me to fly jets, but an old guy named Jack Shipe sat in the right seat of a beat-up old Piper Chero-kee while that airplane taught me to fly all over these mountains."

I said, "I've been flying with you for ten years, and I never knew any of that. I guess that's why you picked Knoxville for this little charade."

He pulled up the before-landing checklist and said, "Yep, if Se-vierville had enough concrete, I would've preferred the anonymity of the smaller field, but the big runway at Knoxville will have to do."

I dialed up the automatic terminal information service for Knox-ville's McGhee Tyson Airport, and we set up for the approach. The tower controller cleared us to land on runway two-three-left using the fictional call sign Disco chose for the first leg of our four-thousand-mile journey. We landed and taxied to Signature Aviation, where we had the *Grey Ghost* topped off with every ounce of fuel the lineman could squeeze into the tanks.

I used a credit card drawn against an account in the Cayman Is-lands in the name of a human who probably never existed. Paying in cash would've been my preference, but a stack of hundred-dollar bills on the counter at Signature Aviation would be far more memorable than a common plastic card. We didn't want anyone behind the counter to remember any of us if an operative of Ontrack Global Re-sources were to show up asking questions. Albeit small, we were leav-ing a trail, but I like to think we were a little better than average at covering our tracks.

We blasted off from Knoxville under visual flight rules, using an-other fictional call sign, and climbed to seventeen thousand five hun-dred feet—the highest legal altitude we could fly without being on an instrument flight plan. The *Ghost* liked the higher, colder altitude much better than the sticky, dense air below ten thousand feet. The engines purred along while burning just under six hundred gallons per hour until we were a hundred miles west of Washington DC.

Disco double-checked our position. "Well, I guess it's time to go official."

I dialed up the Air Route Traffic Control Center frequency, and Disco keyed his mic. "Washington Center, Dairy-Air-five-four-one is one hundred miles west of DC, level at seventeen-five, request IFR clearance to Zurich."

The controller answered without hesitation. "Dairy-Air flight five-four-one, Washington Center, good morning, sir. Squawk three-five-seven-five."

I programmed the transponder, and a few seconds later, the controller said, "Dairy-Air-five-four-one is radar contact over the Kessel VOR. Cleared to Zurich, Switzerland, as filed. Climb and maintain flight level four-one-zero."

Disco read back the clearance, and we finally unleashed the muscle of the Gulfstream as we climbed well into the frozen altitudes, where the turbines loved every breath of the thin, frigid air.

I pulled off my sunglasses and turned to my captain. "Seriously? Dairy-Air?"

He threw up his hands. "What? It's a real thing. I think it's the call sign for the Wisconsin Dairy Association fleet."

Although the *Grey Ghost* had more computers on board than I could count, I manually calculated our fuel burn across the icy North Atlantic. Running out of gas and sliding onto an iceberg held no appeal for me. Thankfully, Disco's and the computers' calculations matched mine, and we'd land with plenty of reserve fuel.

Disco pointed out my window. "A hundred miles or so that way is where the *Titanic* went down."

"You're just full of fun facts this morning, but you should know that talking about one of the worst travel catastrophes in history while traveling isn't comforting for your passengers and crew."

We crossed Lizard Lighthouse and the English Channel eight miles below as the French countryside spread out ahead of us. I wondered how many times my mentor, Dr. Robert "Rocket" Richter, crossed that stretch of water in his P-51 Mustang, escorting WWII bombers to and from their missions against the fascists seventy-five years before. I had boundless faith in the *Ghost*, but there was something comforting about having terra firma beneath our belly instead of freezing salt water. I'm sure the bomber crews and their escorts felt the same.

Descending into Zurich with the Swiss Alps and Lichtenstein as a backdrop was unforgettable. The breathtaking beauty was enough to pull my head out of the cockpit and away from my responsibilities inside the airplane. I'll never forget thinking how much Penny would've loved the view, as well.

"Hey, Sightseer. Do you mind helping me fly the airplane?"

That was enough to yank me out of my awe and back to work. "Sorry, I was—"

"I know what you were doing," Disco said. "It happened to me the first time I flew in here. Beautiful, isn't it?"

"Astonishing."

I pulled up the approach plate for the ILS-14 and ran through the checklist. Although I was tempted to get one more look at the Alps, duty demanded that I keep my nose to the grindstone.

Disco said, "It's your turn to fly the approach and landing, so you have the controls."

I laid a hand on the control yoke and double-checked the instruments. "I have the controls."

As is our routine to ensure positive exchange of responsibility in the cockpit, Disco repeated, "You have the controls."

More than a few airplanes have pranged into the earth because each pilot on board believed somebody else was doing the flying. That wouldn't happen with Disco in the front seat.

Instead of letting the autopilot have all the fun, I hand-flew the *Ghost* down the localizer and glideslope until the wheels gave that ever-so-satisfying chirp as they kissed the runway. The flight had gone off without a hitch, but there were still far too many moving parts to believe we were anywhere near the conclusion of our ordeal with Ontrack Global Resources.

Chapter 11
Party on Azurstrasse

After shutting down the Gulfstream, my first order of business was a secure sat-phone call back to the States. I was pleased to hear Skipper's voice.

"Op center."

"We're safe on deck at our destination. Is there any evidence that our escape was detected?"

She said, "No indication so far. The ladies' departure seems to have worked, as well. The satellites haven't moved, and there's no discernible reaction that I can find from Ontrack Global Resources."

"That's good news. Keep us posted. Now, on to the task at hand. We'll be at OGR in half an hour or less. Roger Dean's reaction upon seeing us should tell us if we successfully snuck away. If we pulled it off, he'll likely be more than a little surprised to see us."

"I wish I could be there to see his face."

I said, "You should've thrown a rifle across your shoulder and joined us."

"Maybe next time."

I asked, "Do we have the ability to run open-channel secure comms between the team and back to you?"

She made a sound I didn't love. "Mmm, not exactly. We can scramble the transmission, but we can't hide the fact that each of you is transmitting something, and as you know, anything transmitted can be tracked."

"That's what I thought. It looks like you'll be blind for this one, but one of us will check in every ten minutes once we make entry. Do you have any idea what our buddy, Roger, drives?"

Skipper said, "He doesn't drive. He is *driven*, and he arrived in a black Mercedes G-Wagon this morning."

"That should be easy to find among the ten thousand other black G-Wagons that are, no doubt, running around Zurich. Thanks, Skipper. We'll let you know when we arrive on-site."

Her voice softened. "Hey, guys . . ."

"Yeah?"

"Be careful, okay? I can't lose anyone else right now."

I begged my brain to come up with anything appropriate, but all I could muster was, "Roger that."

The Toyota Land Cruiser Ginger arranged for us was no G-Wagon, but it certainly wasn't bad. The only weakness was the challenging egress from the third-row seats. Disco took the wheel. Mongo, of course, rode shotgun. Hunter and I took the second row, while Kodiak and Gator climbed into the rear.

Once we were situated inside, Kodiak said, "If we have to bail out, pop the back hatch, and we'll clear to the rear."

Disco checked the mirror. "You got it. Is everybody ready?"

We pulled away from the airport and into late-afternoon Zurich traffic that made rush hour in Atlanta look like a walk in the park. Horns blew, and vehicles jockeyed for position by squeezing into quickly closing holes in traffic lanes, but Disco managed the melee like a pro. It took far longer than expected, but we arrived at the world headquarters for Ontrack Global Resources just after 7:00 p.m. Parking was practically impossible, so the five of us climbed from the Land Cruiser while Disco stayed with the vehicle.

As we approached the double glass doors, Hunter glanced inside and said, "The gig is up as soon as we step into that foyer. I've got two cameras in sight, and there's probably more."

I looked inside, and Hunter was right, so I stuck out my hand.

"Give me your hat and wait here. I'll go in alone. If I can talk my way past security, I'll call you in. If you see Roger Dean leave the building, let me know."

I donned Hunter's hat and pulled it low across my forehead before stepping into the foyer. Once inside, I didn't look up. Having my face appear on those cameras would set off far too many alarms for us to deal with. While keeping my head low, I caught the interior door with my forearm to avoid leaving fingerprints, and I gave the door a tug.

It didn't budge, but a speaker high overhead came to life. "*Kann ich Ihnen helfen?*"

My mother spoke German and taught me the language as a child, but what was coming through that speaker wasn't the German I knew relatively well. The Swiss German spoken in Zurich appeared to lean toward French, a language I did not understand.

In German German, not Swiss German, I said, "I'm here to see Roger Dean."

The voice switched to the German I was more than capable of communicating. "Mr. Dean is gone for the day. Did you have an appointment?"

"No, I don't have an appointment, but Roger is expecting me."

I thought perhaps the familiar use of his first name might buy me at least a bit of a departure from protocol. It did not.

"I'm sorry, sir, but Mr. Dean has gone for the day. I'm afraid you'll have to make an appointment."

I wasn't ready to give up the ruse. "I can't believe I missed him. He told me he'd be here until seven. Are you sure he's gone?"

The voice said, "Again, I'm sorry, sir, but Mr. Dean left his office a few minutes ago. It is now a quarter past seven. He must've believed you weren't coming."

I groaned. "Okay. *Danke, auf wiedersehen.*"

I headed back through the exterior doors and keyed my sat-com. "The guard said Dean left just minutes ago. Did anybody spot him?"

Disco said, "A blacked-out G-Wagon just left the parking garage, but I can't tell who's inside."

I paused for a beat as I considered our options. Hesitation in my world often leads to squandered opportunities, and in many cases, mission failure. With our lives hanging in the balance, every decision could mean the difference between life and ultimate failure.

I gave the order. "Stay with the G-Wagon and report changes."

Disco said, "I'm on him."

Back with the remainder of my team on the sidewalk, I asked, "Did anybody spot a place we can lie low until this thing plays out?"

Kodiak motioned across the bustling street. "I can't read the sign from here, but that looks like a coffee shop to me."

He was right, and the café gave us the perfect spot to hide in plain sight. The Canadian flag pin on the barista's apron made me think we may share a common language, and although her English was accented with unmistakable French, we placed our orders in English.

Two minutes into our wait, Disco reported, "Does anybody know where Dean lives?"

"Stand by," I said as I shucked my sat-phone from a pocket.

Skipper answered quickly. "Go for op center."

"We're going to open-channel comms. Disco is in pursuit of the car that likely contains Dean, but the team is split. The rest of us are in a café across the street from OGR headquarters. Disco needs Dean's home address."

I could hear Skipper's fingers dancing across the keyboard. Seconds later, she said, "Channel is open. Disco, are you there?"

"Affirmative."

She said, "I just sent Dean's address to your sat-phone."

He said, "I don't really have time to look at the phone. I'm headed northeast on the Kornhausbrücke Bridge across the Limmat. Is that the route to Dean's home address?"

Skipper said, "Give me a second . . . Uh, no, not at all. He lives west of downtown."

I could almost taste Disco's frustration when he said, "I jumped on the wrong train. Should I discontinue the pursuit?"

Skipper said, "That's Chase's call, but if you're heading northeast, you're definitely not headed to Dean's apartment."

Something inside my skull didn't share Disco's opinion. "Stay with him," I said. "You're the only dog in the hunt right now, so let's wait and see what you tree."

"Roger. I'll stay with him."

He continued chasing the SUV and calling turns every time they changed streets. After fifteen minutes of Disco laboring to pronounce the street names, he finally said, "This is starting to feel like a surveillance detection route. I don't know if they made me as a tail or they're just being cautious, but we're making a lot of turns, and they feel unnecessary."

As I considered the situation, he said, "Wait a minute. They're stopping on Azurstrasse. If I'm busted, this is where they try to scare me off."

I said, "Drive past and see if you can catch the address. Try to look like a local."

A few seconds later, Disco said. "It's eight one eight Azurstrasse, and it looks like somebody's getting out of the car."

"Is it Dean?"

"It's a man, and he's the right size, but . . . wait a minute. Does Dean walk with a limp?"

Skipper said, "Uh, stand by . . ."

Time dragged on at an agonizing pace until I could hear my heart thundering in my ears. I ground the heel of my boot into the floor, knowing we were hanging Disco out to dry if he was slow playing the drive. Finally, I couldn't wait another second. "Get out of there, Disco."

Before he could answer, Skipper yelled, "Yes! He broke his leg three months ago in a skiing accident. That's him!"

I asked, "What's he doing on that side of Zurich at almost eight o'clock at night?"

Skipper said, "I'm on it. Would somebody spell Azurstrasse for me, please?" Silence consumed the line until she said, "Never mind, you bunch of illiterate knuckle-draggers. I've got it. The house belongs to one Franziska Kobel."

I said, "Keep digging, Skipper. Disco, are you clear?"

He said, "Affirmative. I made the block, and the G-Wagon drove off. It looks like he's headed back toward the river."

"Got her!" Skipper said. "She's forty-four years old, widow of Ulrich Kobel, who was . . . Oh, this is interesting."

"Come on, Skipper. Tell us what you've got," I demanded.

"Ulrich Kobel was the founder and CEO of Euro-Global Com, the last telecom business Roger Dean worked for before leaving to take the VP gig at Credit Suisse."

"That *is* interesting."

Disco chimed in. "That would explain this house on Azurstrasse. It's enormous."

I couldn't hear my heartbeat anymore because the gears in my head were spinning out of control. I said, "I need—"

Skipper said, "I know what you need, and I'm on it. Just give me a second." Moments later, she said, "Okay, got it. Roger Dean, fifty-seven years old, married for thirty-six of those fifty-seven years to the same woman named Maria Dean. Two children, both boys, Roger Dean the second, senior at Princeton, majoring in English literature."

She went silent, and I asked, "What about the other son?"

She clicked her fingernails against the keys loud enough for me to hear. "I can't find him."

"Okay, forget about him. Focus on the wife."

"Yeah, yeah, I am." After a long pause, Skipper said, "It would appear that the lovely Mrs. Roger Dean is on holiday in New York City."

"Oh, this is a gift with a big red bow," I said. "Disco, get back here and pick us up ASAP. We're at the café across the street from the OGR building. It's time to crash a party on Azurstrasse."

"I'm rolling," he said.

Chapter 12
Banging and Clanging

Almost without Disco coming to a complete stop, we climbed back aboard the Land Cruiser and headed to the house at 818 Azurstrasse. Knowing every detail of what we'd discover inside was impossible, but none of us doubted the primary reason the CEO of the world's largest private communications intelligence gathering company was spending time in the home of a wealthy widow while his apparently loving wife was four thousand miles away in the Big Apple.

"How are we going to play this?" Hunter asked as we pulled to a stop two hundred yards from the address.

"I've got an idea," I said. "Let's have a little fun. We've all been to dignitary protection training, right?"

Disco looked at Gator, the new kid. "Nope, not me. How 'bout you?"

Gator shook his head. "Me, neither."

I said, "You've seen Secret Service guys on TV, though, right?"

Our pilot and the new kid on the block nodded.

"Good. Just do what they do, except look meaner. Let's go."

We climbed the steps in a diamond formation like the Blue Angels, and I knocked on the door as if people's lives depended on having it open. Perhaps it did, and perhaps those lives were mine and the people I cared about.

I loved a thousand things about Kodiak, but very near the top of the list was his cool, quiet confidence. He licked the pad of his thumb as if it were a lollipop and smeared the goodness all over the fish-eye lens of Ms. Franziska Kobel's door camera. She'd still see us, but we'd look like spirits floating on the wind.

I thumbed the doorbell repeatedly and continued beating on the heavy wooden door until even I was tired of the noise. After a couple of minutes of my ridiculous banging and clanging, the door opened an inch, and one beautiful blue eye peered through the crack.

"*Kann ich dir helfen?*"

Mongo was first through the door because, well, he was Mongo, and the door had been chained. I was second, but Frau Kobel didn't see me; instead, she saw my United States Secret Service credentials jabbed a few inches in front of her face. Regardless of the language a person speaks, reads, and understands, a badge is still a badge, no matter the dialect.

In German, I said, "Security detail! We're here for Mr. Dean. Where is he?"

Her eyes exploded to the size of silver dollars, and panic distorted her beautiful features. Her stammering reply came in something close to the German I knew. "What? What do you want? Who are you?"

The robe she'd obviously thrown on quite quickly slipped from one shoulder, and Singer gently lifted it back in place.

I softened my tone and continued in German. "Herr Dean is in grave danger, ma'am. We're here to protect him. Please tell me where he is."

Her eyes betrayed her. She glanced down the hallway in an involuntary reaction to my question, and we moved as one—still Blue Angels —down the hall and through the second door on the right, the single door with light spilling from beneath.

As we moved, she called out in a trembling voice, "Roger, these men are here for you. They say you're in danger."

When five commandos come through a door, the scene is difficult to understand from the inside. We were powerful, confident men moving with unmatched speed and precision. Overwhelming force is

the guiding principle in such movement, and we undoubtedly qualified as such a force when Roger Dean looked up from his position on
the edge of Frau Kobel's ornate bed. Only his boxers and six feet of
open floor space separated us from the man who was only slightly less
confused than the woman behind us in Singer's loving care.

Dean leapt to his feet. "What's the meaning of this?"

The upper-class accent I expected from a Harvard man didn't
come. Instead, his New Jersey, tough-guy brogue took over.

Kodiak took a step toward a window with the shade raised a few
inches above the sill. "Oh, Roger, my boy. You of all people should be
more cautious. You're in the intel business. You know better than to
leave a window shade open even a little bit while you're engaged in flagrante delicto with your mistress."

Kodiak held up his phone and waggled it between his thumb and
forefinger. "These things have fantastic video capability these days.
Would you care to see some of the footage I got through this window?
You're in pretty good shape for an older guy."

"What do you people want? Where's Franziska? If you hurt her, so
help me God."

I planted the tips of my fingers in the center of his chest and forced
him back onto the bed. "A decent, respectful person in my situation
would allow you to get dressed to preserve at least a modicum of dignity, but decency and respect aren't terms people usually employ when
they're talking about me. I've got a bit of a reputation for leaving dead
bodies in my wake."

He roared, "Who are you?"

I said, "I'm impressed, Roger. You've got some real chutzpah there,
but unfortunately, I need answers, not attitude, so let's start with
Courtney Kellum, your chief of physical security. Where might I find
Mr. Kellum these days?"

"What are you talking about?"

I glanced at Dean's iPhone lying on the antique nightstand, and we
both lunged for it at the same instant. Relative youth played in my fa-

vor, and my hand reached the finish line first. I snatched the phone with my right hand and Dean's wrist with my left. "Be a good boy, now, Rogey-pooh. Give me that thumbprint."

He yanked and twisted against my grip until Mongo stepped in. "Step aside, boss. I'll rip his hand off for you."

Roger Dean suddenly became far more compliant than he originally wanted to be, and the iPhone's lock screen magically disappeared, revealing the home screen picture of a beautiful woman who was clearly a decade older than the owner of the house in which we were standing.

I tossed the phone to Kodiak. "I'm sure Mrs. Dean's phone number is in there somewhere." I glanced at my watch. "It's just a few minutes past two in New York City. She may be having afternoon tea, but I'm sure she'll take a call from her husband. Perhaps she'd like to speak with the widow Kobel."

Dean threw up his hands. "Okay, that's enough. What do you want?"

"I told you what I want. I want to know where your chief of physical security, Mr. Kellum, is. He's been missing for several days, and we're starting to worry about him."

"He's not missing," he said. "He's sick. He's convalescing at home. And how do you know he's not been at the office?"

I ruffled his hair, exposing the baldness he obviously worked hard to hide. "I know all sorts of things, Roger. I know, for example, your boy—your namesake—isn't making the grades at Princeton that you and Maria expect. What a disappointment that must be. But I'm sure you can make a multi-million-dollar donation to the university, and all will be forgiven."

"Is that what you want? Money? If that's what you want—"

I pressed a finger to his lips. "Shh, Rog. You're embarrassing yourself. We're not for sale."

"Then tell me who you are and what you want. If it's within my power—"

I pressed my finger against his lips again. "No, no, no. We're not negotiating or posturing or any of those other things that work in your little world of corporate spying. Let's cut to the chase, shall we?"

He recoiled from the pressure of my finger against his lips. "Just tell me what you want."

I planted a boot between his bare feet and took up as much of his personal space as my two hundred thirty pounds would consume. "Okay, Roger. Here's what we really want to know. Why are you killing people around me?"

He shuddered as if shaking off an uppercut. "What are you talking about? I don't even know who you are. Why would I try to kill you?"

I couldn't decide if he needed an Academy Award for Best Actor or an elbow strike to the temple.

I lowered my face to within inches of his. "I didn't say you were trying to kill me, Roger. I said you were killing people around me. Don't play games with me. You'll lose, I promise."

He furrowed his brow. "I don't think you know who you're talking to."

"Save it," I said. "I know exactly who you are, where you live, who you're married to, and who you're sleeping with. I've proven I can find you and get to you anytime I want. I mean, look at us, Roger. You're in your boxers, on someone else's bed, all the way across the ocean, and I paraded right on in as if I owned the place."

His face grew redder and more furious with every word. It was clear he wanted to lash out, as I'm sure he did in too many board meetings to mention. His underlings, no doubt, lived in fear of his wrath, but I was nobody's underling, especially not a cheating, corporate espionage clown in Zurich.

I slapped him hard across the face, sending his head spinning to the side.

He roared, "How dare you?"

I gave him one more slap in the opposite direction. "That's how I dare, Roger. I'm not afraid of you, I'm not intimidated by you, and most of all, I'm not impressed by you. Now, you listen closely to every word I'm about to say, and if you have a brain in your skull, you'll heed the warning."

He gritted his teeth in defiance, but that only made me close the distance between us even more. "Listen to me very closely. If anyone around me so much as trips and falls in the future, I'll find you again, just like I found you here today, and I'll tear you into so many pieces, they'll never find all of you. You're going to pay dearly for the deeds you've already done. I'll see to that. But the killing stops this instant. Are we clear?"

To my surprise, he leaned forward until our foreheads were almost touching, and he hissed, "Whoever you are, you've just crossed a line you'll never—"

Before he could finish his toothless threat, I laced a hand behind his neck, lunged backward, and drove his face into the marble-top nightstand, precisely hard enough to crush his nose without rendering him unconscious.

"Look what you made me do, Roger. I'm sure your girlfriend in there will help you shove some cotton balls up your nose to stop the bleeding, but there's nothing she or anyone else will be able to do for you if you and I ever see each other again. Do . . . not . . . doubt me."

The elbow shot I'd longed to deliver came of its own will, almost without my involvement, and Roger Dean melted to the silk sheets of Frau Franziska Kobel's enormous bed.

* * *

Back aboard the *Grey Ghost*, we climbed away from the Swiss Alps and Ontrack Global Resources' corporate headquarters. When we reached our cruising altitude and configured the plane for the long, western passage, Disco turned to me. "Why didn't you kill him?"

I closed the checklist binder and returned it to the slot beside my seat. "Because I don't think he's behind this."

Chapter 13
Technically Naked

In cruise flight, the *Grey Ghost* is relatively autonomous, leaving Disco and me to be little more than systems monitors. Everything about our chief pilot's expression said he didn't care that we were eight miles above the Earth at that moment.

Disco said, "What? Are you serious? We broke into a house halfway across the planet, scared a woman nearly to death, and threatened a naked guy, and you don't think he's the right guy?"

"Technically, he wasn't naked. He *was* wearing boxers."

"You can't be serious. What makes you think he's not our guy?"

"The eyes."

He shook his head and continued ignoring the airplane. "What about his eyes?"

I replayed the scene in my mind. "He didn't know who we were."

"Oh, come on. How could he not know who we are? He deployed a ship to track us down and kill us in the Black Sea. He's turned a madman loose to pick us off, one by one, and leave silver bullets behind. What's going on in your head, man? You're smarter than that."

I'd worked alongside Disco for a decade, and I'd never heard him raise his voice at anyone, especially not me. His confidence left me questioning what I saw in Roger Dean's face from six inches away.

He calmed down, scanned the instrument panel, and asked, "If he's not our guy, then who is?"

I forced my mind back inside the cockpit as I labored to answer that question. "I don't know, but it's not Roger Dean."

Disco rolled his eyes. "I'm going to the head. Do you want anything?"

"From the head?"

He gave me a shove as he climbed from the captain's seat. "Yes, from the head. Perhaps a roll of toilet paper so you can wipe off your glasses and see what's right in front of your face."

I watched him go. "A bottle of water would be great."

I sat alone in the cockpit, poring over every detail of our encounter. A couple of minutes into my musings, I leaned to my left and called into the cabin. "Hey, Kodiak. Please tell me you've still got Dean's iPhone."

He slipped it from his pocket and bounced the device in his palm. "You know it, boss."

"Get up here."

He left the posh end of the airplane and climbed into the working section, taking Disco's seat. He said, "Ooh, look at all this stuff I could screw up. Where's the self-destruct button?"

I snatched the phone from his hand. "They're all self-destruct buttons when *you* touch them."

He studied the panels and controls with the curiosity of a child as I scrolled through Roger Dean's contacts.

I must've said it out loud, but it was intended to be a question only for me. "Why didn't he have security?"

Kodiak said, "Would you take personal security with you to your mistress's house?"

"I don't have a mistress."

"Penny might disagree."

"What are you talking about?"

"She may not have the face of a goddess anymore, but everybody can see the spell the little Russian still has over you."

"I'm not under anybody's spell, Mr. In Flagrante Delicto. Where'd you learn a big word like that, anyway?"

"It's actually three words, and I'm not as illiterate as I look. I read part of a book once, and I liked how those words felt rolling off my tongue. Something tells me the widow Kobel likes the way Roger Dean's tongue—"

I held up a hand. "Just stop."

He chuckled. "I wondered how far you were going to let me take that one. By the way, what did you do to upset Disco? He came through the cabin mumbling and shaking his head like a madman."

Instead of an answer, I said, "Tell me what you thought about Dean."

"What do you mean?"

"I mean, do you think he's our guy?"

"He's not the shooter, if that's what you're asking."

"No, that's not what I'm asking. Of course he's not the shooter. After what you saw in the bedroom, do you think he's behind this whole thing?"

He shrugged. "I don't know. Maybe. But I did notice one thing. His demeanor was entirely different when we accused him of trying to kill us versus when we threatened to call his wife."

"You might make a pretty good psychologist."

"Nah. But I've done enough interrogations to know when you strike a nerve. I noticed something else, too. He never once asked if the widow was all right."

"I noticed that, too," I said.

"You're the psychiatrist, but in my experience, people in dire situations worry about what they love. I got the feeling he loves the flagrante more then he loves the delicto."

It was my turn to laugh. "I'm not sure what that means, but I'm a psychologist, not a psychiatrist."

He climbed from Disco's seat. "No, you're not. I've spent my whole adult life around warriors, so I know one when I see one. You're a fighter, Chase. You're not an ologist of any kind."

Disco dropped a bottle of water into my hand as he squirmed his way back into the driver's seat. "What was that all about?"

"Kodiak and I were having vocabulary class."

"Huh?"

"Never mind," I said as I waggled Dean's iPhone in the air between us. "What do you think of having Skipper try to run down Courtney Kellum with the numbers Dean has in his phone?"

"Kellum's the chief of security, right?"

"That's right. He's the one who's been missing in action, and Dean seems to believe he's sick."

"Couldn't hurt," he said. "And maybe she'll dig up something that makes you wake up and smell the coffee."

I uncapped the water bottle and swallowed half the contents before making the call.

The phone rang several times before the wrong voice answered. "Is operation center."

"Anya?"

"Yes, is Anya Burinkova. Is Chasechka, yes?"

"How many times do I have to tell you that you're the only Anya I know? Your last name isn't necessary. And why are you answering the phone in the op center?"

"Is my turn," she said. "Ginger is sleeping. Skipper is crying. And I am tired from fighting with boy."

"Fighting with a boy?"

"He is man, not boy, but he is not very good fighter with knife. He is very strong and fast though."

"Who? Did somebody attack you?"

"No, silly. Person who said he was SEAL had knife on belt and also one inside boot, so I took from him first knife so I could know if he was good fighter."

I sighed. "You're not supposed to be messing with the security detail. They aren't there for your amusement."

"But he had two knives. Only person who knows how to use them carries two knives."

I surrendered. "How did he do?"

"He is very good learner."

"Anya, you have to leave those guys alone. They don't have time for your classes."

"There is always time to learn to fight better. He made very big mistake by underestimating me, but he learned quickly, and he is now better fighter."

"Okay, whatever. You said Skipper's crying. Is she okay?"

"No, of course not. Her husband is dead. Would Penny be okay if you were murdered? I know I would not be okay if you were gone."

"I get it. Listen, when either of them relieves you, have them call me. I have something I need."

"I can do for you this thing you need."

That felt way too much like the spell Kodiak mentioned, so instead of dancing with the devil, I said, "No, this one requires Skipper or Ginger. Just have one of them call me."

"I will do for you anything you want."

"Just have one of them call me."

I hate it when Kodiak is right. Maybe everybody around me could see everything more clearly than I could. Perhaps I was wrong about everything. Maybe Roger Dean was the guy we should drop off a cliff. Maybe my fingers were still sticky from Anya's honeytrap. Maybe every bad decision I ever made was coming back to haunt me, and that haunting was killing the people I cared about, one by one.

* * *

The jet stream over the North Atlantic blew in our face at well over a hundred knots, so making the continental U.S. without a fuel stop wasn't going to happen. Naval Air Station Keflavik shared a runway with the international civil airport on the misnamed island of Iceland. Greenland is mostly ice, and Iceland is mostly green. I blame the Vikings.

It was Disco's turn to fly the approach and landing, and he made it look easy. My body had no idea what time the clock said it was, but I knew without a doubt that it was bedtime. Disco and I yawned in unison, and he said, "I need a little sleep before . . ."

"Say no more. I'm on it."

The wonderful woman behind the reception desk at the Navy Lodge at NAS Keflavik found four rooms for us, and we crashed as if we hadn't slept in days.

Only minutes after my mind and body succumbed to exhaustion, my sat-phone became the most hated implement I owned. I slapped the device that yanked me from the sleep I needed so desperately and stuck it to my ear. "What?"

"Try not to be so excited," Skipper said. "I'm just following orders from your Russian knife-fighting sensei."

"She's not *my* Russian anything," I growled.

"Yeah, whatever. What do you need?"

I sat up and flipped on the bedside lamp. "I've got Roger Dean's cell phone, and—"

She let out a squeal like a kid on Christmas morning. "Are you serious?"

I wiped the sleep from my eyes. "Yes, why would I make up something like that? Here's what I need you to do . . ."

She cut me off. "Oh, I know what you need. Is it an iPhone or an Android?"

"iPhone."

"Excellent," she said. "Plug your charger into Dean's phone, and plug the other end into your sat-phone."

"Will the cable do that?"

"Yes, it'll do it. Just plug it in."

I fumbled with the cable. "Okay, it's done."

She said, "Hang on a second."

The taps of her fingertips on the keyboard would never get old. Even in my exhausted state, I loved that sound.

Finally, she said, "Oh, this is a gold mine. I've got everything downloaded, and I'll pick it apart. When will you be home?"

"We crashed," I said.

"What? Is everybody okay? What happened? Is the plane okay?"

"Sorry, poor choice of words. Everybody's fine. We just needed some sleep, so we're in lodging at NAS Keflavik."

"Oh, thank God. Get some rest, and I'll glean everything possible out of Dean's cell phone data."

I said, "Hey, one more thing. Are you doing okay? Anya said you were having a tough day."

She sighed. "Yeah, I had a moment, but work helps. I've got Ginger, and she's a godsend. I'm sorry for yelling at you for calling her."

"Never apologize. It's you and me, kid. We go back further than anybody else on the team. We've got each other. If you need time, take time. Ginger is almost as good as the real thing."

She giggled. "Thanks. I needed that. But I'm okay for now. I've got a task, and you need some sleep. I'll see you tomorrow. Oh, and Chase . . ."

"Yeah?"

"I don't say it enough, but I love you. I really do."

"I love you, too, Skipper."

Chapter 14
The One Before the First

Sleep is the closest thing to real magic. We awoke refreshed and ready for whatever happened next. Breakfast was in the Navy mess, and it was the perfect punctuation to the perfect night's sleep. I've been fed by every branch of the U.S. military, and although the Air Force won the prize for quantity, the Navy took home the gold medal for quality.

Home was almost three thousand nautical miles away, but that was well within the *Grey Ghost*'s range, and I didn't care how many satellites watched us arrive. We had far more to discuss than who was spying on Bonaventure.

When we turned south over the continental U.S., the jet stream became far less of an issue, and home felt closer than ever. My anxiety to be home was rooted in two elements. First, I needed to know that Penny, Irina, and Maebelle were safe in their temporary new home, but coming in right behind that tidbit of knowledge was the intel Skipper pulled from Roger Dean's iPhone. Would it tell us anything we didn't already know, or would it only present more questions to which there seemed to be no answers?

Skipper buzzed us into the op center, and we assumed our typical seats around the conference table. She wasted no time bringing us up to speed. "First, and most importantly, Captain Sprayberry made his escape under the cover of a nasty storm lying off the east coast of Florida, and he picked up his three passengers near Bermuda, where they were choppered aboard by our very own Gun Bunny."

A sigh of relief left my mind, if not my lips. Having the three women safely aboard the ship was a weight off my shoulders so massive that I couldn't describe it.

"What about the cell phone?" I asked.

Skipper huffed. "I hate to be the bearer of bad news, but you got the wrong phone."

"What? That can't be true. Dean's thumbprint unlocked that phone, thanks to a little encouragement from Mongo."

Skipper said, "It's *one* of his phones, but not the *best* one. The one that you commandeered appears to be his personal, non-business line. There's nothing particularly interesting on it based on what I downloaded through your sat-phone link last night. If you'll give me the phone, I can compare what I downloaded against what's actually on it. Maybe I missed something, but I'm pretty sure they're going to match."

Kodiak pulled the phone from his pocket and tossed it to our analyst. "There you go."

She snatched it from the air like a hawk and plugged it into her console in seconds. After making a few faces, she said, "Yep, they're identical. The only thing I learned from this phone is two additional phone numbers for Courtney Kellum."

"Speaking of Kellum, have you found him yet?"

She leaned back in her chair. "No, and that pisses me off. I'm pretty darned good at finding people who don't want to be found, but this guy is a ghost. I ran all five numbers I have for him, including the two new ones from Dean's phone, and there's nothing. He's completely under the radar, and I'm running out of ideas."

Anya raised a finger. "May I tell to you something you may not know?"

Skipper raised an eyebrow. "Absolutely. Don't hold anything back."

"This sort of disappearance is taught inside KGB and SVR training. I know how, and I have ability to do this myself. Is effective and very simple."

"Keep talking," Skipper said. "I'm all ears."

Anya said, "I tried to tell to you before. He will now have not only brand-new identity, cell phone, satellite phone, passport, but also new face, hair, and body."

"How do you get a new body?"

"Is very simple. Everyone, give to me shirts."

Everyone in the room looked to me as if asking permission to surrender their clothes, so I led the way by pulling mine off and tossing it to the Russian. She wrapped shirts around her arms and body until Mongo's enormous shirt fit her like a glove. She pulled Clark's Alabama cap from his head, piled her hair underneath, and pulled it snugly over her ears. She moved like a man big enough to wear Mongo's clothes and was instantly barely recognizable.

She said, "He will wear glasses designed to make his eyes appear farther apart or closer together. He will wear prosthetic facial features to obscure or change his cheekbones, chin, size of upper lip, shape of bones above eyes, and size and shape of ears. These changes will make it impossible for facial recognition software to identify him. Is likely his own wife would not recognize him from only feet away. This is common tactic. Even your CIA teaches this, but they are not as good as Europeans."

Skipper seemed to let the show sink in before saying, "If you're right, we're wasting our time looking for him through conventional means."

"Yes, this is correct," Anya said as she shucked off the layers and returned our shirts.

Ginger said, "Let's assume Anya's right and this guy is masquerading as somebody else while running all over the world and directing this op to pick us off one at a time."

Anya said, "Wait. I did not say he was running around. I said this is how he avoided detection when he disappeared. He may be now inside facility, where disguise is not necessary."

Ginger said, "We'll assume that's true. What do we really know about this guy? Have we done a deep dive? Is he the only person miss-ing from Ontrack Global?"

Every eye turned to Skipper, and she bowed her head. "This is on me, and it should be. Normally, I would've done all of that early on and had answers to those questions, but . . ."

"There's no need to apologize," I said. "Everybody understands. That's why we brought Ginger in. How long will a deep dive take?"

Ginger dragged her chair to the console beside Skipper, and her fin-gers went to work. She said, "You go civ. I've got the military side."

"Is anybody going to answer my question?" I asked.

Ginger didn't look up. "Give us thirty minutes, tops. Oh, and this may be terrible timing, but brava to Anya for getting every man in the room to take off his shirt at exactly the same time. That's a trick you simply must teach me."

I pushed away from the table and curled a finger toward the Rus-sian. She rolled beside me, and I whispered, "If you were Courtney Kellum, and you were trying to get back at me, what would be your next move?"

"Is simple. I would continue doing same thing over and over until it stopped working. So far, he is killing people you care about with no consequences. Why would he change anything?"

"I was afraid that was going to be your answer. I'm running low on ideas here. If you've got any suggestions, don't hold back. So far, you're the only one who seems to understand this thing."

The team huddled around Anya and me to avoid disturbing the an-alysts as they plowed into Kellum's background. Almost everyone had a guess or two, but nobody had anything solid to offer until Anya said, "Next person will be active member of team."

I recoiled. "Wait, what?"

"Is simple pattern. First person he killed was maybe patient of yours, yes?"

"Not maybe. It was definitely my patient, Jimmy Fairmont."

"How do you know he was first?"

I shook my head in confusion. "Because he was killed at least several hours before Tony."

Anya huffed in apparent frustration. "Yes, we know this, but we do not know if he was first. Only that he was before Tony."

I froze. "Give me some names, everybody. Think about people outside the inner circle and the circle of my patients in the psych practice."

I scrolled through the contacts in my phone as my heart raced out of control. When Earl's name rolled to the top of the list, I felt my stomach turn inside out. Crushing the call button, I slammed the phone against my ear, silently begging her to answer. It seemed to ring for an eternity until her raspy voice filled my ear.

"Hey Stud Muffin! What's going on? Wish you were here."

"Where's here, Earl?"

"Heck, I don't know. My sexy Cajun king brought me halfway to kingdom come. We're on some island in the South Pacific. You oughta see me in my grass skirt. Baby Boy, you couldn't stand it. Momma's even got one of them coconut shell bikini tops, and it's drivin' my man outta his mind over here."

"So, you and Kenny are okay?"

"Okay? We're better than okay. This is the best vacation I've ever had. We may never come back."

"That's a great idea, Earl. Stay where you are. Or, better yet, change islands every other day or so. It's on me. I'll cover whatever it costs."

"Huh? What are you talking about, Stud Muffin?"

I filled her in on what was happening, and the joy fell from her voice. "Oh my God, Chase. Tony? Please say it ain't so."

"I wish I could, Earl. It's bad."

"I can't believe you didn't let us know so we could come home for the funeral. That poor Skipper. She's gotta be a wreck. I need to be there."

"No. Please stay on the islands. I can't bear the thought of putting anyone else at risk. You're safe over there, so just stay. You've still got the credit card I gave you, right?"

"Yeah, I got it."

"Use it," I said. "Whatever you want or need is on me. I'm serious. I'll let you know when all of this is over."

"Do you know who's doin' it?"

"We've got a pretty good idea, but nothing's solid yet."

She said, "You know when me and Boomer was working for Air America, we got ourselves into some scrapes, so I ain't afraid to—"

It didn't matter what she was going to say next. I cut her off. "Just stay away. That's the safest thing for now. If anything changes, I'll call you, I promise."

"So, that's why you was callin' me? You wanted to make sure I was still alive?"

"No, not exactly. I'm just covering all the bases."

The next words out of her mouth froze me again. "Have you talked to my brother, Cotton?"

Cotton Jackson, Earl's brother, was the owner of the only hands that touched the engines on our airplanes, and the thought of a sniper cutting him down sickened me to my core.

I said, "I've gotta go. I'm calling him now."

Earl said, "Just hang on, Sugar Britches. I'm calling him right now on three-way."

The line rang several times until his unmistakable voice said, "Hello . . ." I breathed a sigh of enormous relief until he said, ". . . this is Cotton. I'm either asleep or too busy to come to the phone. Leave me a message, and I'll call you back when I get time."

"Cotton, it's your sister, Earline. Call me the second you get this. I need to know—"

The line clicked several times before a winded voice came on. "Are you there, Earline?"

"Cotton, thank God! Are you all right?"

"Well, yeah. I'm fine so far as I know. I've got a Continental IO-five-twenty torn down for some old boy who let most of the cylinders overheat, but other than that, I'm doing all right. How's the vacation?"

Clark knocked on the table. "Chase, you need to see this."

I reached for the phone he slid across the table and read the headline from five days before.

Longtime St. Augustine Bridge of Lions drawbridge tender, Charlie Bevins, killed by apparent sniper.

My head felt like someone had driven a spike through my ear. I had befriended Charlie Bevins during my time in St. Augustine. He'd been my local source of intel on the river. I could never talk him into taking cash for helping me out, but he never turned down a bottle of Jack Daniel's Gentleman Jack.

Once again, Anya was right. My patient, Jimmy Fairmont, hadn't been the sniper's first victim, and she was likely right about the next attempt. He was coming after me by walking in his kills, nearer and nearer with every press of the trigger, and I wasn't an inch closer to figuring out who he was or how to stop him.

Chapter 15
Just Because You Haven't

I slid the phone back to Clark and ran my fingers through my hair as a billion scattered thoughts consumed what was left of my mind.

Disco leaned close. "Do you still think Roger Dean isn't behind this?"

"I don't know. So far, I've been wrong at every turn. Whoever it is, he's a dozen steps ahead of me and increasing his lead by the minute."

Clark asked, "Are you calling St. Augustine PD, or do you want me to do it?"

I shook back the fog. "I'll do it. What's that beat cop's name? The big Irish guy who used to work in the Old City?"

Skipper looked up from her console. "Kendrick O'Malley."

"How do you remember everything?"

She shrugged. "Not everything. Just the stuff I think we might need someday."

I dialed the dispatcher. "Good morning. My name is Chase Fulton. Can you tell me if Officer Kendrick O'Malley is still on the force?"

"Yes, sir, but he's not an officer anymore. He was promoted to detective a few years ago."

"That's good to hear," I said. "Is he available to take my call?"

She said, "I can put you through to his office, and you can leave a message if he doesn't pick up."

"Thank you. I'd appreciate that."

A series of clicks preceded a ringtone. "Homicide, Detective O'Malley."

His tone was firm, but he still sounded like he'd just walked out of a pub in Dublin.

"O'Malley, you probably don't remember me, but my name is Chase Fulton. I kept my catamaran at the municipal marina a few years ago."

"Special Agent—but not really—Fulton. Of course I remember you. What a surprise. What can I do for you?"

Uncertain how to proceed, I chose the direct approach. "Listen, O'Malley, I'm actually calling about Charlie Bevins's murder. You wouldn't happen to know who's working that case, would you?"

"Yeah, I know the old boy on that case. He's shite for solving murders, but he's pretty good at rememberin' names. What can I do for you?"

"Are you serious? It's your case?"

He said, "We're a small department here, Chase. You know that. We've got two homicide detectives, and one of us spends most of his time working narcotics. That leaves you stuck with me."

"Before we get ahead of ourselves, can you tell me how many times he was shot and the caliber of the round?"

O'Malley hesitated. "What do you know about this shooter, Chase?"

"Just tell me this. Were there two rounds fired, but only the first one was necessary?"

"Keep talkin'," he said.

"Was it a thirty-cal and two different projectiles?"

Another hesitation. "Chase, I think I'm going to need you to come down and answer a few questions."

"I can do that, but before I do, take a look at a shooting up in Hilton Head. The victim was James Fairmont. Then check out the murder of a detective named Anthony Johnson here in St. Marys."

"Give me a minute."

I could hear his fingers on the keyboard, but the sound was nothing like Skipper's speed.

When he came back on the line, he said. "It's the same MO. What's going on here, Special Agent?"

"O'Malley, you know I'm not an agent."

"Yeah, I know, but you know something about this case. Come on. Out with it."

"How much time do you have?" I asked.

"All the time I need to take your statement."

"I won't give an official statement, but I'll tell you what I know off the record."

"Okay, I'll take what I can get for now, but if I have to subpoena you to catch this guy . . ."

"You're not going to catch him, O'Malley. Nobody with a badge is going to get anywhere near this guy, whoever he is."

"You've got a badge."

"Yeah, I do, and I'm starting to doubt that I'll ever find him either."

He said, "So, this guy's a serial killer. Ain't that the FBI's bailiwick?"

"They wouldn't touch this one with a ten-foot pole and gloves."

"So, where does that leave me?" he asked.

"I'm going to put you on the line with an intel analyst, and she'll give you an authorization code to have the bullets sent to the FBI crime lab for analysis. If yours is like the others, you have one killing projectile and one relatively undamaged, shiny round of the same caliber but very different material."

He huffed. "I wish you'd brought that up before we sent them to the state lab in Tallahassee."

"They've already been analyzed?" I asked. "Are they from the same weapon?"

"You don't know about the second bullet, do you?"

"What about it?"

"Chase, the rifling matches on both bullets, so they came from the same gun, but that's not what makes them interesting."

"What is it, O'Malley? Stop stalling!"

He lowered his voice. "I'll call you back in two minutes from my cell. Is the number you called from real?"

"Yes, it's real. I'll be waiting."

I hung up and turned to Skipper. "Stop what you're doing on Kellum and get the ballistics lab on the phone. I need to know what's going on with those bullets."

Skipper growled. "Give me two more minutes on this, and I'll have everything you need."

I bounced my phone in my palm while awaiting O'Malley's call, and the ringing began exactly two minutes after I'd hung up. "Let's hear it, O'Malley."

He said, "Have you read the ballistics report from the other two victims yet?"

"No, I haven't. Tell me what you've got."

"First, let me make sure I understand what you believe. You think this guy—whoever he is—is killing people you know in an ever-shrinking diameter of importance. Is that pretty much what you think is happening here?"

"Yeah, something like that," I said. "Come on. Don't make me wait any longer."

He cleared his throat. "Do you know anyone named Dennis who might be tied to this thing in any way?"

I closed my eyes and pored over the list of friends, acquaintances, and people I love, but nothing came, so I covered the mouthpiece. "Does anybody know somebody named Dennis who might be part of this?"

Frowns and furrowed brows came back, but no one could name a Dennis.

"I've got nothing," I said. "Do you have another victim?"

O'Malley said, "No, Chase. It's not another victim, as far as I know. It's two words laser-engraved on the undamaged projectile. It's far too wee to view with the naked eye, but under the microscope, it's clear as day. It says 'Dennis Sinned.'"

I wrote the words on a pad and flipped it toward the center of the table. Everyone stared at the page as if I'd written the phrase in Greek, but no one seemed to have any ideas about what it could mean.

I asked, "What else does the ballistics report have to say?"

"Nothing else interesting. We've got the weights and dimensions of the projectiles. Oh, and the metallurgy on the steel bullet."

"Let's hear it."

He said, "I'm outside, and I don't have the report in my hand. That was the reason for the callback. I didn't want to have this conversation inside the department. They'd skin me alive."

"I appreciate the confidence. Tell me what you remember."

He said, "I remember it was forty-one-forty steel, but I don't know what that means."

I tilted the phone away from my mouth. "He said the surviving projectile was forty-one-forty steel. Anybody know what that means?"

Of course it was our resident big brain in a big body who spoke up. "Forty-one-forty steel alloy is a medium carbon steel with a relatively good strength-to-workability ratio. It's essentially iron with about point four percent carbon and a few other elements like chromium, molybdenum, manganese, silicon, and sulfur in extremely small quantities."

He paused, took a drink of water, and continued. "If I remember correctly, its density is just under eight grams per cubic centimeter. It's not as hard as high-carbon steel, but it's still pretty tough with a one ninety-seven on the Brinell scale."

A roomful of zombies stared back at Mongo, so he withdrew a pair of fingernail clippers from one pocket, his switchblade from another, and tossed them on the table. He pointed to the clippers. "It's harder than that." Then he pointed at the knife's blade. "But softer than that."

The reaction around the table said we finally understood what he was talking about.

I asked, "Is there some significance to that particular alloy for a bullet?"

Mongo shook his head. "I suspect he bought or stole forty-one-forty round stock and machined it down to size to precisely fit the thirty-cal barrel. It's hard enough to withstand supersonic impact on any material softer than itself without too much deformation. Honestly, it's exactly what I would make bullets out of if I wanted to send a message like this."

O'Malley said, "I'm glad I got to sit in on that little lecture. I'm not sure if I understood any of it, but now I'll sound like I know what I'm talking about if anybody asks me."

"Everybody needs a Mongo in their life," I said. "Is there anything else we need to know about your case?"

He said, "I think it's quid pro quo time. How about letting me in on what you know?"

Skipper held up a single sheet of paper. "I've got the report from the Fairmont murder, but not Tony's yet."

I took the paper from her and scanned the information before passing it to Mongo. He studied it for a minute and nodded. "Yep, same steel."

O'Malley said, "What about the laser engraving? Any message on yours?"

I rustled the page loud enough to be heard through the phone and said, "Nothing."

"Is that so?" O'Malley said. "If you change your mind and decide to make this a two-way street, you know where to find me. Don't make me subpoena you, okay, Chase?"

I filled my lungs, read the note at the bottom of the brief report, and said, "You're right, O'Malley. I wasn't playing fair. There's a note here that goes into great detail about the depth of the laser engraving. It actually calls it micro-laser engraving."

He said, "Yeah, I think that's the wording the state lab used, as well. What does it say?"

I read the line twice to make sure I had it correct. "It says, 'Drab as a fool, aloof as a bard.' Any idea what that could mean?"

Detective O'Malley said, "Beats me, but would you mind copying me on the report and the one from your man Tony? I'm sorry about that, by the way. I know what it's like to lose a brother."

"Sure thing," I said. "And thanks. I'll let you know when we get the second ballistics report."

"Thanks, Chase. Maybe I won't have to subpoena you after all. Take care, old pal."

I hung up and read through the report again. Finally, I dropped the page on the table. "Does anybody have any guesses on what 'Drab as a fool, aloof as a bard' could mean?"

Clark said, "Fairmont was a Delta operator, right?"

I said, "Yeah, nine years."

"And he was fighting PTSD, right?"

"That's right."

"Was he drab?" Clark asked.

I thought back to our sessions. "Yeah, I guess he could be at times when his demons were beating him up pretty bad, but most people in his shoes would be."

Clark said, "How about aloof? I'm not even sure I know what that means."

I remembered how difficult it had been to get Jimmy to open up and talk about what was going on inside his head. "Yeah, I'm sure a lot of people would consider him to be aloof, but how could the shooter know that?"

Nobody spoke for several minutes until Anya said, "Maybe Dennis is someone your friend Charlie knew. Maybe message was for Charlie and not for us."

"Hang on a minute," I said as I pressed the recall button on my phone.

O'Malley answered on the second ring, and I put him on speaker. "Yeah, Chase? What is it?"

"Where was the sniper?"

"What?"

"Where was the sniper who shot Charlie?"

"Somewhere to the north-northeast, so he had to either be on a boat or on the Usina Bridge over the ICW."

I closed my eyes as I tried to remember the details of the Intracoastal Waterway. "No way he could've been on the bridge. That's gotta be two miles."

"A mile and three quarters," O'Malley said. "Measured it myself. If that's where he was, he's a crack shot. How many guys in the world can make that shot?"

I looked up at Singer, and he said, "Maybe two dozen besides me and Gator."

The new kid shook his head. "Not me. I've never made a shot that long."

Singer lowered his chin. "Just because you haven't doesn't mean you can't."

Chapter 16
Communist Kickball

"Was Charlie married?" I asked no one in particular, and Skipper fielded the question.

"I've already started the background, and yes, he was married to Charlotte Bevins for thirty-two years."

"Can you find a phone number for her?"

"Way ahead of you," Skipper said. "I just sent it to your phone."

I saved Mrs. Bevins's contact to my phone and paced to the corner of the room. She answered quickly and sounded younger than I remembered Charlie being.

"Hello?"

I said, "Hello, Mrs. Bevins. My name is Chase Fulton."

She wasted no time. "If you're calling to try to sell me anything, you're a horrible person, and do not ever call back."

"Mrs. Bevins, I'm not a salesman. I knew your husband several years ago in St. Augustine. I'm calling to offer my condolences."

"What did you say your name is?"

"Chase Fulton, ma'am. I kept my boat at the municipal marina near Charlie's bridge. He and I struck up a kind of friendship."

"What kind of friendship are you talking about, Mr. Fulton?"

"Please call me Chase. Charlie taught me things about the river, and in return, I brought him a few bottles of whiskey."

"Was it Gentleman Jack?"

I smiled. "Yes, ma'am, it was. I don't remember how I found out, but I remember that being Charlie's favorite."

She made a sound that, in another context, could've been a short burst of laughter. "Charlie didn't drink, Chase."

"What? I'm certain I took him several bottles in the few months I spent in St. Augustine."

She said, "And they're all still here in the house. None of them have ever been opened. I remember Charlie talking about you, and he told me a little about you and what you do."

"But that doesn't make any sense," I said. "Why would he accept the whiskey if he was never going to drink it?"

"Chase, I think Charlie really liked you. I remember him coming home back then and telling me about this bright young kid living on a sailboat. He also told me what he was actually doing for you, so we don't have to dance around it."

"That still doesn't explain why he kept letting me bring him bottle after bottle if he was never going to drink it."

"He just enjoyed the time you spent with him. Being a bridgetender is a lonely job. He used to say you always brightened his day every time you came up to the bridge to visit with him. I remember him saying you were friends with that woman . . . Oh, what was her name? She was the mechanic at the marina."

"Her name is Earline, but everybody called her Earl at the End because she kept her boat at the end of the floating dock."

"Yes, that's it," she said. "Earl. Oh, I wonder what ever became of her."

"She's living here in St. Marys now, and she's the happiest I've ever seen her."

"That's so nice to hear," she said. "And I can't tell you how much it means that you would call. Thank you for that, Chase."

I bit my tongue and gathered my courage. "Mrs. Bevins . . ."

"Call me, Charlotte. I insist."

"Okay, Charlotte. I wasn't just calling to offer my condolences, although I am deeply sorry for your loss. I'm sort of working with a team of people who are trying to track down Charlie's killer."

"I don't understand. The police are investigating the murder. Are you working with the police?"

"Not exactly," I said. "It's a long, complicated story, but we believe there may be a connection between your husband's murder and at least two other shootings over the past few days."

"Oh, my. I had no idea. The detective here is a nice Irish boy named Kendrick O'Malley."

"Yes, ma'am. I know Detective O'Malley, and he and I are sharing information. The real reason I called you is to find out if there's anything I can do to help with Charlie's arrangements."

"Oh, thank you, but we had the funeral yesterday, and now it's just me and the grandkids."

"The grandkids?"

"Yes, you probably didn't know this, but our daughter, Caroline, and her husband were killed by a drunk driver a few months ago, so Charlie and I adopted their two boys. Ethan is four, and Levi is almost seven."

My heart sank. "I'm so sorry, Charlotte. I'm not trying to pry into your personal finances, but I know funerals can be incredibly expensive. If you'll let me, I would love to help cover some of those expenses."

"That's so kind of you, but I couldn't accept anything like that. Charlie was a city employee, so I'll get his pension. It's not much, but we don't need much. Our little house is paid for, and we had enough insurance to pay for the funeral."

"I'd really like to send you a little something to help with unexpected expenses. It's the least I can do, really. I've been blessed with a wonderful career that allows us to do little things for special people who come into our lives, and Charlie more than qualifies as a special person."

I was certain her reaction was laughter that time. "Oh, you have no idea. Charlie was quite special. A goofball, really. So many people are going to miss him."

Her words trailed off as tears replaced brief laughter, and I said, "Again, I've been blessed beyond measure, so I'm going to send a little something, and I'd like to start a small college fund for Levi and Ethan, if you wouldn't mind."

She was silent except for an occasional sob. "That's sweet of you, Chase. Thank you so much. I can give you the address if you don't have it."

I copied down the address and the boys' full names. "I'll stick a check in the mail, and I'll have someone contact you about setting up the education accounts. Don't worry, Charlotte. We're going to find the people responsible for Charlie's murder, and we'll make sure they pay dearly for their crimes. If you don't mind, I have one more question."

"I don't mind at all. What is it?"

"Do you know anybody named Dennis who was close to Charlie?"

After a brief pause, she said, "I can't think of anyone. Why do you ask?"

"It's just something that came up in the investigation. Detective O'Malley will probably ask you about it, as well, so if you can think of anyone named Dennis who might've meant something to your husband, please let the detective know."

"Okay. I'll see if I can come up with any ideas about who it might be."

We ended the call, and Skipper asked, "How much?"

"Send her a check for fifty thousand, and get two education savings accounts set up for the boys with fifty thousand in each. That should be more than enough to send them to school by the time they're eighteen."

Skipper looked up at me across her shoulder. "The world needs more people like you."

I waved her off. "The world doesn't know what to do with the one of me it already has. It surely couldn't handle another one."

I reclaimed my seat at the table. "What's the latest on Calvin Lynard? We're still taking him food, right?"

Clark nodded. "Yeah, and we're keeping track of him when he leaves the hotel. I've got one of the security team on him. He leaves the room about two minutes after we take him food. He's done it every time so far."

"Where does he go?" I asked.

Clark said, "He takes most of the food we give him to some other homeless guys, so we've increased the amount of chow we deliver."

Although it shouldn't have surprised me, I was fascinated to hear Calvin was routinely sacrificing the food we brought him for people he cared about.

"I've got an idea," I said. "When all of this is over, let's take a look at setting up something to help Calvin and his buddies. Maybe they just need a chance."

Skipper said, "Got it. I'll make a note, but for now, we need to get out of the charity business and back into the business of stopping whoever's trying to kill us."

I asked, "What do you have on Courtney Kellum?"

"Ginger did the military side, and I took the civilian road, and you're not going to like what we found. Ginger, why don't you go first?"

Ginger said, "I'm going to start on the civilian side, but I won't steal your thunder. Kellum graduated high school in the middle of his class. Academically, he wasn't anything special, but he lettered in three sports. Apparently, he wasn't much of a scholar, but he was a stud on the field. He went to college at Leeds Beckett University, where he played football and studied public education."

Clark said, "Football? That's cool. So, he wasn't afraid to butt heads and rough it up a little."

"Not that kind of football," Ginger said. "It's soccer, but the Brits will lose their mind if you call it soccer."

Clark shuddered. "Soccer? That's communist kickball. What else have you got?"

Ginger continued. "Anyway, he graduated, but just barely. Then he joined the British Army and quickly found himself in the Special Air Service."

Several low whistles escaped the table, and Ginger said, "Yeah, exactly, but it gets worse. The official records for the SAS guys aren't readily available, even for me, so it'll take some time to know exactly what he did in the service. But I did find this picture."

The monitor above her head filled with a photograph of a man in full battle rattle, but every eye in the room shot precisely to the patch on his uniform that said 'Sniper.'

"Well, that's not good," Hunter said, "The dude's SAS and a sniper."

"It would appear so," Ginger said. "But his time in the unit was brief. I don't have any details, but he's not listed as having been honorably discharged, so that could mean they tossed him, or it could mean they lost his records. It doesn't really matter either way because I found our boy in a different uniform."

She brought up another picture, and a chorus of groans rose from the table. Gator scanned the room, almost begging for an explanation.

Kodiak caught Gator's look and said, "Dude was a legionnaire."

"Like the French Foreign Legion?" Gator asked.

Kodiak nodded. "Exactly like that."

I said, "Okay, so Kellum is a serious player, and he can shoot. The checkmarks are adding up in his column pretty quickly."

Ginger said, "Indeed, they are, but that's all I have on the guy from the military side."

Skipper said, "I'll take it from here. Apparently, he spent a little more time in the Legion than in the SAS because he was absent from the planet for thirty-six months or so before he emerged as a security contractor for none other than Credit Suisse at the same time Roger Dean was the VP of international security."

"There's the connection," I said. "Things are starting to make sense for the first time since this all started."

Skipper said, "Kellum came to work for OGR six months after Roger Dean took over as CEO, but there's plenty of evidence that their relationship was more than just professional. Apparently, they vacation together and spend a lot of time together after hours. These guys are buddies, not just coworkers."

I said, "If that's true, there's no way Kellum is pretending to be sick without Roger Dean knowing it's a scam."

Skipper said, "Exactly. If Kellum is behind this, at the very least, Dean has to know about it, and more likely, he's the real force behind it, especially with the expense of the satellites. He's racking up an enormous bill, and I doubt Courtney Kellum has the bankroll to finance that part of the operation."

I leaned back and tried to absorb all the new information. It was becoming increasingly clear that Disco was right and my assessment of Roger Dean was completely off the mark. He had to be behind the scheme. Who else could afford five million bucks a day to rent a pair of satellites?

Ginger said, "It's my turn again. While Skipper was briefing the civilian side of Kellum's life, I did a little more digging and found something interesting."

"I'm all ears," I said.

"I figured that OGR probably didn't start out with a very big security staff, so they probably used a lot of contractors. Financial records in Zurich aren't easy to come by since one of their major selling points for the banking community is anonymity. But just because we can't follow the money doesn't mean we can't follow other trails. Every path I took led me to a few of the same players."

I pulled my notepad toward me.

She said, "I'm still working on figuring out who these guys are, but one dude in particular kept turning up with Courtney Kellum down every rabbit hole I jumped into. Here are a couple of pictures of him and Kellum."

A pair of men appeared on the monitor. In the first picture, they were smoking cigars and drinking something that looked a lot like good bourbon.

Ginger said, "As you can see, that's Courtney Kellum on the left, but I'm still not sure who the other guy is."

"Have you tried facial recognition?" Mongo asked.

Ginger said, "It's running in the background right now, but even with your monster computer, it's likely to take a while to find a match."

"Any guesses who he might be?" I asked.

"I have one, but you're not going to like it."

"Let's hear it," I said. "We don't have to like it as long as it gets us closer to figuring out who's behind this thing."

The picture on the monitor changed to a close-up image of someone's eyes.

"Who is that?" I asked.

She said, "It's our mystery man in the picture with Kellum, but just wait . . ."

A second close-up image appeared beneath the first. The angle was different, but the eyes were almost interchangeable.

"Are those two the same person?"

She said, "It looks like it, doesn't it?"

"I'm no expert," I said, "but they're pretty close."

She zoomed out on the second picture, revealing the full headshot. "This is Roger Dean II. In fact, this is his picture straight from the Princeton University website."

I devoured the photograph inch by inch until the image was burned into my mind. "But that's not him in the picture with Kellum, right?"

She zoomed back into the close-ups. "No, it's definitely not him. You can tell by the small scar in the left eyebrow and the shape of the pupil, but they're very close."

I met Ginger's gaze. "Are you saying this guy is Roger Dean's other son who seemed to drop off the face of the Earth?"

"I'm not ready to make that definitive determination, but at first glance, it certainly looks that way."

The wheels in my head spooled up, and I said, "Skipper, you said Courtney Kellum's wife was still shopping and their son was still at Cambridge, right?"

She spun to face me. "That's right."

"Can you find both of them right now?"

"Not instantly, but I'm sure I can find them in a few minutes."

I stood. "Do it. Who's up for a little snatch-and-grab?"

Chapter 17
Enjoy the Show

Access to the op center at Bonaventure is closely controlled. No one outside our immediate team and family had unfettered access to the room. With the whole team inside and our wives safely aboard our ship a thousand miles away, I was surprised to hear the access notification alarm. It must've caught Skipper off guard, as well. She jumped and spun toward the door before activating the camera. We both relaxed when Dr. Celeste Mankiller's face appeared on the screen and she came through the door.

Dr. Mankiller was a somewhat new addition to our team after we poached her from the Technical Services branch at the Department of Justice. She was our modern-day version of James Bond's Q. We gave her the lab every mad scientist dreamed of, and we paid her extremely well. In return, she developed gadgets exclusively for us that most people would never believe existed. When she had an idea, I made sure she had whatever she needed to bring the idea to life.

As she made her entrance, she stuffed her hands into the pockets of her white lab coat. "I hope I'm not interrupting anything too important."

"Not at all," I said. "We were just planning a good old-fashioned kidnapping."

"Oh, just another Tuesday, huh?"

"Exactly. What's on your mind, Doc?"

She said, "I've been thinking about the satellites that won't go away, and I think I've come up with a way to use them to our advantage."

I motioned to an empty chair. "Have a seat, and tell us a story."

She slipped onto the seat. "Well, if you strip away all the high-tech stuff, each of those two satellites is essentially a camera, a transmitter, a solar panel, and a GPS to drive the boosters that move the satellite." No one made a sound, so Dr. Mankiller said, "This is the part where you nod your head and agree with me." We nodded, and she continued. "Now, this is the part where you play along. If someone can tell that satellite to move to another spot in the sky, what other basic part is required?"

Mongo blurted out, "A receiver!"

"Ding! We have a winner. If those things have receivers, there's a way to talk to them. If I can talk to them, I can send any message or picture you want delivered to whoever's monitoring those things."

I leapt to my feet and ordered Dr. Mankiller to do the same. In her typical timid manner, she stood, and I wrapped my arms around her and kissed her forehead. "You're my favorite genius! You deserve a raise."

Skipper said, "Don't believe him, sister. He's been telling me the same thing for years."

She said, "Yeah, but it's still nice to hear."

"How long will it take to establish comms with the satellite?" I asked.

She reclaimed her seat. "I can't give you an exact timeline, but if you're okay with it, I'd like to focus entirely on that task for now."

"Absolutely," I said. "Everything else comes in second place. Let me know as soon as you figure out how to make E.T. phone home."

"You got it, boss. I'm on it." She headed through the door but stopped before she was all the way out. She stuck her head back inside and said, "One more thing. Thanks for the hottie you sent to babysit me. He's not very smart, but he's pretty to look at, and he seems really anxious to kill somebody for me."

I chuckled. "If you want, you can keep him when all of this is over."

She crinkled her nose. "Thanks, but biceps and blue eyes only get you so far. If he could hold a grown-up conversation, I'd take you up on it, but I'll just enjoy the show while it lasts."

Celeste Mankiller made her exit, and I couldn't stop thinking about just how appropriate her last name was.

Skipper yanked me back to reality. "Got her!"

I stepped behind her, and she said, "Sorry it took so long, but I found Courtney's wife, Gabrielle Kellum. She just paid for dinner with her credit card at Haus zum Rüden in Zurich."

"Excellent. Can you find any routine for her?"

Skipper said, "She does Pilates Monday, Wednesday, and Friday, and yoga every Thursday morning. For the past three weeks, it looks like she bought lunch after yoga at the same café. I think that qualifies as a routine."

"I would definitely call that a pattern. What's today?"

"Tuesday," she said.

"Perfect. Looks like we're headed back to Switzerland. I'll need a safe house, preferably outside the country, but still within five hundred miles of Zurich. We'll need some privacy but good satellite coverage. And don't make it a dump. Gabrielle Kellum sounds like a classy lady. We don't want to make her too uncomfortable. She's an innocent victim in all of this, but she's our best route to her husband."

"I'm on it," she said.

I sat down beside her. "Realistically, how long will it take Celeste to figure out how to talk to those satellites?"

She shrugged. "I'll be honest. I'm ashamed that I didn't come up with that idea. I'll talk with her and see what I can do to help. If I weren't all screwed up in the head right now, I could probably figure it out in twenty-four hours or less."

I laid a hand on her shoulder. "Quit beating yourself up, and take care of you. You're making it look easy. We've got plenty of help on this one. Everybody understands."

"Yeah, maybe, but I'm not ready to give myself the same breaks you guys are so generous with. I still expect myself to perform a little above everybody around me."

"We're all human. Well, maybe not Mongo, but you get the point."

"Thanks, Chase. Now, get out of here. You've got a yogi to kidnap."

I cocked my head. "Like Yogi Bear?"

She shook her head. "No, Boo-Boo. Like Yogi Gabrielle Kellum. Now, skedaddle. I'm busy."

I turned back to the conference table. "I know we don't usually operate with a plan B, but I've got an idea. I'll take Disco, Kodiak, and Gator with me to Zurich and snatch Mrs. Kellum. I want the rest of you to go to New York and tail Maria, Roger Dean's wife. If we blow it with Gabrielle Kellum, we'll snatch Maria and play cards with Dean again."

Clark said, "I've got the King Air, so New York is easy as long as Skipper can give us some particulars about where the lovely Maria Dean might be eating and sleeping in the Big Apple."

"Way ahead of you," Skipper said. "I just sent everything to your tablet and phone."

I turned to Disco. "You up for another trip across the pond?"

"You know it, but I'm starting to feel like an overpaid chauffeur. You have to let me punch somebody in the face pretty soon or I'll start thinking you guys don't love me anymore."

I said, "I'll see what I can do. If all else fails, I'll let you punch me."

Disco nodded. "I'll take it. Thanks. When do you want to leave?"

"As soon as possible. We need to have our boots on the ground in time to scout out the yoga studio and café before Thursday."

He checked his watch. "Give me ninety minutes. If we're going to spend much time in the air over Europe, I need to update the GPS databases in the *Ghost* before we go. I should've done it before our last flight, but things got a little hectic."

"No problem. I've also got a couple of things to take care of before we leave."

Disco headed for the airport while the rest of the team headed out to pack their gear for the next seventy-two hours.

Hunter was the last to leave, and I grabbed a handful of his sleeve as he went by. "Hey, man. Are you okay?"

He tapped his temple with a finger. "Just got a lot going on up here. I'm solid."

I said, "Give me ten minutes to make a call, and then meet me in the gazebo."

He nodded once and headed out the door.

I pulled up a chair beside Skipper and said, "I need a headset and a secure line to the ship."

She pulled the headset from a drawer and plugged it into the console. "There you go. Do you want the bridge or the radio room?"

"I want Penny."

"Oh, that's easy. You don't need a headset for that. I sent her new sat-phone number to your contacts. It's encrypted end-to-end, so you can call her directly from anywhere."

"I'd be lost without you."

She said, "I know, and I feel the same about you."

I parked myself in one of the wingbacks in front of the fireplace in the library. Since the day we moved into Bonaventure, that had been my favorite room. It felt quiet, safe, and solitary—three things I rarely got to enjoy simultaneously in my life.

"Hello," Penny said.

Just hearing her voice made everything better, if only for an instant.

"Hey there. How's life aboard the ship?"

"Hey! I wondered when you were going to call. We're getting used to life aboard, but this thing definitely doesn't qualify as a luxury cruise liner."

"I'm sorry about the accommodations, but keeping you safe is the most important thing right now."

"Speaking of safe, how's it going with the investigation?"

"We're getting closer. We're pretty sure we know who's behind it, and we're taking the necessary steps to get to them."

"Just be careful, Chase. I couldn't bear losing you. How much longer do you think we'll have to stay on the ship?"

"Things are going to come to a head in the next few days. If everything goes as I plan, all of this will be over in less than a week."

She huffed. "When was the last time anything went the way you planned?"

"There's always a first time. How are the others?"

She said, "Irina's mad because she can't join the fight, and Maebelle's teaching the cooks how to make a hundred new dishes."

"The crew will appreciate that. Is Irina really upset?"

"No, she's just pretending, but she does miss Mongo. If you have time, ask him to give her a call. It would do her good to hear his voice."

"I will. Listen, I have to run, but I just wanted to call and tell you I love you. I'll keep you posted as things progress, but I can't promise I'll call every day."

"It's okay. I understand. Just be careful and know that I love you, okay?"

"I will. I promise."

I hung up and sent Mongo and Clark a text to remind them to call the ship, just to check in. They responded almost instantly, and I headed for the gazebo.

When I got there, Hunter was already ensconced in his preferred Adirondack, and I slipped into mine. Neither of us spoke for the first several minutes, and I chose to wait him out.

Finally, he said, "It's quite a life we live, huh?"

"Sure is."

"You ever think about doing something else?"

I tried to show little, if any, reaction. "Sometimes I wonder what it would've been like to play pro ball, and I've got my psych practice. That gives me a break from what we do."

He nodded but didn't say another word for a minute or two. He had something he needed to get off his chest, but I couldn't pull it. I had to wait for him to push.

He tapped his toe against the carriage on which the eighteenth-century cannon rested between us. "I've been taking some classes online and doing a lot of studying with Singer. I'm thinking about going to seminary."

It was impossible to withhold my reaction. "Seminary? Really? What brought that about?"

He sucked on his mustache and crossed and uncrossed his legs several times. "I feel like I'm supposed to be a missionary."

"A missionary? Where?"

He said, "Yeah, you know . . . Remember in the Bible when God told Jonah to go to Nineveh, and he didn't want to go?"

"He wound up in the belly of a great fish, if I remember the story correctly."

He chuckled. "Yeah, he sure did. I guess I don't want to end up in a fish's belly."

"So, are you going to Nineveh?"

He shrugged. "I'm ashamed to admit it, but I'm not sure where Nineveh is . . . or was. I've been brushing up on my Spanish for some reason, so I'll probably end up somewhere in South America."

"Makes sense," I said. "When were you planning to tell us?"

He bounced the heel of his right boot off the toe of his left. "Last week. The day Tony got shot."

I bowed my head and felt the razor's edge of the blade on which we walk sink into my flesh. Every second of every day could've been our last. I tried to imagine the anxiety Hunter carried around inside his chest for the past weeks while trying to make the decision that, in my opinion, wasn't a decision at all.

"Does Singer know?"

Hunter shook his head. "No, just you and me."

I replayed the fun we'd had on and in the water, the adrenaline we shared in more gunfights than I wanted to remember, the moments of utter terror when neither of us believed we'd survive the next hour or minute or even the next second of our lives. I was thankful for every instant we shared, and I loved Stone W. Hunter more than I could love a blood brother.

I said, "Not all battles are fought with bullets and blades. The most important ones are won with faith and love. I have to admit that I'm a little envious of your calling. Most of us never hear ours, or we're making too much noise to listen. You have to answer that call, my friend."

"I should've known you'd understand."

The next ten seconds of my life seemed to last an eternity. I watched my partner, my brother, fly from the Adirondack in a cloud of red mist. The force of the impact rolled the chair onto its side, leaving Hunter on his side with blood pouring from his shoulder, neck, and back. The roaring thunder and blistering crack of the shot pierced my head, and it felt as if I'd absorbed the round. In absolute disbelief of what was unfolding in front of me, I planted my boots and shoved myself from the chair as I instinctually drew my pistol. In the next instant, splinters of oak filled the air in front of me as the second projectile buried itself in the cannon's carriage and I dived on top of my fallen brother to shield him from a third round.

Chapter 18
Assets

The world around me dissolved into a blanket of white billowing foam, with Hunter lying in the center of an ever-expanding crimson pool, his eyes staring up at me as if he were clinging to my very flesh in an attempt to remain on this side of the darkness beyond. The glistening orbs of blood beneath his nose told me his lungs were still drawing and easing. The pulsing, viscous flow from the massive wound said his heart was fighting to force what blood remained inside of his body to his brain. Hunter was one breath, one beat of a dying heart away from eternity, and nothing short of the Almighty could sustain him.

I rolled him onto his stomach, exposing the gruesome wound that had once been his shoulder. I yanked my shirt from my body, pressing the fabric into the unimaginable wound. The shirt was almost instantly soaked, but I kept pressing until I found myself lying on top of him with my full weight, delivering pressure to the wound. If I could've opened my body and poured my blood into him, I would've done it without hesitation, but I was powerless to do anything other than feel the life escaping the body of my closest friend and truest brother.

I yelled with every ounce of breath my lungs could expel, but no one answered. Still screaming like a madman, I held my pistol overhead and emptied the magazine into the rafters of the gazebo. Although I never heard a single round leaving my Glock, the desperate effort worked.

I couldn't focus on the faces that surrounded me, nor could I hear what they were saying, so I yelled out, "Hunter's down! Get a kit!"

Someone shouldered me from on top of Hunter and piled dressings on the wound, each of them turning black in seconds. As my vision cleared, I watched Singer drive a large-bore needle into each of Hunter's arms with bags of fluid hanging from unseen hands.

Time lost is its command of the world around me, and I couldn't distinguish an instant from an eternity. I felt a pair of hands exploring my bare chest and abdomen and a voice crying out, "Chasechka! Where are you hit? Where are you bleeding?"

I slapped her hands away and lunged back toward Hunter. "It's not my blood!"

The sight of two paramedics in blue uniforms came into focus as the flashing lights of the ambulance punctuated the scene. Hunter was on the stretcher, and the siren wailed in continually softening bellows as they disappeared around the end of the house.

When my breath returned, I found myself lying against the carriage of the mighty cannon with Hunter's blood still covering my skin.

Mongo's massive form blocked the light from above. "Chase, are you hit?"

"No. The blood's not mine. Two rounds. First one . . . in Hunter's shoulder . . ."

I felt for the end of the heavy oak carriage. "Second one . . . here somewhere."

Mongo said, "Take a breath. Hunter's alive, at least for now. Singer went with him. Are you sure you're not hit?"

"I'm sure."

I took long, intentional breaths, forcing the air into the bottoms of my lungs until I could finally breathe normally.

"I'm sure I'm not hit. The shots came from across the river."

Mongo held my face in his massive hands. "I need you to think, Chase. How long between the impact and the thunder?"

"I don't know."

"You have to remember. How long? We have to know how far away the shooter was."

"It was a long time. That's all I remember. He wasn't close."

"Can you stand up?" he asked as he took my arm in his hands.

I was on my feet before I realized I'd tried to stand.

He led me from the gazebo and toward the river. "Point to the shooter."

I raised one hand to the east. "He was somewhere around Point Peter."

The peninsula of land between the North River and Point Peter Creek was home to some of the area's most affluent families. It wasn't the kind of neighborhood in which a sniper could climb onto a roof, crack off two rounds, and escape without anyone noticing. Someone saw him. Someone heard him. Someone knew which direction he escaped in.

The hard-rock former SEAL appeared as if from thin air. "Where's that Mark-Five?"

Almost before I could answer, the SEAL, Mongo, and I were racing across the black surface of North River with the throttles of the Mark V buried into their stops. The SEAL braced himself against the helm station and appeared to become part of the boat. The sharper the turns, the more he moved with the vessel. I'd spent hundreds of hours at the controls of the patrol boat, but I would never possess the degree of skill and confidence behind the controls as that SEAL whose name I'd yet to hear. As we drew nearer to Point Peter, I scanned rooflines for any sign they had held a sniper. While I wasted time on a task that would never produce any meaningful results, Mongo scoured the open water of Cumberland Sound. The SEAL, though, with experience and training unlike anything I would ever endure, cast his eyes to the murky shallows and muddy shoreline of the peninsula.

With his attention focused on the surface environment instead of the depth, the SEAL put us aground in four feet of creek water. He threw the shifters into neutral and the throttles to idle and did the last thing I could've imagined him doing. As the Mark V floundered with her keel stuck in the mud, the SEAL dived across the gunwale and into the black water.

Mongo turned to me with disbelief in his eyes. "What's he doing?"

"No idea!" I yelled back. "But we're wasting a lot of time."

Mongo and I turned in unison as the SEAL burst from the water near the shoreline and waded through the mud and muck toward the point. As the depth grew shallower, he picked up his pace until he was in a sprint toward an almost limitless mass of reeds and marsh grass. Although he shared Mongo's impressive muscular bulk, the SEAL didn't share his height. The grass swallowed him as he bolted into dense foliage.

"Is he tracking somebody?" I asked

Mongo squinted, desperately trying to see through the growth. "He's a SEAL. Who knows what he's thinking?"

I shook off my nearly insatiable longing to know what the fireplug of a man was doing and stepped into the helm of the boat. "We're wasting time. I'm going hunting."

The maze of creeks, rivers, and marshland surrounding St Marys was vast, but I knew it well. If the sniper believed he could escape and hide in my backyard, he'd just made the worst mistake of his life.

I gripped both throttles and prepared to yank the Mark V off the bottom with her brute horsepower, but Mongo grabbed my shoulder before I could apply power.

He pointed into the marsh, "Look!"

The SEAL was standing ten feet above the marsh grass on the rusted-out remains of what had once been an antenna. The wiry structure blended in with the surroundings so well that it was all but invisible.

We stared back at the warrior, and Mongo said, "Man, he's good."

"Be careful. If he hears you say that, he'll come sniffing around looking for a job."

Mongo looked down at me and shrugged. That simple gesture

made my blood run cold, and I shoved him hard enough to knock him from his feet and onto one of the crew seats. "Don't do that! Hunter is *not* dead yet. You do not get to do that!"

Instead of crushing me like the tantrum-throwing, fit-pitching child I was in that moment, Mongo spoke barely loud enough to be heard over the twin diesels. "Keep your head about you, Chase. You're our captain, and everybody needs you at the top of your game right now."

The SEAL came over the transom with stalactites of black sludge hanging from his beard. He galloped to the cockpit, leaving a trail of filthy water and mud on the deck behind him. "It was a catamaran."

I shoved a towel toward him. "A catamaran? Like a sailboat?"

He shook his head, sending water flying from his face in every direction. "No. It was a power cat. He ran it aground hard enough to stick the prop in the mud."

"How could you possibly know that?"

He looked at me as if I'd asked him how to tie my boots. "It's simple, man. Once I found the indentations of the twin hulls in the bank, I followed them back into deeper water and found the scar he left on the bottom when he powered off. It was a single screw, the beam was maybe twelve feet or a little less, and the length maybe twenty-five to thirty feet."

I stared at him, unsure if I should believe him or ask him to teach me how to do that. "And you think he took the shots from that antenna base?"

"I know he did. There's powder burns on one of the legs. He had a wide-open line of sight to Bonaventure from there."

His look said he wanted something from me, but I was lost. "What? What do you want?"

He pushed me aside. "Get out of the way so I can chase this guy."

I obeyed, and he powered off the bottom with the muscle of the twin diesels. I tried to imagine the scar the hull of the Mark V left in the mud beneath us and if he could identify *any* vessel by the traces it left behind.

Forcing myself to prioritize and focus, I dialed Disco.

"Yeah, Chase. I just heard. What do you need from me?"

"Get in the air with anything that'll fly. We're looking for a twenty-five to thirty-foot power cat with a ten- to twelve-foot beam and probably a single outboard."

"How do you know?"

"The SEAL."

As we spun to the south, our driver yelled over his shoulder. "Which way would you run if you were the shooter?"

"I'd go south. There are too many dead ends to the north and west."

"What about the open ocean?" he asked.

I gave it some thought. "Maybe, but if you're right about the size and configuration, that's not much of a boat for open water."

He seemed to catalog every piece of information in his head. "Do you have any available air assets?"

"That was the reason for the call I just made. We'll have a plane in the air in two minutes."

Our speed made conversation in normal tones impossible, so we were forced to yell every word until I grabbed the headsets from beneath the panel. The three of us donned the noise-canceling intercom sets. The roar of the world around me sank away, leaving me in relative silence in my ears but drowning in a cacophony of terror inside my head.

With our open-channel satellite comms up and running, Disco said, "Air One airborne over Bonaventure in the Caravan."

The SEAL checked over his shoulder, apparently to make sure I heard our chief pilot.

I said, "Air One, Sierra One. We're crossing the sound and headed for the Amelia River in the Mark-Five. Make a pass over the river south of town and then out the pass to the open ocean."

Disco said, "Roger, Sierra One. I'm headed southwest."

I grabbed the binoculars from the console and climbed on top of the canopy above the cockpit. As I positioned myself to start my visual search for the power cat, it occurred to me that I was missing a bit of information that might come in handy.

Over the intercom, I said, "Hey, SEAL. What's your name?"

"It's Shawn. I shut down the radar so it wouldn't cook your guts up there. You see anything yet?"

"Thanks," I said. "I've got plenty of targets, but nothing that looks like a power cat."

"Keep scanning," he said. "He's got to be out here somewhere."

Disco's voice filled my head. "Sierra One, Air One. Contact! I've got a single outboard power cat approaching Waterman's Bluff. Tell me what to do."

Chapter 19
The SEAL

I scampered down from the canopy and back into the cockpit with Mongo and Shawn, the SEAL. "Break hard right! We're headed to Waterman's Bluff."

Shawn spun the wheel, and the keel of the Mark V sliced into water in the tightest turn I'd ever felt the boat make.

I stepped around him and zoomed out on the chart plotter until the bluff was centered on the screen. "That's where we're going."

Shawn glanced at the plotter as we tore across the surface well above fifty knots. "Got it!"

While staring at the chart plotter, I tried to picture Disco's position relative to the power cat. "Air One, are you armed?"

"Affirmative," came Disco's reply. "I've got a rifle and my sidearm. What do you want me to do with this guy? He's a single."

"Keep him in the boat and off the shore, but don't get shot. If he's our guy, he's well-armed and not afraid to pull the trigger."

"Roger."

I glanced up to assess our position as we snaked through the ever-narrowing confines of the river west of the city. I grabbed Shawn's arm and said, "We're going left in five hundred yards."

Instead of double-checking my directions on the plotter, his eyes never left the water in front of us. Spreading my feet to absorb the steep turn that was quickly approaching, I glanced at Mongo slithering his arm through the sling of his SR-25, .308.

Shawn laid the patrol boat on its side as we swung to the south and into an even narrower branch of the St. Marys River. Mongo shoved himself from the oversized crew seat Earl had built just for the giant. He threw open the weapons hatch and withdrew one of the pair of Ma Deuce fifty-caliber machine guns. Against the wind and angles, he hefted the mighty weapon onto its mount ahead of the cockpit. We were seconds away from intercepting the sniper who'd cut Hunter down, and we were bringing hell with us.

Shawn pointed through the windshield. "Is that your boy?"

I followed his finger to the Cessna Caravan careening out of the sky like a mighty albatross diving on baitfish. "That's Disco."

Shawn focused his attention on the power cat coming into view over the bow. "Tallyho!"

I braced against the console and stuck the binoculars to my eyes. "He's definitely a single. I think he's our guy."

I glanced up at the Caravan. "Get on his bow, Disco. We're going to pinch him from astern and see which way he breaks."

Disco said, "Roger. I'll break away from his turn in case you have to open fire."

"Roger."

Another look across the bow showed the power cat running at what must've been full throttle, but his single outboard was no match for our twin turbo diesels.

I said, "Pinch him, Shawn. I want to see which way he runs."

The SEAL made barely perceptible adjustments to the controls until we were lined up directly astern of the other boat. "Is that big dude any good on that fifty? If this is our guy, he won't go down without a fight, no matter how outgunned he is."

"There's nobody better on that fifty-cal than Mongo. If that sniper so much as winks at us, he'll cut him in half."

Disco continued his dive until the floats of the amphib were mere inches above the surface. I could almost see the wheels churning in Shawn's head as he calculated the closure rate and adjusted our speed.

The Caravan screamed toward the bow of the power cat as we closed from astern. Everything was happening fast, and the sniper was only seconds away from having no choice but to break in one direction or the other.

I threw down the binoculars as we tightened the grip on our prey. He was almost close enough to touch, and I couldn't wait to pin him to the deck and make him beg for the life I'd never let him keep.

The man in the power cat finally checked his six and saw the eighty-foot, fifty-ton, gun-metal grey patrol boat bearing down on him, and his next move wasn't what I expected. Instead of breaking right or left, he chopped the throttle and spun the wheel hard over, bringing his vessel to a dead stop in the center of the river.

Shawn gave the order. "Brace! Brace! Brace!"

Mongo planted a heavy boot behind the fifty-cal mount, and I drove my palms into the console as the SEAL threw the transmissions in reverse and crushed the throttles. The bow of the Mark V dived like a submarine, and the stern bucked into the air as our forward momentum was converted to vertical motion in the pitch.

When every piece of the enormous vessel came to rest, we lay abeam the power cat with Disco and the Caravan roaring only inches overhead. The instant I regained my footing, I lunged around the SEAL with my rifle at high ready, but instead of hurdling the gunwale and devouring the filthy bastard who'd shot Hunter, I met a hurdle I couldn't overcome.

Shawn planted a powerful arm against my chest, stopping me in my tracks. I had, at times in the past, run through Mongo when he tried to hold me back, but with the SEAL's strength, it was like wrestling with a boulder.

He looked up and wrapped a hand around my rifle. "I'm taking this one. They can't afford to lose you. Hold the boat, skipper." Shawn ripped the rifle from my hands and bounded over the gunwale in one motion. Mongo was back on his feet with the Ma Deuce trained on the much smaller boat.

I ran to the rail to watch Shawn handle the shooter. The speed and efficiency of motion he used was astonishing. Without a single word, he had the man face-down on the deck and had him flex-cuffed in seconds. Once the sniper was completely under control, Shawn tossed a line from the power cat over the rail of the Mark V, and I made it fast around a cleat. There was no chance of this guy escaping, no matter what happened next.

Disco circled overhead in a tight turn to the left, watching the spectacle unfold fifty feet away. Between the roar of the Caravan's PT6 turbine, the growl of the twin diesels of the Mark V, and Shawn's unstoppable force on deck, the sniper was clearly overwhelmed.

I climbed onto the gunwale with my pistol in hand, begging for any excuse to execute the man where he lay, but to my utter surprise, he offered no resistance. Instead, he lay perfectly still, whimpering like a terrified child.

"Get him up!" I yelled. "Let him see my face."

Shawn clawed the man's neck and yanked him to his feet with the muzzle of his rifle buried in his ear. Instead of the hardened face of a seasoned warrior, the man wore the look of a mortified hostage. His eyes were enormous, and his lips quivered with every jerking breath.

"Who do you work for?" Shawn growled.

I yelled, "Watch him. He's sandbagging."

The performance continued, and the man spoke between gasps of feigned terror. "River . . . uh, Valley. I drive . . . a truck."

"What's River Valley?" Shawn hissed as he pressed the muzzle deeper into the man's flesh.

"A paper company . . . in Yulee." He seemed to choke on the words, but his act was convincing.

Shawn yanked a wallet from the man's pocket and tossed it up to me. "What's your name?"

"Gary . . . McDonald. I didn't steal this boat, I swear. I just bought it."

I flipped open the wallet, and the name matched the driver's license and several other cards inside.

"Tell me your address," I yelled, and he blurted out exactly what was printed on his license.

I yelled, "Where's the rifle?"

"What are you talking about? I ain't got no rifle. I got a pistol in the truck, but I ain't got no rifle." His tone seemed to transform from fearful into misunderstanding. "I ain't done nothing wrong, I swear. I can show you the bill of sale. I just bought this boat."

I studied the scene beneath me. The boat was clean and dry, just like the man in Shawn's grasp. No mud, no muck, and no salt water.

I said, "Take his hat off."

Shawn yanked off the man's cap, exposing a head of dry, disheveled hair.

The SEAL ran a hand through the man's hair and shook his head. "He hasn't been wet."

I lowered my pistol and ground my boot into the combing of the gunwale. "Damnit! Cut him loose." With my Secret Service credentials held open in front of me, I said, "We're sorry, sir. You're not the person we're after. Have you seen any other boats like yours on the water today?"

Shawn cut off the flex-cuffs, and the man rubbed his wrists. "Yeah, there was another one crossing the sound a couple hours ago. It was blue, though. You guys scared the crap out of me. What'd this guy do?"

"He's a serial killer. Let's go."

I hopped down from the gunwale, cast off the line from the smaller vessel, and eased the boat around until the stern ladder was poised for Shawn's return. He climbed back aboard, and I took one more look down at the power cat. McDonald was waving his arms and yelling something.

I turned to Shawn, and he said, "Give the guy back his wallet."

I shoved several one-hundred-dollar bills into the wallet and tossed it back to the man. He caught it, gave me a finger, and motored away.

I looked up at the Caravan. "Keep hunting, Air One. This one wasn't our guy."

"Roger. Air One is on the hunt."

Shawn handed back my rifle. "I suck at failing, boss."

I hung my head. "Me, too. Take us back to the pass. We'll loiter there in case Disco spots anything, but I'm afraid this one's a bust."

He stepped to the helm and said, "Roger."

On our way toward Fort Clinch, I rang the op center.

When Skipper answered, I said, "What's the word on Hunter?"

"He's in surgery, but he lost a lot of blood. They called in a surgeon from the Mayo Clinic in Jacksonville. She's coming by helicopter, and she's supposed to be one of the best trauma surgeons in the country."

I said, "That's good news, I guess. Our op was a bust. Wrong guy."

"Yeah, I've been listening on the sat-com. He's gone, isn't he?"

"Probably. If Disco doesn't pick him up in a few minutes, we'll head to the hospital. Have you got anything else for me?"

"We got the ballistics report from the bullets that killed Tony."

"Same gun?" I asked.

"Yeah, and there's another cryptic message."

"Let's hear it."

She said, "This one's really weird. It says, 'We panic in a pew.'"

I groaned. "What could that possibly mean?"

"Maybe it's a reference to the church fire. I don't know."

"Maybe. Keep me posted if you get any updates on Hunter."

"Wilco. And Chase?"

"What is it?"

"You didn't hurt the guy in the boat, did you?"

"No. Shawn kept me from getting to him."

"Who's Shawn?" she asked.

"The SEAL."

Chapter 20
Home to Mother

Disco flew a search grid for half an hour, but there was no sign of another boat fitting the description of the power cat.

"I'm calling it," I said. "Let's get back to Bonaventure and check on Hunter."

Shawn brought us about, and seconds later, we were on plane at sixty knots, headed for the North River.

He pulled his headset mic close to his lips. "Maybe it's none of my business, but how'd you score a Mark-Five?"

I said, "It was a gift from the guys up at the submarine base."

"Kings Bay?"

"Yeah. It was grounded on the hard when we got it, and both engines were garbage. It had apparently been sunken, so it wasn't much more than scrap."

"Who rebuilt it?"

"We've got one of the best diesel mechanics and metal fabricators you've ever seen, but you probably won't meet her."

He raised an eyebrow. "Her?"

"Yep. But don't get too excited. From a distance, it's tough to tell that she's a woman, and it's even tougher up close. To top it off, she's married to an insane Cajun who kills people for fun and buries them a hundred feet deep."

"Sounds like my kind of guy," he said.

"I don't know what language he speaks, but it's nothing resembling English."

"We had a guy like that on the Teams. He carried a knife that looked like a sword, and he could cook anything out of nothing. Those Cajuns are something else."

"Kenny's the only one I've ever met, but if they're all like him, I think one might be enough."

Shawn backed the vessel into the boathouse as if he'd done it a thousand times, and I ran him through the fueling procedure.

I said, "We've got two fifteen-hundred-gallon tanks buried near the house. They feed this pump and the one out by the maintenance building. If you guys need diesel, help yourselves. I told your team leader about the gas pumps at the airport. If you use those, make sure you don't put avgas or JP-6 in your Suburbans."

"That could be interesting. Hey, listen. I'm sorry about what's going on, and I'm even more sorry I didn't pick up that sniper. One of us should've seen him."

"Listen to me. Mongo and I were fifty feet away from the antenna base you found in the marsh, and neither of us saw it. What happened to Hunter isn't your fault, nor is it the fault of anybody on your team. Don't carry that one around. It's not yours."

He grimaced. "Still . . ."

I squared up with him. "If it were your fault, I would've come down on your team leader so hard he'd still be digging himself out of the ground. This is my team and my responsibility. I appreciate and respect your attitude, but don't let it shape what you do in the coming days. Clark likes to say 'Embrace the suck and soldier on.'"

Mongo and I picked up Disco at the airport and found Clark and Anya in the surgical waiting room. They stood when we walked in, and I shook my head.

"We didn't catch him. Have you heard anything from the surgeons?"

Clark raked vending machine Honey Buns crumbs from his beard. "Nothing yet."

Gator and Singer came through the door, and Singer said, "I just saw the surgeon."

"What did he say?" I asked.

"I didn't talk to him. I just saw him through a window. He was changing scrubs. That probably means he's coming out to talk to us."

A narrow door in the back of the waiting area opened, and a man and woman, both in clean scrubs, came into the room. We turned as they approached, and the man said, "The family seems to be expanding."

I took that as a positive indication since I doubted he'd dispense bad news after a jovial comment like that.

Clark said, "There are more. How's Hunter?"

The man said, "I'll let Dr. Margolis bring you up to date."

The lady, who appeared to be in her fifties, with short, dark hair and glasses, said, "I'm Virginia Margolis, and I'm the chief of surgery for the Mayo Clinic in Jacksonville. I'm board-certified in—"

I said, "We trust you, and we don't need your credentials. Tell us about Hunter."

She sighed. "Mr. Hunter, as you know, suffered a traumatic large-caliber gunshot wound to the right shoulder, neck, and upper back. The damage was devastating, but thanks to the nearly instant reaction by someone to apply massive pressure and start IVs, he is likely to survive."

A collective sigh of relief escaped us, and Dr. Margolis said, "Let me caution you. There are no certainties in treatment following a wound such as the one Mr. Hunter sustained."

She paused and cupped her right hand over her left shoulder. "The projectile completely destroyed the glenohumeral joint, upper third of the humerus, scapula, clavicle, and three cervical vertebrae, C-four, five, and six. That's essentially every bone in the right shoulder, upper arm, and lower neck. The soft tissue associated with the all of these bones and joints is essentially destroyed, as well. Fortunately, the spinal cord was not severed. If it were, Mr. Hunter would've arrived at the morgue instead of the ER."

I stood in awe and disbelief, and it appeared everyone shared my feelings. "Is there . . . Can you . . . I don't even know what questions to ask."

Dr. Margolis said, "It's okay. I'll answer them anyway. I believe Mr. Hunter will survive. Dr. Carter and I are not reconstructive surgeons. We, along with the two other doctors still in the OR, are trauma surgeons. It's our job to stabilize him so the other surgeons can reconstruct what the gunman destroyed. We will do everything that can be done to stop the trauma and keep your friend alive. He's a long way from being out of the woods, and he will remain in a medically induced coma for some time."

I heard a hissing noise and turned to see Singer with his eyes closed and his lips whispering a prayer that was, no doubt, the expression of relief all of us felt in that moment.

Dr. Margolis said, "I'm sure you have a thousand more questions, but we need to get back in there. We've still got a lot of work to do."

They disappeared back through the small door, and we collapsed into our seats. More thoughts poured through my mind in those few minutes than should've been possible. The prevailing emotion was endless fury when it should've been abundant thanks, but I wanted nothing more than to tear the soul from the man who'd killed Charlie, Jimmy, and Tony, and nearly killed the best friend I'd ever know. Rage boiled where gratitude should've dwelt, and vengeance beckoned where mercy should've reined. When my hands finally ceased their trembling, I said, "If it were any of us lying on that table in there, we all know Hunter would be the first man out the door to find the shooter. We owe him nothing less. Our brother is in the hands of God and those doctors. It's time for us to go to work."

* * *

We reconvened in the op center, and I issued the orders. "Disco, Anya, you're with me. We're going to Zurich, and we're going to roll up Gabrielle Kellum. Skipper, did you find us a safe house yet?"

"I'm still on it, but I'm coming up dry."

"I know I told you to find someplace comfortable, but the time for courtesy is long gone. Find me a hole in the ground if that's all there is. I no longer care who we have to hurt. We're taking these people down, and they will rue the day they put us in their sights."

Fists struck the table like thunder, and I continued. "Clark, you're taking Mongo, Kodiak, and Gator to New York. Roger Dean's wife, Maria, is no longer a contingency target. I want you to take her, regardless of what happens in Zurich. Bring her back here or find a safe house. It's up to you."

Clark nodded, and I turned to Dr. Mankiller. "Celeste, where are you on the comms with the satellites?"

She held her thumb and forefinger a fraction of an inch apart. "I'm ninety-nine percent of the way there."

"What does that mean?"

She withdrew, almost shrinking in her seat. "I can do it, but—"

I growled. "No buts! You can do it, or you can't."

Her tone softened even more. "Yeah, I can do it. The thing is, I found a way to capture the satellite video feed back to Singe Voir in Paris."

My heart tried to leap from my chest. "How far back can you go?"

"I don't know. Maybe a thousand hours or so."

I closed my eyes, threw my head back, and thanked God for Dr. Celeste Mankiller. When I forced my mind back into the room, I said, "That means we can see Hunter's shooter."

Celeste nodded enthusiastically. "Yes, that's exactly what it means. I've already got it queued up."

"Why didn't you say that?"

"I tried, but you . . ."

"Never mind. Just show us."

The large monitor came to life with a still shot of a blue power cat nestled at the edge of the marsh grass off Point Peter.

Celeste said, "I can run this back and show you where the boat came from on the backside of Cumberland Island near the Dungeness Dock."

"What about before that? Can you show us where he originally came from?"

"I tried, but the cloud cover wouldn't allow me to see how he got to Cumberland Island."

She started the video, and we watched in horror as the gunman climbed from the boat, crossed the mud and marsh grass, and climbed the remains of the antenna.

"Is there a timestamp?" Singer asked.

Celeste said, "Yes, but not an overlay. The video file is timestamped in the code, so I can extrapolate it, but it's not displayed."

She ran the video forward and stopped it again. When the video began moving, the sniper patiently sent two rounds toward Bonaventure, and it felt like both of them pierced my chest. I caught myself breathing hard. "Please tell me we can see him run."

She sped up the video as the shooter made his way back to the boat and headed straight for the pass into the Atlantic. The video showed the Mark V racing south out of the North River at the same time the power cat exited the pass and continued due east into the ocean.

"Where's he going?" Gator asked.

Celeste said, "I don't know."

She sped up the video again until the small boat was no longer visible on the screen. "He motored out of the satellite coverage area. I'm sorry I couldn't get any more."

I said, "It's okay, Celeste. I know exactly where he's going. He was running home to Mother."

Chapter 21
A Better Perspective

I yanked my pad from the bin beneath my spot at the table. "How long will it take for you to match a position with a time for the moment he left the satellite coverage?"

Celeste said, "Maybe a minute."

"Do it."

She pulled her laptop close and worked furiously. When she looked up, she said, "He was thirty miles due east of the St. Marys Pass two hours and six minutes ago."

"Calculate his speed from the time he left the pass until he dropped off the satellite."

Without hesitation, Celeste said, "Forty-two knots."

I closed my eyes and let the calculator in my head try to catch up. "That means he could travel about eighty-six miles, right?"

"Yes, if he maintained that speed, but a boat that size in the open water is a death trap."

"Maybe not," I said. "I just pulled up the sea state, and it's less than three feet swells a hundred miles off. It wouldn't be a comfortable ride, but it's possible."

"Tell me what you want," Celeste said.

"I want a satellite view of the ship he rendezvoused with."

Before Celeste could answer, Skipper said, "I'm on it."

Disco leaned against the table. "The Mustang can do eight times his speed."

I had Don Maynard, our airport manager, on the phone seconds later.

"Hey, Chase."

"Don, I need you to pull out the Mustang and make sure the tanks are topped off."

"No problem. When do you want it?"

"An hour ago."

Nothing else he could say would change anything, so I clicked off and asked, "How's the satellite imagery coming?"

Skipper said, "It's going to take at least forty-five minutes to have a usable satellite in place."

Controlling my whirring mind wasn't easy, but things were falling into place. "Work with Celeste. Since she can talk to the satellites OGR is using, maybe you can find a way to hijack them and move them to where we need them instead of where *they* want them."

Disco was already on his way to the door, so I stood to follow. "Clark, get your team moving to New York. We need to roll up our bargaining chips as soon as possible."

"What about Zurich?" Clark asked.

"We're chasing down that boat first. If we can get an ID, Captain Sprayberry and the *Lori Danielle* can take care of the ship while we keep our feet dry."

When Disco and I arrived at the airport, *Penny's Secret*, my P-51 D-model Mustang, was gleaming in the midday sun, and Don was pulling away in the fuel truck. Disco checked the fuel while I ran through the remaining pre-flight checklist. I couldn't let our desire to get into the air as quickly as possible outweigh the necessity of the pre-flight checks. Ninety-nine percent of our flight would take place over the open Atlantic, and ditching the Mustang wasn't something I wanted to include in our afternoon.

I started the massive Merlin engine and watched flames belch from the exhaust as we taxied from the ramp. I caught a glimpse of Don on the ramp, waving his right hand in a pistol formation with his thumb and index finger.

"What's he trying to tell us?"

Disco said, "I guess you didn't notice the fifty-cal rounds in the wing during your pre-flight, huh?"

"Good ol' Don," I said. "You may have a tough time keeping my finger off the trigger if we find that guy."

Disco huffed. "You may have a hard time beating me to that trigger."

We blasted off and climbed due east from Bonaventure over the seemingly endless blue of the Atlantic. With the gear in the wells and the prop dragging us through the hot air with all of its might, the airspeed indicator showed three hundred twenty knots. That made Disco's projection of eight times the gunman's speed right on the money.

I configured the sat-com and called Skipper. "Sierra Ops, Sierra One. Any news on the satellite?"

She said, "Negative, Sierra One, but we're still on it."

"Roger. We're airborne and thirty-five miles offshore."

She said, "Roger. I'm tracking you. Advise if you make contact."

"Wilco. Have someone get on the horn with Captain Sprayberry and get the ship headed toward us. We're going to have our hands full, and we can use all the help we can get."

"You got it," she said. "Element two will be airborne in minutes."

"Tell them I said happy hunting.'"

"Will do."

With no radar aboard the Mustang, we were relegated to scanning every direction with nothing more than our eyes. Shrimp boats and cargo freighters dotted the seascape, and we even spotted a few sailboats, but after forty minutes in the air, we still hadn't spotted anything resembling a thirty-foot power cat blasting its way to the east.

I called home again. "Sierra Ops, plot the likely position of the target against our position, and give me some directions."

It was Celeste's voice that filled my ear. "Five degrees right and twenty-three miles will put you over his calculated position if he didn't change course or speed."

I made the heading change and reduced the power to not only conserve fuel but to also slow our speed from five miles per minute to a slower loitering speed for our search grid.

If Celeste's calculations were correct, we hit the spot seven minutes later.

"We should be on target," I said. "What do you show?"

Celeste said, "That's it. If nothing changed, he should be directly beneath you."

Disco leaned from side to side, peering through the canopy in search of our target. "I got nothing. How about you?"

I said, "A pod of dolphins at nine o'clock and a freighter at four, but that's it."

"What do you think changed?" he asked.

"Three options," I said. "He either slowed down, changed course, or got picked up by his support ship."

I made a slow turn, giving us a 360-degree view. "I'm starting a grid. We'll work fifty miles east and west and a hundred miles north and south."

Disco said, "That sounds good to me. If you get tired, I'll be glad to do the flying."

"Yeah, take it for a while, if you don't mind. You have the controls."

"I have the controls," he answered.

"You have the controls."

With my hands and feet free, I allowed my body to relax for the first time since I pressed the throttle forward back on the ground. We flew the north-south track at fifteen hundred feet until we'd worked our way fifty miles east. Nothing we spotted looked anything like the power cat or a support ship capable of launching and recovering such a craft.

I said, "I'm surprised how empty the ocean is this far offshore."

"Me, too. Are you ready to work west?"

I glanced off the right wing, where home and my life belonged. Hiding my wife aboard what many would describe as a ship of war was not an action I ever believed I would be forced to make. Scouring the limitless bounds of the Atlantic Ocean in search of a lone gunman who likely killed my dearest friend and brother was not a task I ever dreamed possible. The life I led imposed demands like none other—demands of my time, my body, and my very soul. Enduring such demands is an undertaking no man should have to bear, but the preservation of my family, my team, and ultimately, the liberties that make America the greatest nation in the history of the world, falls onto the shoulders of common men and women like me and the selfless professionals around me who look to me for direction. How I came to stand on such ground will forever be a mystery to me. The force that deposited me into the life that is mine will never reveal itself, but I will grind whatever grist the mill requires to preserve the lives of the people I love, the ideals I hold dear, and the country that will forever be my home.

"Chase, I asked if you're ready to turn west."

Disco's voice pulled me from my stupor, and I said, "No. The Gulfstream is flowing about four knots to the northeast. Take us that direction, and reestablish a grid adjusted for that current."

Disco put us in position to continue our search, and I reclaimed the controls. We searched for another half hour until I was minutes away from calling it off and heading west.

Disco's voice pierced the silence like a bolt of lightning. "Contact! Ten o'clock, maybe two miles."

I leaned left and followed his line of sight to a white speck on the floor of blue. "I see it. Coming left."

I lowered the nose and accelerated until the speck became a spot, and then a shape, and then a blue and white power cat with a single outboard engine.

"That's it!" Disco yelled. "We found it!"

I pulled the power back and descended to a hundred feet above the water as we made our first pass from stern to bow.

"Did you see anybody on board?"

Disco shook his head. "Negative. Make another pass."

I flew a maneuver a crop duster might make and reversed our direction, taking the boat down our left side—this time from the bow to stern.

"There's nobody down there," I said. "Does that boat have a cabin down below?"

Disco said, "I don't think so. Maybe he fell out and it finally ran out of gas. The engine isn't producing any thrust."

"You're right. It's either out of gas or shut down. That means the shooter is either shark bait or he's safe and sound aboard another vessel that picked him up."

Disco pulled his shoulder harness tight against his body. "I have the controls."

I surrendered the airplane back to him and tightened my straps. Whatever he was about to do was going to be extreme, and sitting behind a man who'd spent his life at the controls of an A-10 Warthog was exactly where I was meant to be in that moment.

He added power, increasing our speed across the water until we had the momentum he needed to fly the coming maneuver. At two hundred knots, he said, "Here comes the Gs!"

He raised the nose sharply, sending my body sinking into the seat and the blood rushing away from my head. I squeezed and performed the breathing technique to allow my body to manage the excessive G loading.

We performed half of a loop and found ourselves upside down and diving back toward the water. Our speed built as the small boat grew larger and larger with every foot. We flew directly over the boat, giving us the perfect vantage point to study the vessel.

With the boat behind us, Disco performed half of a roll, returning us to upright flight.

I shook my head, regathering myself. "It was definitely empty, and how about letting me know next time you're going do something like that?"

"Something like what? I was just getting us a better perspective."

"Is that what that was?"

"That's what I call it," he said. "That thing is a hazard to navigation, don't you think?"

"Absolutely."

Without another word, Disco, the A-10 driver, made his presence known. The turn back to the target made my crop duster maneuver look like child's play, and we rolled in on the boat at just under two hundred knots. The three-second burst of fifty-caliber rounds nearly cut the boat in half, but he was far from finished.

We flew another pass to make sure we hadn't stirred somebody up who we hadn't seen on deck, and Disco said, "Still nobody, right?"

"Still empty."

He made a second gun run and splintered what remained of the boat. The parts that didn't sink wouldn't be large enough to cause any damage to a vessel this far from land.

"What now, boss?"

I reported our position and what we found to the op center and said, "Let's go home. We're wasting our time. Even if we see a dozen ships, there's no way to know which one our shooter's on. We can't sink all of them."

We climbed away from the wreckage and poured on the coal. Zurich was calling, and the longer we spent on a fishing expedition, the worse the exhaustion would be for the coming mission half a world away.

Chapter 22
Focus

Landing the Mustang is an exercise in obedience. She must be flown precisely by the prescribed numbers, or she makes me look like a fool. When flown as the manufacturer specified, based on thousands of hours of test flights, she is docile and impressive. When flown outside that envelope, she is a spiteful child. On that day, I let my mind wander during the approach and landing, and I paid the price. Saying *Penny's Secret* bounced would be the equivalent of saying the *Titanic* took on a little water. When she bounced, I shoved the throttle forward in a desperate attempt to keep her in the air long enough to prevent the next bounce from becoming catastrophic. The powerplant spinning the enormous propeller of my Mustang was the 1,490-horse-power Rolls-Royce Merlin 12-cylinder beast originally built by Packard. An engine of that size produces more torque than most pilots ever have to deal with. Adding full power not only increased the RPMs, it also increased the torque exponentially. That caused the airplane to roll left as if trying to twist itself in half. It was suddenly like riding a raging bull in the dark without anything to hold on to.

The best pilot I'd ever know sat five feet in front of me with a collection of controls nearly identical to those I had in the back seat, but before that day, I never remember him touching the controls except when we agreed for him to do so. That well-established streak ended that day.

He didn't yell, panic, or give me any reason to believe we wouldn't survive the next few seconds of our lives. He simply grasped the controls and spoke in a smooth, confident tone. "My airplane."

Releasing the controls wasn't easy while the left wing was plummeting toward the runway and the propeller was clawing at the air in an attempt to keep the airplane any distance above the concrete.

Disco smoothly rolled the wings level, adjusted the throttle, and tamed the beast. A few seconds later, we were climbing away from the airport in perfectly coordinated flight, with everything happening in a predictable, systematic manner. Everything except my pounding heart, that is.

As we turned onto the downwind leg of the traffic pattern, Disco said, "Would you like to try that again, or shall I do it?"

On my second attempt, I forced myself to get Zurich, New York City, Stone W. Hunter, and the sniper's boat out of my head, at least temporarily. The landing wasn't great, but both mains touched down simultaneously and stayed on the runway. I let the tail wag a little before landing the third wheel, but Disco never had to get involved.

We taxied to the ramp, where Anya and Singer stood beside the Gulfstream IV *Grey Ghost*. The embarrassment from my failed landing, still rumbling in my chest, exploded when I realized I'd done it in front of Anya, but I don't know why.

I parked the Mustang beside the *Ghost*, and Don was on his way before Disco and I crawled out. He towed the plane back into the hangar, and Anya watched it go.

To no one in particular, Anya said, "Is sometimes difficult to tell difference between crash and landing."

I pretended not to hear the jab and stepped beside Singer. "I guess you noticed that I didn't assign you to either team, huh?" He nodded, and I said, "That was intentional. If you want to stay here with Hunter, that's what I want you to do."

He twisted the toe of his boot against the concrete. "I guess I should, but if you think you'll need a hand in Zurich, I'm all yours. They say he's going to be in a coma for a while."

"Are you packed?" He nodded again, and I said, "Let's go to Switzerland."

Disco came from the hangar with a bag and handed out protein bars and bottles of water. "Is Singer going with us?"

I started up the steps and into the *Grey Ghost*. "I figured an extra pair of eyes and hands wouldn't be a bad idea."

Disco followed me into the cockpit. "Singer's eyes don't qualify as a regular set, so having him on board changes the game."

As we taxied out, Disco said, "That satellite of theirs is going to see us leave."

"I don't care anymore. Let them watch. Within the next forty-eight hours, I plan to broadcast a livestream of Roger Dean's and Courtney Kellum's wives in our custody, so it won't matter if they saw us leave."

He turned to face me. "Don't forget how important it is to stay focused. I can save an airplane when you get distracted, but there's a lot more at stake here than just a flying machine."

"You're right about all of it. Thank you for taking control."

"Don't thank me for that. I didn't do it for you. I'm my favorite person, so I did it to protect myself. You and the airplane staying alive are just a bonus."

When we reached our cruising altitude, Disco unbuckled his harness. "I'm going to make some coffee. Do you want anything?"

"Coffee sounds good, but why don't you get a couple hours of sleep if you can? We're six hours behind schedule, and we'll need to be on our game when we hit the ground."

He said, "In that case, I'll start the coffee for you and grab a couple of hours."

"Thanks. I'll wake you up if anything goes off the rails."

Ten minutes later, Anya stuck her head into the cockpit. "I have for you coffee."

I reached up and took the cup. "Thanks. Is everything okay back there?"

She glanced back into the cabin. "I am only person not sleeping."

THE SCORPION'S CHASE · 163

I nodded toward the captain's seat. "Come on in. The view is better from here anyway."

She slithered into Disco's seat and seemed fascinated by the array of instrumentation, switches, and controls. "This is not like small airplane."

I chuckled and took the first sip of my coffee. "No, it's a little different, but the basics are the same."

She caressed the yoke with her fingertips. "Perhaps you can teach to me how to fly this airplane someday."

I watched her hands slide across the controls with delicate precision. "Thanks for working this one with us."

"You do not have to thank me for this. I am always happy to work with you. Tell me about Penny. Is she frightened?"

"It's kind of weird talking about my wife with you."

"It is not weird. She is wonderful person, and she is very good for you. I know you must worry about her in times like this."

"I've never had another time like this, but you're right. I'm concerned about her. Of course I don't want anything to happen to her, but I also hate having to hide her away on a ship."

"You have instinct for taking care of people," she said. "This makes you very good person. You were kind to me. You were maybe first man who was ever truly kind to me without expecting for me to . . . you know."

"Yeah, I know. I was kind to you because you weren't an immediate threat to me. I'm glad I didn't shoot you."

"You did shoot me. I have now only nine toes because of this."

"I guess you're right, but you have to admit that you were an immediate threat at that moment."

"I would not have let you drown that night. I only needed to control you."

"You're good at that."

"I am good at what?" she asked.

"Controlling me."

She huffed. "This is not true. If you believe it is true, it is only because you want to be controlled."

I chuckled. "Who's the psychologist now?"

"I am now Doctor Anya, yes?"

"Absolutely."

We watched the world race eight miles beneath us for a while before I asked, "Where do you go when you're not working?"

She turned and watched me for a long moment. "Before I answer this question, I am thinking if this is really question you meant to ask."

I scanned the instrument panel while I thought about what she said. "Don't overthink it. I just wonder where you go and what you do when you're not working with us or the DOJ."

"Job with DOJ is officially finished, but unofficially, there is still one thing I must do before it will be finished in my mind."

"That sounds like a vigilante operation."

She nodded. "Vigilante is maybe correct word. I must cut head from beast, and it will not be something Attorney General will sanction."

"Need any help?"

Her smile said a thousand things before she spoke. "This means so much to me that you would offer. Thank you, but I must do this one alone, or maybe only with Gwynn."

"If you need me, I'm just a call away."

She studied me intently. "I wish that was truth."

I sighed. "If you need me for the mission, I'm just a phone call away."

Her smile returned. "Yes, this I know is truth from you."

"So, are you going to tell me where you go and what you do when you're not working?"

"I have business on island of Bonaire. Is adventure business. We take people on rides through desert on all kinds of vehicles. We have four-wheelers, Jeeps, motorcycles, and side-by-sides. We have helicopters for seeing of sights tours. We have also two diving boats. You will come to Bonaire and bring Penny. Everything I have is yours. You can dive and fly and ride in desert. Is so much fun."

"I'm happy to hear that. I hope it's going well."

"It is, but company does not need me. I have very good people who can do everything without me."

I said, "So do I."

She glanced over her shoulder. "Yes, you do, and if you want me to be one of those people again, I would like this very much."

We sat in silence for almost an hour as the turbines whined and pushed us through space and time at ten miles per minute. Without a word, she climbed from the seat and stepped back toward the cabin, but before she left, she leaned down and reached across my body until her face was only inches from mine.

I froze, and she chuckled. "Relax. I am trying to take your coffee cup, silly boy. I brought it to you, so I should take it away."

I lifted the cup and slid it into her hand.

She leaned even closer, kissed my cheek, and whispered, "I will always love you, my Chasechka."

Disco made his return to the cockpit while we were somewhere over the iceberg-dotted North Atlantic. "How you doing up here all by yourself?"

"I'm all right. How was the nap?"

"Restless," he said. "I was afraid you'd replaced me with an Eastern European captain."

"Nothing like that. She brought me coffee, and we had a nice conversation."

I briefed him on our position and condition, and he said, "It's your turn to get some rest, but don't invite that Russian girl. Flying together is one thing, but napping together is quite another. Remember . . . focus."

Chapter 23
Anything with Nothing

Zurich welcomed us like the invisible trespassers we were. No one seemed to notice or care that three Americans and a Russian emerged from a conspicuously grey Gulfstream business jet in the middle of the night and melted into the city the Romans named Turicum before the Alemanni and the Franks claimed the town as a debaucherous getaway for their royalty. The ill repute came to an end in the sixteenth century, when Zurich became a center of the Protestant Reformation under the pious hand of Huldrych Zwingli. I cared little about the history except for the small piece of it I would create when I reformed Gabrielle Kellum's religion with a good old-fashioned snatch-and-grab.

Disco and Anya shared a taxi to an address two blocks away from our hotel while Singer and I waited for the city bus. When the authorities began piecing together the hours leading up to the abduction of one of the city's fair maidens, I didn't want our foursome to earn an honorable mention in the investigation.

The hotel was pleasant but not posh, and our watches showed a block of time had been stolen from us as we soared across the Atlantic. Our bodies disagreed, but forcing ourselves to sleep was the only way to set our internal clocks to Zurich time and become part of the local aura.

Although back home beside our giant, I was little more than average sized, in Zurich, my six-foot-four-inch frame towered over most of the Europeans going about their lives. I didn't want to stand out, but genetics didn't seem to care what I wanted. Hiding beneath a nondescript cap and dark glasses provided some anonymity, but I was anything but inconspicuous. The blonde Russian and the demure, retired Air Force colonel seemed to draw no attention at all. Our sniper, though, with familial roots somewhere in Central Africa, didn't exactly disappear against the pale sea of Anglo-Saxon Switzerland.

"Maybe I should drive," Singer said. "Nobody pays any attention to the driver."

My Canadian driver's license and fictional name on an actual credit card scored us a sedan with nicely tinted windows, and we accepted Singer's offer to play chauffeur.

Our tablets showed the likely route Gabrielle Kellum would take from her home in the suburbs, to the yoga studio, and finally, the café. We drove the route four times, memorizing details of traffic patterns, signal light timing, and pedestrian crossings, and especially the locations of every camera along the route.

Disco said, "I realize I'm just the pilot, but this is starting to look impossible. The only inch of this route that's invisible is immediately around Kellum's house."

I said, "Have no fear, my friend. You're far more than just a pilot, but you have to keep one thing in mind. We've done so much for so long with so little that we're now qualified to do anything with nothing."

"What does that mean?" he asked.

Singer chuckled behind the wheel. "That means Chase has a plan."

"I've got the makings of a plan, but it's not going to be easy. Anya, how do you feel about playing dress-up?"

She gave me a smile. "Is wonderful game, and I am very good at it. I like this plan already."

We drove the route three more times and spent an hour scouting the area surrounding Kellum's substantial property.

Singer said, "I think the only reasonable place to hit her will be that stretch of road by the river about half a mile from the house. If we play it right, it could look like a car accident."

I pictured the location in my head and let the scenario play out. "That could work if there are no witnesses, but it'll be a small window."

"That's better than no window at all," Singer said.

"You're right, but if we miss, she'll be in her garage less than a minute later, and we can't risk getting spotted on Kellum's security cameras."

"Why not?" Disco asked. "You said you didn't care if they watched us leave St. Marys in the plane. Why do you care if they see us at Kellum's house?"

"You've got a point, but I don't want to deal with the local police. If we set off a camera and the cops show up, what are you going to do then? We need to get in and out as quickly and as quietly as possible."

Anya said, "I have maybe better plan than either of yours. Instead of taking her inside city and me driving her car away dressed as Mrs. Kellum, we can sneak inside her car at café and let her drive us into garage."

Disco said, "I think there's one more possibility that we're overlooking. Just because she went to yoga and lunch at the same time for the past two weeks doesn't mean she'll do it tomorrow. What if she blows it off and goes shopping or doesn't go out at all?"

"I thought about that," I said. "And I think we need to tail her from home, just in case she changes her routine." Heads nodded in silent agreement, and I asked, "Do you think we should rent another car and leapfrog?"

Anya said, "I do not think this is necessary. Even though her husband is chief of security, I do not think she will look for someone following her."

I said, "Here's the plan. We'll wait near the house tomorrow morning and tail Gabrielle Kellum when she leaves her house. If a window opens up for us to take her on the road, we'll do it, but if not, we'll put two of us inside her vehicle and let it play out back inside the garage. We're all good with this idea, right?"

Singer said, "Under the circumstances, I think it's the best shot we've got."

"I agree," I said. "Let's head back to the hotel."

Singer put the sedan into drive, and we made our way back toward the center of the city.

Skipper answered on the second ring. "Good morning. How's it going over there?"

I said, "We've got a plan, and we've run the route several times. We're good to go. How about Clark's team in New York?"

She said, "They're on-site and conducting recon. Clark said they can probably take her tonight."

"Good. The sooner, the better. We'll have Gabrielle Kellum rolled up by early afternoon tomorrow. Any word on Hunter?"

"Yeah, a couple of things. The doctor from the Mayo Clinic was wrong about Hunter's spine. There *was* some spinal cord damage. On top of that, his right arm is in bad shape. The veins and arteries in the upper arm and shoulder were so badly damaged that they may not be able to save it."

"The whole arm?"

"Yeah, it's not looking good. He's still in critical condition, but he's stable."

"That sounds like a contradiction of terms to me. How can he be stable and critical?"

She said, "I had the same question, and the doctor said it means that although his injuries are horrific, he isn't getting worse."

"I guess that's good. So, what's next?"

"The next step is a consultation from a neurosurgeon about his spine. After that's resolved, they'll begin reconstructive surgery. They'll start with the major bone structure and move to tissue repair and transplant in time."

"Is he awake?"

She said, "No, not hardly. Waking him up with his right shoulder missing would be a terrible idea, so they're keeping him in a coma for now."

"All right. Keep us up to date on any changes."

"I will. Do you need anything from me?"

I said, "Are you having any luck repositioning the satellite?"

"Not yet, but Celeste is still on it."

"Please tell me you're certain we can feed video and audio to the satellite and that it'll get back to OGR."

"We're confident about video, but audio might be an issue. Satellites aren't designed to listen. They're designed to watch. But we can get by that by feeding text streams to the receiver."

"That's good enough," I said. "What else?"

She cleared her throat. "We dug the second bullet out of the cannon carriage, and Celeste examined it under her massive microscope."

"What did you find?" I asked.

"It's another phrase that doesn't make any sense."

"Let's hear it."

"It says, 'Ah, Satan sees Natasha.'"

"Natasha?" I said. "Do you think he's talking about Anya?"

Skipper groaned. "I don't know. That seems like the logical assumption, but at this point, I'm out of ideas."

"Hang in there," I said. "I know you're struggling, but if we're going to catch the people behind this, we need you clearheaded."

"I know. I'm with you," she said. "It's just starting to wear on me."

"Me too, kiddo, but we'll get through this one together. We always do."

"Yeah, we will," she said. "I've got a question for you if we're not on speaker."

"It's just you and me."

It took her a minute, but she finally asked, "Do you ever think about that day when you, Clark, and Anya saved me from that house in South Beach?"

I swallowed the lump in my throat as the old film reel played in my head. "Sure. I think about it sometimes. That was a bad day."

"Bad day? Not for me. It was the best day of my life back then.

That day was going to end with me either being dead or being free, and thanks to you, I'm still alive."

I said, "I didn't mean it the way it came out. It was a bad day for Anya, and in some ways, for me, too. Getting you out of there was one of the greatest victories of my life, and I'll always be grateful that we plucked you out of a terrible situation, but watching Anya bleed out in the back seat of that car was one of the worst things I've ever experienced."

She said, "I understand. I've watched the dashcam video of Tony's murder a thousand times, and it gets worse every time. I was just thinking that if you hadn't gotten me away from that place all those years ago, I would've never had to watch the man I love die on the street like that."

The psychologist wanted to explain why she was harboring those feelings, but instead, the real Chase Fulton—the one behind the façade of a warrior, behind the diplomas and license, the one who would always love Skipper as if she were my own little sister—took the reins. "Hundreds, if not thousands of people are alive today because of you. You've saved my life more times than I'll ever be able to count or thank you for. You're one of the best covert operations intel analysts who's ever lived, and the world is a better and safer place because you're in it."

I paused only long enough to let those words sink in. "Sometimes I think about walking away and leaving all of this to somebody else, and then I think about the people I love and who love me. Are their lives better because I'm alive and doing what I'm meant to do? Every time I get selfish, I think about how Penny smiles when I come back from some godforsaken corner of the world and how you wrap your arms around all of us every time we drag ourselves home beaten and bruised. I think about those little moments, and one of the most comforting, assuring, and strengthening things in my life is hearing *your* voice in my ear when I'm taking fire from every direction and running out of bullets. As long as I can hear your voice, I know I'm still in the fight and you'll find a way to get me home when lead stops flying. Skipper, I love you, and I always will. You are more than the one person you see when you look in the mirror. You're part of all of us, and to us, you're the reason we have the strength and fortitude to spit in the face of evil wherever it rears its ugly head. You're the reason we survive and succeed when others fail and fall."

"How do you always know exactly what to say?"

I chuckled. "I just make it up as I go along, and I tend to get lucky every now and then."

I could almost see her smile through the sat-com. "Me too, big brother."

Chapter 24
Showtime

Our boots met the ground of Zurich long before the morning sun made her glorious entry over the towering Alps, resting as they had for eons, just southeast of the celebrated city. The crisp, cool morning breeze tasted somehow different than the humid, clinging air of coastal Georgia, where I drew most of my early-morning breaths. The undeniable beauty of the European landscape would soon wake and lay in peaceful, stoic reminder of ages come and gone, when Christian knights wielded swords of gleaming iron on the backs of Spanish steeds, with their banners held high and their hearts devoted to a crusade grander than they could fathom. Just like those fearless, chain-mail-clad invaders, I believed myself to be on the noblest of pursuits, doing whatever the task required and paying whatever price that was demanded of me to drive my spear through the heart of evil. Although I carried no banner and hid behind no shield, I was no less devoted to my destiny than those brave men of old who bent a knee only to the Almighty.

The suburban location of Courtney and Gabrielle Kellum's home gave us more-than-ample spots from which to hide and wait for the car to emerge from the sealed garage and through the towering gates of the palatial grounds. We made our choice at the direction of the man who knew more about hiding than anyone I knew.

Singer's skill and experience lying motionless for hours at a time, with his finger lingering patiently above a trigger, made him one of the finest surveillance minds on the planet. Our position to the east of the house would make us all but invisible when the sun rose in the cloudless sky.

Singer, Disco, and I drank coffee from the plastic lids of our thermoses, but Anya enjoyed her morning tea from a dainty porcelain cup decorated with roses and ivy scrollwork.

"Where did you get that cup?" I asked.

"Is my cup. It is part of a set that is very important to me. You would not understand."

"I wasn't attacking you. I just wasn't expecting to see a formal setting for predawn tea."

She cradled the delicate cup as if it were priceless. "Someday, I will tell to you why this cup is so important to me, but not today."

"I look forward to it," I said.

Anya checked her watch. "Why are we up so early? Yoga does not begin until ten a.m."

"Maybe yoga isn't her first stop. Maybe she has a date for morning tea from her own special cup."

Anya blew across the surface of the golden liquid. "Is very possible. They love tea in Switzerland."

The third cup of coffee did little to lighten the weight of my eyelids. My body and mind were still lingering in American Eastern Standard Time, and with any luck, I would wake up the next morning in that time zone.

"Contact." Singer's baritone was commanding, even when spoken softly, and everyone in the car responded by staring through the waning darkness toward the entry gates.

"Who is that?" Disco asked.

Singer snatched the night-vision binoculars from the seat and stuck them to his face. "I don't know, but whoever it is, he has the gate code. And now . . . so do we. It's ten twenty pound."

The driver of the unmarked van waited for the massive gates to swing inward before driving through as if he were the master of the estate. He followed the sweeping driveway around the stone house and parked out of sight of the street.

"He didn't open the garage," Singer said, "but he looks like he knows what he's doing."

"It could be Courtney Kellum," Anya whispered.

Singer said, "It's possible, but why would he park outside?"

We watched in anxious anticipation until both front doors of the van opened almost simultaneously. Two men emerged and opened the large double doors at the rear of the vehicle.

Singer said, "Neither of those guys is Kellum. They look like workers of some kind."

A few seconds later, they climbed inside the van through the back doors and emerged with a shovel, a rake, and a broom.

Singer's shoulders relaxed, and he lowered the binoculars. "They're gardeners."

I said, "Even though the coffee doesn't get the credit, I'm awake now."

Disco stretched and yawned. "I didn't want to admit it, but I was drifting off, as well."

Anya raised her cup. "See? This is why tea is always better. I am completely awake and focused while you boys are lazy and slow."

"That's pretty aggressive," I said. "Lazy and slow?"

Anya grinned. "Okay, maybe not lazy, but definitely slow. We can have footrace if you would like." She stared toward the ceiling of the car for a moment. "For only Chase is footrace. For rest of us is feet-race."

"Oh, she's got jokes," I said. "Just because I have a prosthetic that's far superior to your mere flesh and bone doesn't mean it's okay to pick on me."

"Is funny joke," she said. "See? My English is good enough to make language joke."

I rolled my eyes. "Your English is far better than you pretend it is."

Singer reeled us back in. "Lights."

Our eyes flashed immediately to the house, where two large windows glowed with an interior light.

"That must be the kitchen," Disco said.

The sun made its first appearance of the day as we stared toward the pair of windows, and a single shadow brushed left to right.

I followed it with singular focus. "Is that her?"

"Could be," Singer said, "but we don't know how many people are in the house."

Disco scoffed. "There's room for a couple hundred in that place. It's bigger than Bonaventure."

I said, "I'll bet it doesn't have an op center like ours, though."

Disco said, "The chief of physical security for the world's largest sig-int company lives there. He may have an op center to rival the Pentagon."

I said, "What if Courtney Kellum really is inside that house with some horrific illness? Roger Dean could've been telling the truth. He was pretty convincing."

Disco said, "I've replayed the encounter with Dean in my head a thousand times. He was shocked at first, but he calmed down and even got a little belligerent as it played out. You're the shrink, but nothing about his reaction made much sense to me."

I said, "He's clearly a type-A personality. He's used to being in charge, and when we surprised him, he instinctually worked out of the initial shock and tried to claim the high ground. We rattled him with the threat of telling his wife about the widow Kobel, but outside of that, he wasn't afraid of us."

"What do you think that means?" Disco asked. "Do you believe him about not knowing where Kellum is?"

"I've been working on that," I said. "I think he believes Kellum is convalescing, but I could be wrong. It's possible that he's solid enough to fake it. I wish we could play that scenario out again and I could shove a pistol in his mouth. That tends to squeeze all the cockiness out of a man. They rarely lie when they're choking on a gun barrel."

He said, "If Clark successfully snatches Maria Dean off the street in New York, we'll be able to scare the truth out of Roger."

Anya said, "Wait a minute. You said this Roger Dean person is having affair with a widow named Kobel, yes?"

"That's right," I said. "We caught them in the middle of an episode of in flagrante delicto, as Kodiak likes to call it."

I never remember seeing Anya blush before that moment, but I'm certain that's exactly what she did. To add a cherry on top, she even giggled. "That is funny phrase, and I like it."

When she'd collected herself, she said, "If Roger is no longer in love with Maria, he may have a very different reaction than we expect when we threaten to kill her. He may see it as way out of marriage he does not want."

I chewed my bottom lip. "I hadn't considered that, but you may be right. Let's hope Courtney Kellum feels differently about his lovely bride. He's the one we really need to rattle."

Singer did it again. "Contact!"

This time, his tone wasn't as calm as before, and that tone meant only one thing. It was showtime.

One of the four garage doors slowly rose, spilling light from inside and casting the long shadow of what we would soon learn was a metallic blue Range Rover.

Singer kept his foot off the brake pedal and instead held the parking brake in place to keep the brake lights from illuminating the trees behind us.

He handed the binoculars to Anya, and she raised them to her eyes. "That is her, but she is early. I guess Chase was right again. She must have date for morning tea."

The gates swung open again, and the Range Rover turned right out of the driveway. We waited until Gabrielle Kellum rounded the first turn in the road before we pulled from the tree line. Catching her wasn't a challenge, but keeping her in sight once we encountered morning rush-hour traffic might become an issue. I suddenly wished

I'd rented a second car just for that problem. Like all of us on the team, Singer possessed far more skills than his primary function of hiding and pressing a trigger. Pursuit driving fell well within his impressive skill set.

We followed at a comfortable distance, with our recently obtained knowledge of the route giving us the confidence to avoid closing in on our prey. Patience was the key until opportunity presented itself. Then, and only then, would we pounce. The catch would be the easy part. Getting Gabrielle Kellum aboard the Gulfstream and out of the country had the potential to be far more troublesome. We didn't have the luxury of thinking that far ahead at that moment. A mission like ours required unmatched precision and focus, and it was likely that our very lives depended on our success. Failure, should we lose focus, would likely be nothing short of fatal.

"Here comes the first traffic circle," Singer said. "And it's full."

The sun was above the trees, and the European night gave way to the ever-brightening day. Commuters filled the streets as the sun filled the sky, and our first significant challenge of the day lay only seconds ahead.

I handed Anya my phone. "Zoom in and get a clean shot of the license plate."

She braced the phone against the windshield and clicked twice. At only slightly slower than the speed of light, I sent both pictures bouncing through space and back to the op center.

My sat-phone promptly rang, and I said, "Good morning!"

Skipper sounded as if she were bright-eyed and ready to work, even though it was still the middle of the night back on the East Coast of America.

"No time for good mornings," she said. "I ran the plate, and it comes back to a German company called Freiheit, GmbH. Freiheit means *freedom*, right?"

"Yes, it does. I've got a big ask for you."

"Let's hear it," she said.

"You don't have any way to track that Range Rover if we lose her, do you?"

"Let me get back to you on that one. I need to do some snooping around, but I'll have an answer for you in a few seconds."

I glanced up as we approached the traffic circle, with two cars and two hundred feet between us and the Range Rover. Just as Singer observed, the circle was indeed full, but instead of slowing to merge into the circle, Gabrielle accelerated, sending one car swerving toward the inside lane and horns blowing furiously. She then yanked the Range Rover furiously into the inner lane. Singer tapped the brakes and merged into the congestion, never taking his eyes off of our target.

I expected Gabrielle to take the second exit from the roundabout and continue toward downtown Zurich, but she continued around the circle, and Singer slapped his palm against the steering wheel. "She's running an SDR."

"We should've expected a surveillance detection route," I said. "She's the wife of a security freak."

Singer said, "We're busted if we chase her. I'm getting off."

We took the second exit as if we had no other agenda, but Disco and I spun in our seat, desperately trying to keep an eye on the Range Rover.

Singer stared into the mirror. "What's she doing?"

"Still coming around," Disco said. "She's back in the outside lane."

Singer pulled into the parking lot of a café and positioned us between a pair of delivery trucks.

Disco said, "I'm losing her."

Singer rolled to a stop. "Don't worry. She'll drive by us in fifteen seconds, and we'll fall back in behind her."

Disco said, "But she must've made us already."

Singer shook his head. "She didn't. It was just a standard SDR. It's exactly what I would've done."

Our sniper was wrong, but only by three seconds. Gabrielle made her appearance back on the road in front of us, and the chase was on again.

"Well, I guess we learned a little something about Mrs. Kellum, huh?"

Singer said, "That's okay. She may be married to a pro, but we *are* pros."

Chapter 25
Sniffing Anya

"Yes! I can absolutely do it!"

I had forgotten I was on the sat-phone with Skipper until her excited declaration rang in my ear. "You can track her?"

"You bet I can. You've heard of OnStar, right?"

"Sure. That's the button you push for emergency roadside assistance or whatever, right?"

"Yeah, exactly. Well, they have an upscale version of that in some European countries, including Switzerland. It's called Euro-Star-Elite."

"Sounds fancy."

"Not really. Just expensive," she said. "It's the same as OnStar but with a few hoity-toity bells and whistles. I guess they'll bring you some Grey Poupon mustard if you run out. I don't know. Anyway, I found a back door into their database. It was some really chintzy firewall garbage they threw up. It was a joke even for a rookie hacker, but that doesn't matter. I'm in, and I'm tracking the lovely Mrs. Gabrielle Kellum as we speak."

"You get a gold star by your name, little Miss Super Analyst. We're tracking her, too."

She said, "I know. I can see you."

I pulled the phone away. "Stay with her, but don't risk getting busted. Skipper's tracking the Range Rover through their version of OnStar."

Singer didn't have to say a word. The satisfied smile on his face said more than enough. He lifted his foot from the accelerator and let us drift back a few car lengths. Tailing her closely was risky, but without a second car to play leapfrog, it had been our only choice. My favorite analyst just became that second car we needed so badly.

We tailed her loosely for ten more minutes until Skipper said, "It looks like she's pulling into a car park, but it's not the yoga studio."

"What's a car park?" Singer asked.

Before Skipper could answer, Anya said, "Is what Americans call parking lot, but rest of world calls car park."

Singer rolled his eyes. "Yeah, well, there are two kinds of countries on Earth—the kind that use the metric system and the kind that've been to the moon and never lost a war."

Anya laughed. "Soviet Union was going to moon, but they learned there was no vodka there, so they went instead to liquor store."

Singer slowly shook his head and locked eyes with me in the mirror. "You just had to bring her, didn't you?"

Skipper said, "The car park is your next left."

"Next left?" I asked.

"Yeah, turn right now," she said.

"There's nowhere to turn right now. The parking lot is behind us."

"Hmm, there must be a slight delay in my tracking. Yeah, I show you past it now."

Singer made the U-turn, and we drove past the lot and scanned it for the blue Range Rover.

"Got her," Singer called out, and we followed his outstretched finger to the back corner, where Gabrielle Kellum was stepping from her SUV.

Anya said, "Let me out."

I ran through the pros and cons of putting Anya on Gabrielle on foot and said, "Don't engage. Just follow and report."

The Russian nodded and pulled the door latch before Singer rolled to a stop. She leapt from the car and used both hands to pull her long, blonde hair forward around her face, then she disappeared between parked cars as Singer made the block.

We found a spot about a hundred feet from Gabrielle's Range Rover and backed into it. The area was bustling with pedestrians and vehicles of every description. We could've hidden an elephant in that environment.

"Where'd they go?" I asked.

Disco said, "I didn't see Gabrielle, but Anya turned the corner to the left."

"I've got an idea," I said.

Disco and Singer turned to face me, and I said, "What if we take her right here in front of God and everybody?"

Disco looked out the window, "There's a thousand people out there. There's no way we can pull it off without a hundred witnesses."

Singer raised a finger. "Wait a minute. When Chase gets that look, something weird is about to happen."

"I'm okay with weird," I said.

Skipper was still on the sat-phone, but she was on speaker, so I asked, "Can you unlock the doors with your Euro-Star back door?"

"Sure. I can start the car if you want."

"Oh, really? Can you disable it, too?"

She said, "I don't know. Give me a minute."

While Skipper was exploring her capabilities through the Euro-Star network, I said, "Hey, did either of you smell Anya?"

Both men recoiled, and Disco said, "What are you talking about?"

"Did either of you smell her? Is she wearing perfume today?"

Disco and Singer sat with their mouths hanging open until I said, "Sorry, that was a weird question. Here's what I want to do. I want to put Anya inside that Range Rover before Gabrielle gets back."

Disco said, "Ah, now it makes sense. No, I don't think she's wearing perfume, but sniff her seat."

Before I realized how ridiculous that suggestion sounded, I leaned forward and inhaled the upholstery of the seat where Anya had been for the previous several hours. Then, it hit all of us simultaneously, and we burst into the laughter of twelve-year-old boys.

Disco made a telephone with his thumb and pinky finger against his face. "Hello, Penny. Chase is sniffing Anya's seat again." He pretended to hang up. "She told me to shoot you in the face."

"That's reasonable," I said.

Skipper came back on the line. "Uh, what's going on in that car?"

"You don't want to know," Singer said. "Can you disable the car?"

"Yes, I can do anything Euro-Star can do except for the Grey Poupon."

I keyed up the sat-com. "Anya, are you there?"

"Yes, I am here. She is inside shop buying coffee. I am on street pretending to look through window at jewelry. I found diamond tennis bracelet you should buy for me."

Disco whispered, "You did sniff her seat. Buying her diamonds is the least you can do."

I silently threatened him with a raised fist, but he didn't back down. I said, "Get back here as quickly as you can. We'll have the Range Rover unlocked when you get here."

"I am coming, but do not forget about bracelet."

"Okay, Skipper. Pop the locks."

She said, "Here we go. Watch for the lights to flash."

We stared at the SUV until the fog lights blinked.

"Nice work," I said. "How about the alarm?"

"I took care of that, too."

Anya jogged around the corner of the building and directly toward the SUV. "Is it open?"

I said, "Yes. Find a place to hide, and don't move until I give the word."

She checked across her shoulder as she stepped beside the SUV. An instant later, she was inside and invisible. "Okay, I am hidden."

"Please tell me you're not wearing perfume," I said.

"This is strange question, but no, I am not."

"Good. We're going to let her drive away, and as soon as we find the right spot, we'll disable the vehicle and you'll take over."

Gabrielle returned, coffee in hand, and climbed inside her Range Rover without looking for stowaways. We followed her from the parking lot and turned toward the center of Zurich.

Singer said, "I like this plan, in theory, but finding a place to disable the vehicle in this traffic is going to be challenging."

I said, "Oh, ye of little faith. Trust me. I've got a plan."

He huffed. "If I didn't trust you, I'd be broke and working for somebody else."

Gabrielle disappeared into the massive sea of automobiles. Although we never saw an SUV of exactly the same color as hers, keeping track of one particular car in that chaos was like watching one raindrop and ignoring all the others.

"Please tell me you've still got her, Skipper."

"Relax. When was the last time I let you down? She's got one of ours in that car, and I'm finished losing operators."

Singer accelerated and probably broke a few European traffic laws, but our prey was back in sight and turning onto the road beside the river, where I envisioned the perfect spot for our little game of Russian guess-who.

We turned behind her with only one other car between us. It was a small white car that looked more like a child's toy than a real car, but it navigated the winding road surprisingly well. We lost the Range Rover a few times around curves, but she was headed directly for the yoga studio and right into my hands.

I asked, "What's going to happen when you disable the car, Skipper?"

She said, "I've been researching that very question, and the answer is perfect. It will gradually slow the car to twenty-five kilometers per hour and issue a warning to the driver on the internal data screen. She'll have three minutes to pull over, and as soon as the car comes to a complete stop, it won't move again until I set it free."

I said, "As soon as you see an opening, pass that thing masquerading as a car."

Singer wasted no time, and we were in front of the toy car in seconds.

"Get ready, Skipper. We're coming up on the spot."

She said, "Just say when."

I peered through the windshield until the Y in the road came into focus, and I said, "Shut it down!"

An instant later, Skipper said, "Done. She should start slowing now."

We continued following, but she didn't change speed.

I said, "Something's wrong. It didn't work. She's not slowing down."

"That's impossible," Skipper said. "The command was accepted . . . Oh, crap."

"What? What's happening?"

She said, "I should've known. The terrible firewall was just the first line of defense against hackers. The real deterrent is in the transmission code. The system is running a self-diagnostic protocol before it transmits the command."

"Can you get around it?"

"I'm trying."

Everything inside of me wanted to yell at her to hurry up, but nothing I could say would create more pressure than she was already putting on herself, so I focused on the few remaining elements of the operation I could control. "Anya, click if you hear me."

The micro transmitters Dr. Mankiller installed on each of our jaw-bones gave us the ability to communicate via our sat-com. The tiny device acted as both speaker and microphone, sending and receiving vibrations through the bones of our skulls and the short distance between our jawbones to our sat-com radios hidden in a pocket.

Anya clicked her tongue against her teeth twice, broadcasting a sound that mimicked clicking a push-to-talk button twice in rapid succession.

I said, "Hold your position. Skipper's working on getting that car stopped as quickly as possible. Are you okay?"

She clicked twice more.

A thousand doubts and even more questions poured into my mind. *Should I have sidelined Skipper and put Ginger at the helm in the op center? Would Skipper ever recover to become the analyst she'd been before Tony's murder? Had I led my team into a train wreck of an operation halfway around the world, only to end up—"*

"I'm back in!"

Skipper's voice sent a calming wave of reassurance washing over me, and I scanned the road ahead. "Don't shut it down now. There's no place for her to pull over."

"Tell me when," she said.

I closed my eyes and replayed the route in my mind. The river road was narrow and winding. Forcing the vehicle to stop on the road could be catastrophic, and I wasn't willing to risk a collision. We were already doing too much to draw attention without adding a rendezvous with the local police into the mix.

Skipper said, "Make a call, Chase. She's approaching the yoga studio."

Singer said, "We've got another wrinkle. She's turning into the parking garage instead of the studio parking lot."

Skipper said, "Chase, you have to make a call. If she gets inside that garage, I'll lose satellite coverage, and Euro-Star won't work."

"Let her go," I said. "We'll take her when she comes out after the yoga session."

Singer turned right across from the parking garage and found a relatively quiet spot.

I said, "Anya, we're directly across the street from the parking garage behind the row of evergreens. When Kellum is clear of the car, come to us."

Her response didn't come.

"Anya? How do you hear?"

Nothing.

"Anya, comms check, over."

Still nothing.

Chapter 26
Chasing the Mailman

"This isn't good," I said. "The garage must be messing with our sat-coms."

Singer said, "Does that mean Skipper can't unlock the Range Rover?"

Skipper answered before I could. "That's exactly what it means, but unlocking it isn't the problem. If Anya is inside, she can get out by simply unlocking the doors from the inside, but that will likely set off the car alarm."

"How about cameras inside the garage?" I asked.

Skipper said, "How should I know?"

"Because you know everything."

"I don't know why Tony had to be murdered . . ."

I had to come up with some way to get her refocused, but nothing was jumping into my head.

Disco, on the other hand, had the perfect response. "None of us knows yet, but with every step we take, we're getting closer and closer to an answer, and I'm sure I speak for the whole team when I say we'll do everything necessary to find the men who are responsible and put them on their knees at your feet."

Everyone held their breath for the next few seconds until Skipper said, "I know. Now, let's get back to work. I say we give Gabrielle Kellum enough time to park, leave the car, and get into the yoga studio before we make another move. Anya knows what she's doing. She won't do anything unexpected."

That sparked a round of laughter, and I said, "When's the last time Anya did anything anyone expected?"

"Okay, you've got a point, but what I meant was, she won't do anything to screw up the operation."

"Skipper's right," I said. "Let's give the clock a little time to tick, then we'll find the Ranger Rover and either get Anya out or keep her in place until Gabrielle finishes the class."

"Sounds good to me," Singer said, and Disco nodded.

The seconds passed as if the world had stopped turning, and my impatience swelled beyond my willingness to sit still. "I don't like it. Let's get in there."

Apparently, mine wasn't the only limit that had been exceeded. Singer shifted the car into gear and pulled into the traffic. We made a U-turn a few hundred yards beyond the parking garage and accelerated back toward the entrance. Singer cut across two streams of traffic and hit the entry lane. The extra speed we carried into the turn sent us onto the curb as we made the turn. The electronic arm loomed like the lance of a charging knight, and we slid to a stop only inches from the bar. Singer thumbed the round glowing button above the string of text none of us could read. The result of the push was identical to what would've happened in any public parking garage back in the States. The machine produced and expelled a barcoded ticket with a timestamp, and our sniper yanked it from the slot.

The bar rose as if propelled by a marauding horde of sloths. When it was barely high enough to clear the roofline of our rented sedan, Singer hit the gas, and the tires barked on the smooth concrete deck. He yanked the wheel to the right, and we began our rise up the gently sloping ramp toward the second floor. A massive convex mirror hung suspended by a steel bracket at the top of the ramp, giving us a fish-eye view of oncoming traffic. No one appeared in the glass, so we made the turn and continued accelerating up the ramp. At the next turn, the big round mirror told a very different story. Coming from the opposite direction was a blue Range Rover, and my heart nearly leapt from my chest.

I pointed into the mirror. "What's she doing?"

Singer gripped the wheel and crushed the accelerator. With a rapid spin of the wheel, the nose of the car shot to the left, and the rear tires lost their grip on the concrete. The Range Rover passed us in a blur, only giving me time to see that there was a woman behind the wheel, but I couldn't see anyone else in the vehicle.

I feared Anya had spooked Gabrielle, sending her running for any safe haven. If Anya was still in the vehicle, she was well hidden, but I couldn't reconcile the idea of Gabrielle running if our favorite Russian was still in the car.

Singer's maneuver continued to develop as the rear of the car drifted sideways until we were headed back down the ramp. As the rear tires came in line with the front pair, they once again found purchase, and we rocketed around the corner, headed back for the entrance.

"Any ideas what's going on?" I asked as I thrust my feet into the floorboard and braced myself against the door.

Singer said, "I don't know, but after that powerslide, our cover is definitely blown. This may have just become a high-speed car chase."

As we approached the exit gate, to my surprise, the Range Rover slowed until the mechanical arm rose to the vertical position.

"She must have a prepaid transponder for the garage," Disco said.

Singer gave no opportunity for the gate to fall. We were only inches from the Rover, and we followed her onto the street and back in the direction we'd come. If Gabrielle Kellum was running, she was running toward home, and we couldn't let her get there. Between the gardeners and security cameras, taking her at home was out of the question.

My brain went into overdrive, and I called out, "If we're going to PIT them, the Y in the river road is the best spot."

Singer's response came as a simple nod as he maneuvered through traffic to stay as close as possible to our target. Sixty seconds into the pursuit, the sat-com receiver activated the bone conduction device in my jaw, and an undeniably Russian voice filled my head.

"Chase, is Anya. I am driving Range Rover, and she is unconscious on back seat."

Singer's aggressive foot came off the accelerator, and he checked me in the rear-view mirror.

I asked, "Is she hurt?"

"Maybe her neck is little bit uncomfortable when she wakes up, but no blood or broken bones. I was gentle."

Disco chuckled and shook his head. "She choked her out, didn't she?"

"Sounds like it," I said.

I keyed the sat-com. "Do you remember how to get to the airport?"

Anya said, "This car has GPS."

"Good," I said. "Slow down and drive like a local. We'll meet you at the airport."

Singer said, "It might be a good idea to put one of us in that car with Anya. If Gabrielle wakes up, God only knows what might happen."

I relayed the idea to Anya, and she said, "This is not possible. She will not wake up. I gave her injection so she will sleep for hours."

"You could've mentioned that earlier."

"You did not ask. You only asked if she was injured."

I said, "In that case, we're back to meeting you at the airport."

Before Anya answered, Skipper's voice appeared. "Hey, Chase? Sorry to interrupt, but we've got action in New York."

"Let's hear it."

She said, "Stand by. I'll patch the signals."

A few seconds later, Clark said, "You there, Chase?"

"Yeah, I'm here. We've got our target, and we're headed to the airport. What's your sitrep?"

"We've got her," he said, "but she's a handful. I don't like the idea of taking her to a safe house unless it's remote."

I said, "Skipper, are you still on?"

"I'm here. And I don't have any safe houses that are remote enough to qualify. It looks like the hangar back here in St. Marys is the best option."

"I agree," Clark said. "We'll be at the airport in twenty minutes."

As I listened to the ordeal play out, I was reminded of the old line about the dog who finally caught the mailman and then had no idea what to do with him.

I said, "I've got a better idea. Where's the ship?"

Skipper said, "They're patrolling The Bahamas for the boat that picked up the sniper, but they're coming up empty."

I said, "Pull them off and send them back to Bermuda. This thing has two possible outcomes. The first, and best for us, is a total surrender, but I doubt that's in the cards. More likely, they'll bring the fight straight to our front door, and I'd much rather have the door be a steel hatch aboard a warship than the wooden front door of Bonaventure."

Clark said, "And that's why you're in charge, College Boy. I like it. That's a two-and-a-half-hour flight for us. No problem. Can the Gulfstream make it?"

Disco already had his phone in his hand, and he was calculating like crazy. "We can make it. It'll be close, but we can do it."

"Disco says we can make it from Zurich. It'll be eight hours for us."

Clark sang, "Baby, let me take you on a sea cruise."

"No, please don't sing to us. There's only so much pain we can endure."

Skipper said, "Speaking of enduring pain, I have an update on Hunter."

"Let's have it," I said.

"The neurologist examined him and conducted some sort of test to determine how badly his spinal cord is damaged and if it can be repaired. The damage is severe, but the good news is that he's a candidate for nerve transfer or nerve graft. They'll do the surgery today."

I shivered at the thought of someone piecing Hunter's spinal cord back together. "Did they say anything about the likelihood of success?"

She said, "Yes, and it's not great. There was a lot of nerve damage, so it'll take several hours, and each graft has about a fifty-percent chance of being successful. If it were only one or two nerves, the percentage would go way up, but apparently, nerves heal incredibly slowly, and with so much trauma in one region, there's a greater chance of infection. So, we just have to pray and trust."

"Thanks for the update. What are we doing for security at the hospital?"

"Shawn, the SEAL, is on the door at night, and two former Force Recon guys are on the day shift. The police chief offered, but I made the decision to use our guys instead."

"Good call," I said. "One more thing. Can you disconnect the Range Rover from the Euro-Star system?"

"I'm not following. What do you mean?"

I said, "We need to hide the car from anybody who can track it."

"Oh, yeah. That's simple. Just tell me when."

"Do it now."

"Done. Anything else?"

"All that's left is to get your butt to Bermuda and bring Ginger, Dr. Mankiller, and that SEAL."

"The SEAL?" she asked.

"If this thing goes south, we're going to need every serious fighter we can muster to survive it."

She said, "Aye, Captain," and the line went dead.

We arrived at the airport and drove to the foot of the airstairs. Disco was the first one out of the car, and he had the canopy rigged over the stairs in no time. It's not easy to hide an unconscious body being carried up the stairs of an airplane, and that sort of behavior tends to catch a lot of attention. Fortunately, for us, the Gulfstream was parked so that the door was facing away from the terminal, so the task only re-

194 · CAP DANIELS

quired waiting until no one was taxiing by before we hefted Gabrielle Kellum aboard the *Grey Ghost*.

Anya stuck the Range Rover in long-term parking and disconnected the battery just in case Skipper hadn't completely severed the electronic link between the SUV and Euro-Star.

Ten minutes later, we climbed away from Zurich and over Eastern France. As we leveled at forty-two thousand, I pulled out my pad and calculator to double-check the computer's calculations. The airplane and I came to the same conclusion at the same time, and I turned to the captain. "We're not going to make it."

Chapter 27
To Just Be

"I see that," Disco said. "How about up or down?"

After several minutes of trying to understand the controller's French accent, I learned that winds were stronger than forecast at every flight level above twenty-four thousand. So, I went fishing for a nice long piece of concrete with jet fuel somewhere on the Atlantic Coast.

"How do you feel about Brest?" I asked.

Disco cocked his head like a confused puppy. "Uh, is this some sort of loaded question?"

I gave him a playful shove. "No, you pervert. Brest Bretagne Airport."

"I may have misunderstood the original question, but my answer remains the same."

I made the request, and the French controller cleared us for a rather steep descent into what had become our fuel stop.

The weather was gorgeous, and it was easy to believe I could see halfway across the Atlantic. "I've never landed in France. Do you mind if I log my first one today?"

"She's all yours," Disco said.

We touched down like a boulder falling from a mountaintop.

"What was that all about?" he asked as I finally got the bouncing jet under control.

"That was me forgetting that we still have almost full tanks of fuel on board. We weigh a lot more than I expected."

He shook his head. "You're supposed to be good at this."

"I didn't break anything."

He glanced over his shoulder into the cabin. "I'll bet at least one of our passengers is unconscious after that crash."

"It wasn't a crash, and *one* of our passengers was already unconscious."

We refueled and repeated our climb-out procedure back into the flight levels. When we reached our cruising altitude, both the computer and I were much happier with the fuel burn calculations.

I put my pad away and said, "It looks much better this time."

Every sailor remembers the first time he lost sight of land on a voyage. It doesn't matter if that first time is aboard a dinghy or an aircraft carrier, there's something both magically freeing and terrifying about that moment. I had thousands of hours of flight in my logbook, and dozens of those hours were over open water, but every time I looked outside the windscreen and saw nothing except blue in every direction, I felt small and insignificant. Perhaps the soul needs those moments to realize and understand how precious everything is and how thankful we should be for every breath and every tick of the clock. The moments when I felt powerful and meaningful were the times at which I experienced my greatest failures. I believe every man should experience massive failure and ultimate freedom, and sometimes, those two moments occur simultaneously.

I re-earned my wings when I finessed the *Ghost* onto the runway on Bermuda. When a passenger can't feel the instant when a seventy-thousand-pound flying machine is transformed into one-hundred-twenty-mile-per-hour rolling machine, that's when a landing was *with* the airplane instead of *to* the airplane. My landing at L.F. Wade International Airport was one of those landings, but Disco, ever the critic, said, "If that's the best you can do, I guess we'll have to take it."

We taxied to the transient ramp and asked for permission to keep one engine running to provide climate control for sensitive cargo. Permission was given, and we kept the hatch sealed against prying eyes.

As if we'd planned the arrival down to the minute, Clark landed almost before we set the parking brakes on the *Ghost*. He taxied and parked alongside us, but he couldn't leave either engine running without the propeller spinning, so he called for an auxiliary power unit. It was delivered and connected in minutes, and we became prisoners inside our sarcophagi, awaiting the arrival of a warship that shouldn't exist and a helicopter that would become our magic carpet from a tiny dot in the middle of the Atlantic to the deck of what would become a horrific crime scene in only hours.

Barbie "Gun Bunny" Brewer, former U.S. Army AH-64 Apache pilot and current flight operations officer aboard the Research Vessel *Lori Danielle*, came to a hover and touched down like the consummate pro she was. The highly modified Bell 412 helicopter in her hands looked like a civilian version of the military Huey that gained well-deserved fame and respect during Vietnam, but behind the gleaming paint job was a machine with capabilities far beyond those of its military brother. The most notable difference was the General Electric M134 Minigun affixed to a gimbal, pivoting mount just inside the sliding side door. That feature alone made the chopper the deadliest airship on the island of Bermuda, but that gun in the hands of the door gunner, Ronda No-H, was a force multiplier of magnificent proportions. Ronda didn't miss, but that was far from the limit of her ferocity behind that electric rotary machine gun. Not only did she never miss her target, I'd never known her to spare any ammunition. To her, elimination of a target meant total annihilation of that target and everything within its immediate environment. I was no stranger to being pinned down on a beach by an overwhelming force, but the sound of those rotor blades and the buzz of that Minigun meant survival for me and the team, although, for the aggressors who thought they'd won the battle, they meant nothing short of a meeting with their maker.

When darkness fell on the island, we transferred our sensitive cargo, and as many of us who would fit into the Huey, and Gun Bunny climbed away on her first shuttle run back to the ship. The second load consisted of Skipper, Singer, Dr. Mankiller, and me—relatively unburdened compared to the first hop. The Huey leapt from the field and climbed into the night sky for the twenty-minute flight to meet the *Lori Danielle*.

Skipper sat on the edge of the deck with her feet hanging out the side of the chopper. The Atlantic lay black beneath her feet as she stared into the star-speckled sky.

"It's beautiful, isn't it?" she seemed to say to no one, or perhaps the man she loved whose soul lived somewhere beyond those dancing crystals of light hanging from the heavens.

She bowed her head and gripped the edge of the deck as if she were an instant away from throwing herself into the endless abyss below. I instinctively slid toward her as I prepared to grab any part of her that I could reach if she offered to take the final leap.

But she didn't. Instead, she raised a hand and wiped a tear from her eye. Looking over her shoulder, she motioned for me to sit beside her, so I slid onto the door rail and let my boots come to rest on the skid.

She looked up at me, and I said, "You know . . ."

She pressed a finger to my lips and laid her head against my shoulder. I laced an arm around her and held her as we flew across time and space. We didn't need to speak. We only needed to be . . . and nothing more.

The lights of the ship came into view, and I silently wished we could fly through the warm night air until the sun showed herself on the eastern horizon, but we had begun a quest that was illegal in every jurisdiction and immoral in most. The quest demanded more from us than anyone should be forced to pay, but the price was small compared to the value of the lives around me.

We touched down on the motorized tracks that would haul the chopper from the helipad and into the hangar bay, and we stepped from a world of stone and earth and into a world of steel. The strength of the vessel beneath our feet had been earned from the time spent in the hands of the shipwrights who bolted and welded her together, piece by piece, under immense pressure, heat, and force. The men and women around me had endured no less in the crucible and forge and on the anvil that built us. We were hardened and formed and weathered to withstand all that an enemy could pour onto us, but what I was about to do burned hotter than any forge I'd ever waded through and stung harder than any blacksmith's hammer could ever strike. I was about to cross a line onto a battlefield from which there was no retreat, and for the first time in my life, I considered asking another man to drink the cup I was given.

I stood on the helipad with the wind whipping through my hair and against my skin, and I watched Clark Johnson, the man who'd taught me how to live when my body demanded to die, the man who would've crushed me if a moment of doubt about my character or will had crept its way into his head, a man to whom I would forever owe my life. I'd seen him do things most men could never comprehend, and I'd seen him emerge victorious from ungodly battle, time after time, until his body had given everything it possessed in those moments. I'd carried him from firefights no one should've survived, and he'd done the same for me. We had become more than brothers. We'd become the things of legend, and I had learned everything I knew about life plunged into certain death from that man. If I lacked the fortitude to finish the final round of a fight someone else began, I knew beyond all doubt that Clark Johnson still held that fire within his soul to threaten the unthinkable in the name of protecting and defending the innocent, but in that moment, I wasn't certain I did.

When the rotors whined to a silent stop, Clark turned from the rail and met my gaze as if staring into the depths of all that I am. We strode toward each other until we were within arm's reach, and he grabbed a fistful of my shirt. "You good, College Boy?"

I drew in the deepest breath my lungs could hold and slowly let it escape my lips. "Are we doing the right thing?"

He glanced into the sky above our heads. "Don't ask me, brother. I don't get to decide what's right and wrong."

"What if I can't do it?"

He pursed his lips, took a breath even deeper than mine, and shrugged. "Then fly your weak ass back to St. Marys, look into Hunter's eyes, and tell him you're not man enough to keep the promise you made to him."

Chapter 28
The Israeli Connection

Learning from Clark Johnson was never easy, but every lesson was unforgettable. He was absolutely right, and he knew better than anyone on Earth how to motivate me to do what had to be done.

Sick bay aboard the *Lori Danielle* is a better and more capable hospital than most people will ever walk into on dry land. On that night, there were three unique but equally important missions taking place simultaneously. The first involved Dr. Shadrack, the ship's physician.

I met the doctor beside a hospital bed containing the unconscious Gabrielle Kellum. He had his stethoscope firmly placed inside his ears and the bell pressed to the patient's chest.

"Is she okay, Doc?"

He tucked the stethoscope into the pocket of his long white coat and nodded. "You guys did a good job on both of them. They're going to be fine. I'll make sure of that."

"That's good news," I said. "I guess it's time to let you in on the plan, huh?"

"That'd probably be a good idea. What are you planning to do to these ladies?"

"Hopefully, nothing," I said. "If things go well, I'll only need to prove that we have them."

"How often do things go well?"

"Touché. Let's wake them up one at a time and have a conversation with them. What we're doing isn't exactly legal. Oh, who am I kid-

202 · CAP DANIELS

ding? What we're doing here isn't remotely legal, so if you'd prefer not to be involved, I understand, and our medics will handle the whole thing if you want to step aside."

He pulled off his glasses. "Chase, the captain briefed me on what's going on, and I'm in. Which one of them do you want to talk with first?"

"Let's start with Maria Dean, but I think we should restrain her before we wake her up. I plan to film every detail."

He said, "Consider it done. Get your camera crew down here, and let's get to work."

I left sick bay and made my way to the bridge, where the second mission was well underway. "Permission to come aboard the bridge?"

Captain Sprayberry looked up from the radar screen and shook his head. "How many times do we need to go through this? It's your ship, Chase. You don't have to ask permission to go anywhere you want when you're aboard."

I shook my old friend's hand, and a junior officer placed a cup of coffee on the console beside me.

I picked up the cup and said, "Thank you."

Barry stopped my hand before I could bring the cup to my lips. He pulled the steaming mug from my grip and spun it around until I could read the word "CAPTAIN" stenciled on the other side. "It may be *your* ship, but it's *my* coffee."

He took a sip, and the young officer delivered a second cup, sans stenciling.

"Where are we headed?" I asked.

He cradled the mug in his hands and motioned toward the chart plotter. "Southwest, back toward places that fly a flag I can recognize. But we may have a small problem."

When Captain Barry Sprayberry calls something a small problem, most other men would classify it as a near catastrophe.

He said, "We've got company."

"Company?"

He touched a blue symbol on the plotter. "This little guy's been trailing us for two days."

"Trailing you? You can outrun everything on the ocean. How's he trailing you?"

"Oh, we're outrunning him, but he's a persistent little bugger. It appears he can make about thirty-eight knots, and that's not bad for a conventional ship. The problem is that he always seems to know where we are, and he patiently approaches, no matter where we go. I've never let him get within visual range, but I have a hunch that your shooter may be on board that vessel."

I studied the plotter. "He's three hundred miles away."

"That's right. And that means he's less than nine hours away from us if we were to heave to."

I asked, "How long would it take to intercept him if we matched his speed precisely and set a collision course?"

Barry nodded at the junior officer who delivered our coffee, and the man went to work on the chart plotter.

A few seconds later, the officer looked up. "I have an intercept solution, Captain."

"Let's hear it."

"Matching the other vessel's speed over ground exactly, we'll intercept in four hours forty-two minutes, sir."

My watch reminded me that my body believed I was still in Zurich, so I ignored it. "Do it."

The captain nodded. "Make way to intercept matching the target vessel's speed over ground."

The junior officer said, "Aye, sir," and turned toward the helmsman. "Helm, make your course two-five-eight degrees and speed over ground three-six knots."

The helmsman echoed the command and programmed the helm station.

I said, "I've got a radio if anything changes."

"I'll let you know," the captain said.

I set mission number three in motion when I met Dr. Mankiller in the combat information center, which looked a lot like the op center back at Bonaventure.

I said, "Bring whatever you need to make our blockbuster film down in sick bay."

"I'll be right there," she said. "We're all set here to broadcast to the satellite whenever you're ready."

On the way back to sick bay, I found the team in the mess. I stuck a piece of roast beef between two slices of bread and said, "It's show-time. I want Gator and the SEAL with me. What's your name again?"

"It's Shawn—the same as it was last time you asked."

"Apparently, sucking up to the boss isn't something SEALs do," I said. "Come with me, Shannon."

I didn't check to see if he cracked a smile, but he had just guaranteed that I wouldn't call him Shawn anytime soon.

As we approached the hatch, I heard Kodiak ask, "What do you think that's about?"

Mongo answered, "It's about Gator seeing how Chase reacts and Chase seeing how Shawn reacts."

I heard chairs scraping the deck as we stepped through the hatch, and there was no question in my mind that sick bay was about to get more than a little crowded.

Fifteen minutes later, Celeste had her cameras, microphones, and lights in place and ready to roll. The SEAL and Gator stayed behind the cameras, and the rest of the team shoved their way into any piece of deck they could claim.

I asked, "What's going to happen when she wakes up, Doc?"

"She's probably going to be equal parts confused and pissed off."

I checked my watch, even though I had no idea which time zone I was in, and nodded to Celeste. She pressed a few buttons and gave me the rolling signal with an index finger.

Dr. Shadrack twisted a syringe into Maria Dean's IV line and depressed the plunger. Then we waited, but not long.

Maria blinked and tried to raise a hand to shade her eyes from the offending light from overhead, but the cushioned restraints prevented either hand from moving more than a few inches. When the realization of her situation occurred, she trembled. "Where am I? Who are you people?"

I leaned close. "Who and where we are isn't important. The fact that we have you is all that matters."

When terror overcomes a person, it makes its presence known in the eyes, and Maria Dean's eyes said she'd never been more terrified in her life. "Why are you doing this? What do you want?"

I laid a hand on her arm. "Relax, Mrs. Dean. You're not in any danger yet. What we want is for your husband to understand exactly how important it is for him to give us the information we want immediately."

A flash of something came across her face. It could've been defiance or maybe relief. "Do you know who my husband is?" That question was a gift wrapped in gold paper and tied up with a beautiful bow.

"I know exactly who your husband is. In fact, I had a conversation with him at eight-eighteen Azurstrasse in Zurich just a few days ago. Do I need to tell you who owns the house at that address?"

She stopped pulling against the restraints and tried to stare me down. "You're with the Israelis, aren't you?"

"If I were, how would that make you feel?"

A commotion stirred behind me, and I turned to see Clark leaving sick bay. I didn't have to guess where he was going. Skipper would have her contact at Mossad on the phone in seconds, and we'd know exactly why theirs was the first name Maria Dean pulled out of her hat.

She scowled. "You don't look like a Jew, but if you're in bed with those filthy animals, you can do with me whatever you want. Roger will never tell you a single word, but he will hunt you down like the dog you clearly are, and he'll tear you limb from limb."

"That's enough of the hollow threats, Maria. You're in no position to be so bold."

To my utter disbelief, she laughed. "There's no place you can hide. There's no place Roger won't find you and kill everyone you know. You can't escape him, and his enemies never live to tell their story."

I smiled down at her. "Perhaps I should've captured Franziska Kobel instead of you, Mrs. Dean. Maybe *she's* the love of his life."

She hissed, "You're a dead man, and you're not even smart enough to realize it yet."

I turned away. "Put her back out. I'm done with her for now. Let's move on to the next one."

Dr. Shadrack screwed another syringe into the IV line, and Maria Dean was fast asleep in minutes.

Celeste said, "Great stuff. I got everything. Do you want to upload it to the satellite?"

"Not yet. We may want to do a little creative editing before we share secrets, and I want to know what the Israeli connection is."

"Skipper and Ginger can manage that, I'm sure. Do you want me to set up to shoot Gabrielle Kellum next?"

I said, "Let's move the mountain to Mohammed instead."

We spent a few minutes repositioning our prisoners until Mrs. Kellum was situated perfectly in front of Celeste's camera and Maria Dean was sleeping it off in the next compartment.

I asked, "Is everybody ready?"

Nods and thumbs-ups gave Celeste the signal to start recording and Dr. Shadrack to bring our second hostile witness to testify before the jury.

Her reaction was nearly identical to Maria Dean's when she batted her eyelids against the glaring lights. "What's happening? Where am I?"

The psychologist that the University of Georgia created inside me took a different approach with Gabrielle Kellum. "Hello, Gabby. Tell me where your husband is."

She squinted and jerked against her restraints, so I put on my best face of frustration and said, "You're wasting my time, and I'm an extremely impatient man. Where is your husband?"

With her eyes squinted until they were almost closed, she spewed the company line. "He's at home. He's been very sick."

I blocked the light with my skull and stuck my nose only inches from hers. The obscenity that came out of my mouth made it clear that I knew she was lying. "Your husband is not at home, Gabrielle. In fact, you no longer have a home. I killed your gardeners and burned your house to the ground. And surprise, surprise . . . your dear husband, Courtney, was nowhere to be found."

"No! Please, no."

"Begging for mercy from me will only prove to you that I have none to give. I'll ask once more before this becomes entirely unpleasant. That is, unpleasant for you, of course. For me, I plan to enjoy every second of it. Where is Courtney Kellum?"

Tears exploded from her eyes as resolution melted into submission. "I don't know where he is, I swear. I don't know. Why did you have to burn down my house?"

I laughed in her face. "How nice of you to care so deeply about your two gardeners. I'm sure their families share your grief over the loss of such a beautiful home . . . not to mention their fathers and husbands."

A voice came from behind me, and I turned to see Ginger standing among the gathered operators. "We found the third satellite."

Chapter 29
Battle Stations?

I turned to Celeste. "Kill the camera, and edit out everything after Ginger came in."

She shut down the lights and cameras, and Dr. Shadrack stepped in to check on his patient.

He asked Gabrielle, "Are you hungry?"

She jerked against her padded cuffs again. "Yes, I'm hungry. Now, get me out of these restraints."

The doctor motioned toward me. "You'll stay in the restraints until he says we can take them off."

I spun before leaving sick bay. "Feed them, and keep them awake or asleep at your discretion. If they become problematic, use whatever means necessary to control them."

Gabrielle jerked her head toward me. "Both? Who else did you kidnap?"

I stepped back beside her bed and glared down at her. "You don't get to ask the questions, but there's one thing you should know. If the other person gives me the information I need, you have absolutely no value to me . . . just like your gardeners."

Tears came. "Why did you have to kill them?"

I smiled. "I didn't *have* to kill them. It was just a little bonus for me."

She sobbed. "Please, just tell me where we are."

I stooped closer. "First, you tell me where your husband is, and maybe I'll tell you where you are. See how that works?"

The sobbing continued. "But I don't know where he is."

"Stop crying," I ordered. "You're not in any immediate danger. You're not hurt. You're just uncomfortable. Do you understand?"

She ignored the command to stop crying, but her speech grew less choppy. "No, I don't understand. I don't understand any of this. Why do you need to know where Courtney is?"

"Look, Gabrielle. I don't want to be a monster, but make no mistake. I'm capable of becoming the worst nightmare you can imagine. You need to understand the position your husband has put you in. I'm not the kind of man who negotiates. In this room, you have no rights, and you have only one possibility of surviving this ordeal. You *will* give me what I want, or I'll find someone who will. It's that simple."

"You don't have to do this," she said, her body trembling.

I gritted my teeth. "Yes, I do, and your husband is the reason I have no choice."

"Why are you so cold? What happened to you to make you this way?"

I grabbed the rail so hard the entire bed shook beneath her, and I roared. "Because your husband killed four people I love, and he did it as a sport to taunt me. He underestimated me. In his wildest imagination, he never thought his beautiful wife—the mother of his children—could end up in my hands, but look where you are. You're strapped to a bed in my world—a world you never knew existed, a world from which you will never escape unless you deliver your husband, the murderous bastard that he is, to me."

The sobbing grew stronger. "But you'll kill him. I can't . . ."

The smile of a demented maniac came to my face. "Oh, no, Gabrielle. I won't kill your husband. Death is the most merciful punishment in existence. What I will do to him will make him beg for the demons of Hell to leap from their fiery pits and save him from my wrath."

She collapsed beneath the unimaginable burden of my threat, and that's exactly where I wanted her to spend the coming hours.

Celeste followed me from sick bay and stopped me in the corridor. "I didn't get any of that on camera."

I wiped the sweat from my brow. "Good. That performance was for her, not Courtney Kellum. It's impossible to simulate the fear she'll display next time she's on camera. I don't like doing that to her. She's innocent in this, but so were Charlie, Jimmy, Tony, and Hunter."

She pressed her lips into a small, horizontal line. "Chase, you're not really going to . . ."

I placed a hand on her arm. "When you go back up to the CIC, I want you to look at the unimaginable agony behind Skipper's eyes. There is no line I will not cross to avenge that agony, but I promise you won't have to see it."

A tear welled up in her eye. "I don't know how you do it, but I'm so glad there are people on Earth like you."

I gave her arm a squeeze and fell in step with Ginger.

Inside the CIC, Skipper sat with the entirety of her focus directed into the screen in front of her.

I planted myself in a chair beside her. "Tell me."

"I did it again," she said. "I missed the movement of the third satellite."

I leaned toward the screen. "Do you know where it is right now?"

She nodded and pointed straight up. "If we were lying on our backs on the helipad, we'd be looking right at it."

"They're tracking the ship?"

"Yes. That's how the ship in The Bahamas knows exactly where we are."

"Have you told Captain Sprayberry?"

"No, of course not. Everything comes to you first."

I gave her the opposite of the sadistic grin I'd shown Gabrielle Kellum. "You didn't miss anything. You let them play right into our hands. Knowing that they'll come to us instead of us hunting them down takes a load off my mind. You're a genius. Excellent work. Keep it up."

She furrowed her brow. "What? No, that's not how this works. You don't get to patronize me. Tony's dead, and there's nothing I can do about that, but you of all people don't get to pretend like I didn't screw up. No. I won't take that from you, Chase Fulton."

I continued smiling. "If I were patronizing you, I'd tell you that it's okay and that anybody would've missed the movement of the third satellite. That's patronization, and that's *not* what I'm doing."

"I mean it, Chase. You need to treat me the same way you'd treat me if this were a normal op."

"That's exactly what I'm doing. Celeste has some video that needs to be uploaded to the satellite. I need you to make that happen as soon as possible. I think I'll go up on deck and wave at that third satellite."

Back on the navigation bridge—after asking permission again—I briefed the captain on everything. He listened intently until I was finished, and he had only one question.

"Battle stations?"

"That's your call," I said, "but my men are going to be armed to the teeth and ready for a fight."

"Your ship will be the same."

"Tell me what you know about the ship we're intercepting."

He scratched his two-day growth of beard. "She's a hundred-meter boat, maybe a little more. She's fast for a conventional ship of her size. I don't know the skipper yet, but there's no outward indicators that she's a warship of any kind."

"Do we show any outward signs of being a warship?"

He rubbed his hand across the console as if caressing the mane of the Kentucky Derby winner. "We do not."

"Keep talking," I said.

"She's configured like an oilfield tender, but I have a sneaky feeling she's more than meets the eye."

He lifted his cup, and I wondered how many gallons of coffee he drank every day.

The captain said, "She changes her AIS ID every twelve hours or so, but we're pretty good at keeping an eye on people who are following us around the open ocean."

"How long before we intercept them?"

"Mr. March. What is our time to intercept?"

"Ninety-four minutes, sir."

Barry waved a hand. "Ninety-four minutes, sir."

"How dangerous is she?" I asked.

He shrugged. "There's no way to know until we provoke her enough to fight back."

"What if I told you I could guarantee they won't fire a single shot?"

He raised an eyebrow. "I'd be concerned that her captain was planning to ram us."

"He'll do neither, but I need you to slow down."

He narrowed his gaze. "Why?"

"Did you ever watch *Star Trek*?"

"I've seen a few episodes," he said.

"Remember when the captain would give the order to put the shields up?"

"Yeah, I remember."

"I'm going to put our shields up, Captain, but it'll take me at least a couple of hours."

A gleam came to his eye, and a mischievous grin followed. "Wanna have a little fun with 'em?"

"This is going to be good, isn't it?"

He said, "Yes, it is. You asked if I watch *Star Trek*, so now it's my turn to ask if you read Patrick O'Brian."

"Of course I do. Every good sailor loves the Captain Aubrey books."

He said, "In that case, Scotty, you go work on those shields, and I'll play a little game of sitting duck."

"Deal."

As I left the bridge, I heard the captain say, "Mr. March, where is our closest downstream hazard?"

I was intrigued. *Is the captain about to hide behind a rock in the middle of the Atlantic?*

My interest froze me in my tracks, and I became an eavesdropper.

Mr. March asked, "What do you mean by downstream, Captain?"

"I mean, if we turned off the engines, how long would it take us to hit something?"

The young officer hesitated. "Uh, I don't know, sir. That's not something I've ever tried to calculate."

Barry growled. "In that case, Mr. March, you can consider this a learning opportunity." The next words out of the captain's mouth were spoken over the comms. "Engineering, Bridge, this is the captain. Main engines all stop, and cool them as quickly as you can without breaking anything. Bring the number-two generator online to provide essential power only. Prioritize CIC, weapons, bridge, and the galley. Warm the number-three generator, and maintain rapid main engines start readiness."

I liked everything I heard, and I could've been convinced our master and commander was Captain "Lucky" Jack Aubrey reincarnated just for that mission.

I followed the weapons systems officer through the hatch and into the combat information center.

Skipper immediately asked, "What's going on with the power?"

Weps took his seat at the weapons control station and brought his console to life as if no one else were in the room, and I reclaimed my seat beside my analyst.

"Don't worry. The captain has everything under control. He's playing a little game of damsel in distress. He killed the main engines and set us adrift as if we'd suffered some sort of catastrophic engine failure."

She asked, "Why?"

"Because I need enough time to establish communications with our adversary to let them know where their beloved next of kin are being held against their will."

"Oh, that's kind of sexy," she said. "Who knew Captain Sprayberry was such the tactician?"

Weps said, "You should've seen him in his glory days. There's never been a better ship handler. He could make a destroyer dance like a ballerina."

Skipper asked, "Was he a coxswain?"

"Nope. He's the only officer I've ever seen who could outthink an admiral and outdrive every helmsman in the fleet. If those guys want to turn this into a shooting war, you'll see what the captain can do."

I tapped on the console. "Have you sent the video yet?"

Skipper resituated herself in front of the screen. "I sent it just before you walked in, but I built in a little time delay and bounced it around outer space like a pinball so they wouldn't know exactly where it's coming from."

"Good thinking," I said. "We'll keep up the ruse until we know Kellum and Dean have seen the video. We don't want to show our hand too early."

Skipper pointed toward a flashing bar on the secondary monitor to her left. "Oh, goody. It looks like they got the message, and they want to have a conversation."

Chapter 30
Before the Lions

The flashing bar on the edge of the monitor seemed to hypnotize me, and I felt as if I were living in both the past and future simultaneously. The best possible outcome for me would be the unconditional surrender and confession by everyone involved in murdering the people around me. In that scenario, the two women I held captive could simply walk back into their lives and forget their ordeal aboard my ship, but in my experience, history rarely allowed the best possible outcome to occur. I had no choice other than to play my hand as aggressively as possible and force a submission at any cost.

"What are we about to see?" I asked.

Skipper said, "I don't know, but it won't be a face-to-face. It'll be a still image or a piece of video."

"Why not a face-to-face?"

"That's not how this type of satellite works. We can send files, but not live video and audio."

I said, "That seems odd, but I'll have to trust you. Let's see what they dropped in our inbox."

She clicked on the flashing bar, and my heart pounded in anticipation of what I was about to see. Part of me wanted to watch Roger Dean or Courtney Kellum yelling into a camera with spittle flying and furious threats echoing through the air, but instead, I saw a typed message, innocuous and plain. I leaned toward the screen and across Skipper to read the words, but she shoved me back into my chair. "Get off me. We're not in eighth-grade computer lab. You have your own monitor over there."

She did whatever was necessary to display the text on the screen in front of me.

Chase Daniel Fulton, #1 Bonaventure Way, St. Marys, GA 31558. DOB 22 January 1974.

I skipped over the rest of the biographical data the writer used to demonstrate how well he knew me, and I continued reading the heart of the text.

You have made the worst decision of your life, and I know everything there is to know about you. You will immediately release my wife into the custody of the nearest European police agency. If you wish to surrender to that agency, feel free to do so; however, that will not keep you alive one second longer. You will die the most horrible death imaginable, and I will laugh while I'm slaughtering you. If you fail to immediately release my wife, I will kill every member of your family and everyone you've ever loved. You will, of course, die either way, but if you possess a shred of compassion for your family and loved ones, you will deliver my wife, completely unharmed, within the next thirty minutes. You may now consider yourself to be a Christian in the Colosseum before the lions, and I am the emperor.

I read it twice more, turned to Skipper, and smiled. "He has no idea where we are."

She returned the icy smile. "He clearly does not, but he's done his homework on you."

"Anybody with a computer could collect that data on me or anybody else in five minutes, so none of that scares me."

"What does scare you?"

"Losing Penny."

The instant the words left my lips, I felt like the worst human who'd ever spoken a word. Everything inside of me wanted to say something to take back those words that had to feel like flaming daggers to the woman who'd watched her husband fall victim to a murderous madman.

Instead of the next words coming from *my* mouth, they came from hers. "I pray you never have to feel the realization of that fear."

She laid her head against my shoulder, and we sat in silence, holding each other for a long, silent moment.

When she finally spoke again, the words came only as a whisper, but their ring was a sounding klaxon horn. "Nobody signed the letter."

I sat up and glared back at the monitor. *Whose words were those? Whose threat? Whose vow?*

Skipper said, "It has to be Kellum, right?"

"Maybe, but how can we know for sure?"

"We could call Roger Dean."

I let the idea bounce around inside my skull. "Can you make it look like the call is coming from Maria's cell phone?"

"Sure. Are you ready now?"

I picked up the handset. "Make the call."

The phone rang twice, and Roger Dean said, "I was just about to call you. I just got off the phone with Courtney. Are you okay?"

We had our answer, but we also had an opportunity, so I said, "Listen closely, Mr. Dean. Right now, your wife is alive and unhurt—"

He exploded. "You listen to me! If you so much . . ."

I laid down the handset. "Cut the connection."

Skipper didn't hesitate, and the line was dead in an instant. "I guess we got our answer, huh?"

I said, "Yeah. It's definitely Kellum's note, and at the very least, Roger Dean knows we're serious."

She said, "I think he got that message in Zurich."

"I still don't think Dean is behind this thing. He may be involved, but he's not the mastermind."

She scoffed. "Well, you certainly dragged him into it if he wasn't already. In case you haven't noticed, we've got his wife tied to a bed down in sick bay."

"I noticed," I said. "Call him back."

She hit the keys, and I lifted the handset.

Dean picked up immediately. "You little son of a—"

Skipper cut the connection again, and we waited.

Sixty seconds later, we tried again.

That time, Roger Dean was no less angry, but he was at least quieter. "What do you want?"

"I told you what I wanted when I caught you with your girlfriend in Zurich. Where is Courtney Kellum?"

"You have no idea who you're—"

Click.

Skipper chuckled. "You're going to keep doing this until he complies, aren't you?"

I shook my head. "Nope. He gets one more chance. Let's do it."

She dialed, and Dean answered, "Why do you keep—"

I interrupted. "Don't open your mouth again except to tell me where Courtney Kellum is. If you say anything other than that, I hope you enjoyed the video of your wife because that's the last time you'll ever see her alive."

He said, "Look, I'm a reasonable man. We can talk through this."

I swallowed my rage, if only for a moment. "You may be a reasonable man, but I am not. I'm a man who's been pushed beyond all limits of rationality, and now I'm responding in kind. Four people are dead. Four people I cared about."

Skipper snapped her head toward me, and I held up a finger. The look on her face didn't change, but she would soon understand the reason for my exaggeration.

"I will avenge their murders. Your wife is alive and unharmed for now, but she means absolutely nothing to me. She's merely a means to an end, and that end is you telling me where to find Courtney Kellum in the next ten seconds."

He coughed. "I understand. I do. But I don't know where Kellum is, and that's the god's honest truth. But I will help you find him. If he's behind the murders of your friends, he's gone completely rogue, and he is not acting as an agent of Ontrack Global Resources."

I looked to Skipper and silently asked what she thought I should do next. I was a stranger in a strange land, and I needed some directions.

With her look of confidence, she nodded once, and that was the reassurance I needed.

"Mr. Dean, I'm tempted to hang up, slit your wife's throat, and send you the high-def video, but I'm going to give you and her one opportunity. When I hang up, you will find your chief of physical security. I will call you back in exactly thirty minutes. If you do not have a set of ten-digit grid coordinates of precisely where Courtney Kellum is, your window of opportunity will close, and any rationality you *think* I might possess will dissolve in your wife's blood. Thirty minutes, Roger, and not a second more."

Skipper cut the connection. "Why did you tell him there'd been four murders?"

"Because I want them to believe their attempt on Hunter was successful. I don't want them trying again."

"Good thinking. Are you really going to kill Maria Dean if he doesn't come through in thirty minutes?"

"I don't know, and *that's* what scares me the most."

She shivered. "Please don't. I think she's innocent in all of this."

"You're probably right, but so was Tony."

Skipper closed her eyes and rolled with the punch I'd just delivered. "Why don't you go talk to her? At the very least, she deserves to know what's really going on."

"You're right. I'm going to do exactly that, and you're coming with me."

"What? No! I don't do that. I'm an analyst. I'm . . ."

It was my turn to press a finger to her lips. "Shh. Bring a picture of Tony."

I was prepared to drag Skipper into sick bay with me if it became necessary, but fortunately, she relented.

We walked through the bay and into Dr. Shadrack's office. "How are they doing, Doc?"

He looked up from the chart he was studying. "They're both awake, and they've been fed."

"Is Maria Dean coherent enough to have a conversation?"

He stood. "Oh, yeah. She's quite chatty. As a matter of fact, I was planning to talk with you about her."

I lowered my chin. "Chatty, huh? About what?"

"I'll put it this way. Hanging her life over Roger Dean's head probably isn't the best carrot you could choose."

"Is that so?"

He slipped into his lab coat. "Come with me."

We followed him across the bay and through a curtain, where I nearly collided with Mongo standing like a statue, his arms crossed and his jaw set.

"Sorry, big guy. I didn't know you were in here."

He didn't speak. Instead, he simply nodded.

Dr. Shadrack said, "The guards were my idea. Kodiak is with Mrs. Kellum in the other room. I had their wrist restraints taken off so they could eat, and I didn't want to risk either of them trying anything stupid."

I stepped beside Maria's bed. "Did you get enough to eat, Mrs. Dean?"

She glared up at me with fury burning in her eyes, and I couldn't tell if the welling tears were fear or anger.

She said, "I don't know who you are, but taking me and Gabrielle was the worst decision you could've made. Our husbands are dangerous men."

"That may be true," I said, "but I need to ask you some questions. First, do you know what your husband and Courtney Kellum have done?"

She stared through my face. "They've done far too many unthinkable things for me to have *any* idea what you're talking about."

"In that case, I'll bring you up to speed. They killed four people who are extremely important to me."

Mongo flinched behind me, and I turned to give him a wink. He pretended to ignore me, but the relief in his eyes said he was pleased to know Hunter was still breathing.

Maria, on the other hand, didn't react, so I pulled up a stool and sat beside her to avoid looming over her. I held out my hand toward Skipper. She slipped me her phone, and I turned the screen to face Maria. "This man's name is Anthony. He was the brother of one of the men who brought you here." I rolled aside and motioned toward Skipper. "And he was her husband."

I gave her time to take in Tony's face.

"Roger Dean and Courtney Kellum murdered him in the middle of the afternoon. Everybody you've seen in the last twelve hours loved him, and any one of us would gladly give up our own life to bring him back."

Maria's eyes betrayed her, revealing a chink in her armor, and I pounced. "Every one of us will wade through Hell to avenge Anthony's death and the murder of the other three men who we revered and respected."

Maria didn't take her eyes off Tony's picture. "Are you sure?"

"I'm certain."

She glanced down as if making the weightiest decision of her life. When she met my gaze again, the rage she'd borne toward me was still roaring in her dark eyes, but I was no longer the target. Her ire was instead directed a thousand miles away at a man she once loved.

Chapter 31
A Woman Scorned

I passed Skipper's phone back to her and whispered, "Go find Singer, and have him relieve Mongo."

She slipped the phone into her pocket and left the curtained-off space without a word.

I rolled my stool back beside Maria's bed at the same time Dr. Shadrack stepped into the space. "Skipper tells me you may need a private compartment."

"That's a good idea," I said. "Can you make that happen?"

He slid back the curtain and motioned for a medic to join us. The young man hustled to us, and the doctor said, "Let's move Mrs. Dean into number three."

"Yes, sir."

Soon, we were ensconced in a space that wasn't as big as the curtain area, but it was quieter. Mongo blocked the door with his bulk, still standing his post like the lifelong soldier he was.

Singer arrived and replaced the giant. It wasn't security that concerned me. Singer was there to listen and keep me from falling into a trap.

I began. "All right. We've got a little privacy now. Tell me about your husband."

She eyed the sniper. "Does he have to be here? I don't think I represent much of a threat."

"He stays," I said. "Start talking."

She resituated herself in the bed and tugged at her ankle restraints. "Can't we take these off? It's obvious we're on a ship. Where would I go?"

"We'll see about the shackles when you start telling me what I need to hear."

She exhaled with a huff. "Roger hasn't been my husband for a long time."

"You're divorced?"

"Not legally, but practically. He's been sleeping with his whore from the bank for years."

"Are you talking about Franziska Kobel?"

She seemed to gag at the mention of her husband's lover. "He thinks he's so smart. I've got enough to bury him a thousand times over. That's why he won't give me a divorce. He knows I'll drag him through mud so deep he'll be lucky to afford an efficiency apartment."

"Your marital issues aren't my concern. I believe your husband is involved in a plot to murder people I care about, and probably me, too. If you can't give me information about those murders, you're of absolutely no use to me."

With a sly smile, she said, "Let me guess. You threatened to kill me if he didn't turn himself in, and he threatened to hunt you down. Sound familiar?"

"Keep talking."

"Think about it. Roger hates me. He hates every penny I spend, every friend I have, and everything in my life that remotely brings me joy. Go ahead and threaten to kill me. He'll play along and make you believe he loves me, and he'll fall apart if anything happens to me. Go ahead and let him suck you in. That's what he does to people. But don't think for one minute that Roger Dean doesn't want you to put a bullet in my brain. Nothing would please him more, and nothing would solve more problems for him than me being dead."

I fed everything about Maria Dean into my brain—her words, her facial expressions, the tone of her voice, her every detail. "Let's say I believe you, which I've not decided yet. What can you give me that'll put me face-to-face with the man who's actually pulling the trigger?"

"What do you know about Ontrack Global Resources?"

I rolled away a few inches. "I know it's the largest private intelligence gathering company in the world. I know it's worth somewhere around a billion dollars, and . . ."

She let out a laugh that caught me completely off guard and I paused.

"What?"

She said, "At most, the company is worth a hundred million, and that's stretching it. The billion-dollar figure Roger likes to throw around is based on accounts receivable that he'll never collect. When you do business with the Kremlin, Hamas, Hezbollah, ISIS, and the PLO, good luck strong-arming them into writing a check that doesn't bounce."

"What makes you think your husband is doing business with people like that?"

"I own fifty point four percent of Ontrack Global Resources."

"Interesting. How did that come about?"

"I think it's time we talk about these shackles. Don't you?"

"First, I want to hear how you became the majority shareholder in OGR."

"My father put up the money to start the original company that became OGR. Roger thought his lawyers were clever enough to dilute my father's share when he began operating as Ontrack Global Resources. Well, that's not exactly accurate. There was a transition period in which Roger operated as Spyglass Industries, but that was short-lived. Ultimately, when my father passed away, Roger believed he would become the full owner of the company, but my father was smart. His original agreement with Roger contained a clause providing for my father's share of the business to be placed in a trust with a trustee to operate in his interest should Roger ever take the business in a direction my father didn't approve of."

"Let me guess," I said. "Your husband took the business someplace your father would never approve."

She nodded. "And guess who he named as trustee upon his death."

"You're a remarkable woman, Mrs. Dean. I'm impressed. Your husband can't divorce you because you'd either force a sale or take control of OGR. Why haven't you filed for divorce yourself?"

Her smile returned. "Because I've been waiting for a situation exactly like this one. Roger has grown more and more arrogant as the years have gone by. He's reached a pinnacle at which he feels invincible . . . godlike, if you will. But I've always known the day would come when he stuck his finger in the wrong face, and I'm now convinced that face is yours."

I stared into her eyes—eyes that said she was both telling the truth and looking forward to watching Roger Dean plummet from his ivory tower.

While I was letting the information go through the tumble-dry cycle in my brain, Skipper stuck her head into the room. "Twenty-six minutes, Chase."

I stood. "Give me your hands, Mrs. Dean."

She jerked away. "No! What are you doing?"

"I'm restraining you while I make a phone call. When I get back, we'll talk about getting you out of all the restraints and into a cabin where you can be a little more comfortable."

She hesitantly offered her hands, and I laced the leather padded bands around her wrists.

"It won't take long, and I'll be back soon."

She said, "Can I make one request?"

"Sure."

"Where are we?"

I said, "We're right in the middle of you picking sides. I'll see you in a few minutes."

I hooked Singer's sleeve as I passed, and he followed me into the corridor.

"What do you think?" I asked.

In his quiet, confident tone, he said, "Hell hath no fury like a majority shareholder scorned."

I returned to my chair in the CIC beside Skipper, and she placed the call at precisely thirty minutes past the time we ended our previous call with Roger Dean. It rang several times, and I almost believed he wasn't going to answer. That would've made for an interesting power play, but he finally picked up.

"Yes."

I wasted no time. "Let's have it, Roger. Where is Courtney Kellum?"

He said, "You have to believe me. I don't know where he is. I can't find him. I need more time."

I'd made a billion decisions in my life, but I'd never struggled with one any more than that one in that moment. I wrestled with my options and finally settled on the only reasonable conclusion. I laid the receiver on the console and said, "Cut the line."

Skipper obeyed, and Roger Dean was left holding a phone in his hand and listening to dead air.

I handed my phone to Skipper. "I recorded my conversation with Maria Dean. Give it a listen, and then we'll talk about it."

She started the playback, and I yawned as if I hadn't slept in days.

Singer mirrored my gape and said, "We all need some sleep."

"Where's the rest of the team?" I asked.

"I think everybody crashed except Kodiak. He's still guarding the other woman."

"Gabrielle Kellum," I said.

"Yeah. Her name was in there somewhere, but I couldn't drag it out."

"Go get some sleep."

He said, "What about you?"

"I'm going downstairs to send Kodiak to bed, then I'm headed for the rack myself."

Skipper said, "Will you please tell Dr. Shadrack to hit the sack, as well? He's been up a long time."

I pointed at my phone. "Keep listening. We'll talk about that conversation in the morning. At least, I think it's still sometime in the middle of the night."

Skipper checked her watch. "Do you really want to know?"

After making my way to sick bay, I found Dr. Shadrack drifting off in his office. I knocked on the door and startled him.

"Oh! Hey, Chase. Sorry, I've been up a while."

"Me too, Doc. Let's put our guests to bed and then get some rest ourselves."

I don't know what he drew into the pair of identical syringes, but it did the trick. Both women were out within seconds, and I removed their restraints.

I asked, "Do you have another room where we could park Mrs. Kellum?"

"Sure. The room next to the other one is open."

We rolled her into the adjoining room and turned out the lights.

I said, "We should put a guard on the doors."

The doctor said, "Joseph is on shift for five more hours. He'll keep an eye on them. We can secure the hatches, and he can watch them on the monitors. If they do anything other than sleep, he'll wake me up."

"Don't let him wake you," I said. "Have him come get me."

"Whatever you say. I'll leave orders for more sweet-dream meds every four hours."

I don't think I've ever felt anything better than slipping into bed and wrapping my arms around my sleeping beauty. She nestled against me and said, "I wondered if you were ever coming to bed. Is everything all right?"

I wanted to tell her the truth, but instead, I said, "Everything's fine."

I believed sleep would take me in minutes, but I was wrong. Everything about my world was inside out, and I felt like I was lost in a hurricane. Penny's soft breath against my skin reminded me of everything that was important, and I finally forced my eyes to close and my mind to stop churning. The coming hours would demand more of me than perhaps I had to give, and I couldn't face them without at least a few hours of merciful sleep.

Chapter 32
Thinking Like a Pirate

When I pulled my boots back on six hours later, the world was a different place, and I was a changed man: refreshed, invigorated, and sharp.

Penny came through the door to our cabin with a pair of steaming cups, and I accepted mine with enthusiasm.

"Good morning, sleepyhead. I was beginning to wonder if you'd ever wake up."

I took my first sip. "Mmm, that's good. Thank you. I guess my body needed the rest. Is everybody else up?"

"They're waiting for us in the . . . wait a minute. It'll come to me . . . Mess hall."

"Nautical terms may not be your strong suit, but it's nice to be together again."

"I know what you mean. I didn't like running off without you."

"Let's have some breakfast."

She waved a finger. "No, no, no. It's not breakfast. It's morning chow."

"Indeed, it is."

Just as promised, the team was elbow-deep in their platters of eggs, bacon, biscuits, and gravy.

Kodiak was first to acknowledge our arrival. "Mornin', boss. Do we get to shoot anybody today?"

I shrugged. "Maybe. The day's still young."

"That's what I like to hear," he said as he dived back into his chow.

I took my seat beside Skipper and bumped shoulders with her. "Did you get any sleep?"

She wiped her mouth. "Oh, yeah. It felt great. How about you?"

"I just woke up."

She laid down her fork. "I checked on Gabrielle and Maria this morning. Shawn the SEAL is babysitting them while they eat. Gabrielle is a mess."

"What do you mean?"

"She's scared, like anybody would be, but I get the feeling she really has no idea what's going on."

"Good. That's how we need her. I'm a little anxious about how willing Maria Dean is to jump in the boat with us."

She scooped a forkful of eggs. "I think Singer's right. She's a woman scorned, and she sees all of this as a way to get her pound of flesh."

"We have to take advantage of that, right?"

"Absolutely. In fact, I don't see any reason to delay. I think you should pull everything out of her you can and go to work. This thing is beginning to drag on, and everybody's nervous about being the next victim."

I flinched, and Skipper asked, "What was that about?"

"I have to talk to the captain."

"Relax, College Boy. Clark already did that. We're still playing lost at sea, and our pursuers are laying off about seven miles."

"Oh, that's how it is, huh? Now *you're* calling me College Boy?"

She giggled. "I'm just doing my job and taking care of all of my boys—not just the one who went to college."

"It's starting to sound like you don't need me around at all."

"Oh, no. That's not true. We need somebody to blame when things fall apart."

"It's nice to be needed," I said. "Let's get to work."

The bridge was my first stop, and for the first time, I didn't ask permission.

Captain Sprayberry turned and growled. "What are you doing on my bridge?"

I threw up both hands and backpedaled. "You said it was my ship."

"I'm just messing with you. Did you finally get some sleep?"

"I did. And you?"

"Enough," he said. "I guess they told you our Peeping Tom is laying off and drifting with us."

"Skipper told me."

He said, "I assumed somebody would brief you. So, what's our plan?"

I propped against a console. "How long would it take for us to be ready to fight with full power restored?"

"We're keeping the main engines warm and ready to start. We can have them up to temperature and producing full power in about two minutes, but we'll have maneuvering power in seconds after the command. We have generator number two running at idle and ready to produce full power in fifteen seconds. Ultimately, we can be ready to fight inside two minutes."

I asked, "Would it decrease that time if we ran the main engines at idle?"

"It would, but they produce enough heat at idle to register on their scope if they're scanning us for a heat signature."

"I'm okay with that," I said. "It'll look like our engineers are repairing the fake breakdown."

He picked up a handset. "Engineering, Bridge. This is the captain. Bring both main engines on line at idle and cycle as necessary." He listened for a few seconds and laid down the set. "Done. Are you expecting a fight?"

"I plan to start one," I said. "While I'm gathering kindling to start the fire, I'd like you to make it look like we've restored a little power and make way toward our adversary. Let's see what he does."

"You got it," Barry said. "We're still at battle stations, and the crew just rolled over, so we're fresh, feisty, and ready for a fight."

"Keep me posted on how the other ship reacts, and give some thought to breaking down again a little more dramatically."

He gave me half a grin. "Now you're thinking like a pirate."

I made my way down to sick bay and stuck my head into Maria Dean's room. "Today's the day, Maria."

"The day for what?"

"The day you get to tell the world about Roger Dean. But first, I want to know about the Israelis."

"What about them?" she asked.

"Why did you assume I was with them when we first woke you up?"

"Mossad has been trying to trap Roger for several months. He sold some information to Hezbollah, and they found out about it. Roger has a great many enemies, but the Israelis are at the top of the list."

I stepped inside her room. "That doesn't explain your hostility toward them."

"I don't harbor any hostility toward them. In fact, my mother's maiden name was Atali."

"You're Jewish?"

"I guess one quarter Jewish, but I'm not observant. I attend mass sometimes."

"So, you're Catholic?"

She shrugged. "I guess if I'm anything, it's Catholic."

My mind was racing, and the thought of involving Mossad in the operation excited me to no end.

"I've got an idea, Maria. If I can put you on the phone with a high-ranking official inside Mossad, will you lay out your plan to cooperate with them once you're CEO of Ontrack Global Resources?"

"Wait a minute," she said. "I never said I was interested in cooperating with anybody."

"Mossad is the answer to both of our problems. If they believe you're willing to play ball with them after you take command of the company, they'll do anything we want, and I think you and I share a common enemy."

She studied me as if dissecting my brain. "What will you ask them to do if I convince them OGR will be a friendly organization when I'm in the CEO's chair?"

"I'll ask them only to find and take your husband into custody."

"He won't go without a fight."

"Fighting a Mossad snatch-and-grab team rarely ends well, Mrs. Dean."

That brought a smile to her face, and a cold chill ran down my spine.

She said, "Sure, get them on the phone. I'll talk to them, but don't waste my time or theirs if you can only get a field agent on the phone."

"If I can't get the director on the line, I'm certain we can get his deputy."

"I heard someone call you Chase. Is that your name or just what you do?"

"Both."

She didn't appear amused. "Tell me, Chase. Who do you work for?"

"The good guys whose checks don't bounce."

She examined the ceiling for a moment. "And do you decide who the good guys are, or do you simply trust the people who claim to be the good guys?"

"In this case, Mrs. Dean, it's starting to look like you just might be the good guys."

"Not from Roger's perspective."

I stepped from the room and called the CIC. "Skipper, I need the Mossad director on the phone."

"You don't want much, do you?"

"I'm serious. Mrs. Dean has agreed to partner with him when she's the CEO of OGR."

"Are you serious?"

"I am. If you can't get the director, find his deputy, and put them on the phone with Maria Dean."

"Do you realize what this will do for us?" she asked.

"Yeah, I know exactly what it'll do, and that's precisely why I want to get it done."

"You're a genius," she said.

"Only part of the time. Can you make it happen?"

"You know I can."

I stepped into Gabrielle Kellum's room. Her eyes were closed, but her breathing was too irregular for her to be asleep.

"Mrs. Kellum, are you awake?"

She opened her eyes and shrank into the pillow. "What do you want?"

I tried to keep my tone as gentle as possible. I'd terrified her the last time we spoke, and I wanted to try a different approach. "I don't want to hurt you. I have no reason to hurt you. I simply want to know where I can find your husband."

"And if I don't help you, you're going to kill me, right?"

"I don't want it to come to that, but ultimately, it's up to you."

Tears began to make their way down her cheeks, and I fought back the urge to take advantage of her fear.

"All you have to do is tell me where I can find Courtney Kellum, and I'll take you home."

"Home? You burned down my home."

The monster I'd threatened to be clawed behind my eyes, but I fought him back. "You're a wealthy woman, Mrs. Kellum. Rebuilding a home anywhere you want is well within your reach."

"Why did you have to burn down my home?"

"Just tell me where your husband is, and this will all be over as soon as we verify the information you give us."

"He's gone," she whispered.

"Gone where?"

"I don't know. He told me to act like everything was normal."

"What do you mean?"

She made no effort to wipe her tears. "He's done this before, but nothing like this has ever happened."

"He's done *what* before, Mrs. Kellum?"

She spoke through trembling lips. "He told me to say he was terribly sick if anyone asked. He's been gone for almost two weeks, I think. I don't know what day it is."

"Do you have any way to get in contact with him?"

She shook her head. "No. He says knowing where he goes puts me at risk. I guess he was right. I guess he meant I would be at risk from people like you."

"Look at me, Mrs. Kellum. If you knew where your husband was, would you tell me?"

Her forehead turned to parallel rows of furrowed flesh. "My God, yes! I don't want to die. You have to believe me."

"No, I don't have to believe you. That's a choice I'll make. But before I do that, I've got two more questions. First, does anybody at OGR know where your husband is?"

She nodded in sharp, abbreviated motions. "I'm sure Roger Dean knows, but—"

"Is there anybody else who would know where he is?"

"I don't know. Why are you doing this to me? What did Courtney do to you?"

"That brings us to my second question. Does your husband shoot?"

She shook her head violently. "What?"

"Does he shoot? Is he a hunter or a long-range shooter?"

"Why does that make any difference?"

I held my breath and let my face turn red. "Don't make this any more uncomfortable than it has to be. Is your husband a long-range shooter?"

She whimpered, "Yes. He hunts in Africa every year, and he always kills something."

"Okay, I've got only one more question, and then we're done. Do you know if he reloads his own ammunition?"

Her crying became powerful. "He does. He brags about his bullets bringing down big game in one shot. Why? Why does any of this matter?"

I stood. "Mrs. Kellum, your husband is on a killing spree, and he's murdering people close to me. I'm going to stop him, and if you don't help me find him, you're as guilty as he is."

She cried harder with every breath. "I swear to you, I don't know where he is. I'll give you Roger Dean's phone number and address, but I swear I don't know where Courtney is."

"I'll take that information," I said, and I jotted down the number and address through her gasps. I laid a hand on the side of her bed. "Listen to me. You can stop crying. No one's going to hurt you. I'm moving you to a cabin on the ship where you can be more comfortable. Your meals will be delivered, and you'll have access to a television, a chair, and a real bed. You're safe . . . for now."

She grabbed my hand. "You're going to kill him, aren't you?"

I squeezed her hand. "Only if he forces me to." If possible, her wailing increased, and I said, "Calm down, Mrs. Kellum. There's one more thing you need to know." Her sobbing slowed, and I said, "We didn't harm your gardeners, nor did we burn down your house. When all of this is over, you still get to go home."

Chapter 33
Don't Get Dead

When a ball begins rolling in my world, it accelerates at an unimaginable rate. The ball that was the mission to find, capture, or kill Courtney Kellum rolled faster and further out of control with every passing minute, and I loved everything about the flaming pace.

Skipper handed me a headset. "You'll want to take this one."

I slipped the headset onto my ears and covered the microphone. "Who is it?"

"Just say hello."

I nestled into my seat. "Yes?"

A deep, heavily accented voice rang in my ears, and I recognized it immediately.

"Hello, Mr. Fulton. It is Dovrat Rabin with Israeli Mossad. It has been too long, my friend."

I'll never understand how a simple kid from Georgia, who should've been playing baseball somewhere, ends up on the telephone with the director of one of the world's foremost intelligence agencies.

"Hello, Director Rabin. So nice of you to take the time."

"Do not be ridiculous. I always have time for you, especially when you bring gifts like today's. You must tell me how you came into partnership with Mrs. Maria Dean."

"I'm afraid I don't have time for the whole story, Director, but I trust that you're satisfied with her information."

He let out a hearty laugh. "Time, indeed. Next time you are in Israel, perhaps."

"Next time, sir. I promise."

He said, "Now, back to Mrs. Dean. Are you confident that she will become chief operating officer of Ontrack Global Resources upon her husband's demise?"

"Quite certain, sir. My analyst has confirmed every detail, and there's absolutely no question."

"And what would you have me do with Roger Dean?"

I cleared my throat. "I wouldn't presume to dictate Mossad activity, Mr. Director."

"Please, Chase. You are being ridiculous still. You must call me Dovrat. Do you call the director of your CIA by his title?"

It was my turn to laugh. "I have a few select names for him, and none of them include his title."

"Yes, I have no doubt of this, but administrations come and go in America. Your party will soon be back in the White House, and the world will be a safer place for both of us."

"If the world becomes a safer place, Dovrat, you and I will be out of business."

"The world will never be so safe as to eliminate the need for men like you and me. Now, back to my question. What will you have me do with Roger Dean when we invite him for tea?"

"Again, Director, I'd never be so bold, but if I were to invite him over for coffee, I don't think I'd ever let him leave."

"Great minds, my friend."

I said, "Forgive me for being so forward, but when do you expect to . . ."

He said, "You're never too forward. I have six officers en route to his office as we speak. They will deliver my invitation, and no one declines my invitation."

"I've always respected your efficiency," I said. "If you'd do me one courtesy, I'd be in your debt."

"Name it."

"If your officers engage Roger Dean in conversation, perhaps they could persuade him to tell me where I might find his chief of security, Courtney Kellum."

"Quite the conversationalists my officers are. I am sure the subject will come up, and you will have your answer within the hour."

"Within the hour?" I said. "That *is* quick."

"We are a small country, surrounded by factions who want nothing more than to rid the Earth of me and my countrymen. We don't have time to—as you say in the States—dillydally."

I asked, "You don't happen to have any naval assets in the Western Atlantic, do you?"

"Unfortunately, I do not, but I am certain your government does."

I said, "My government is never as cooperative as yours in these matters, so I'll handle it without a carrier battle group in my pocket."

"Oh, how I miss the days of my youth. Savor the thrill, Chase. Soon, you will be relegated to watching the game from the sidelines, and after a man has tasted the game face-to-face with his foe, the sideline is a wretched place to be."

We ended the conversation, and I called the team into a huddle while I was still on the field.

The CIC was smaller than the op center back at Bonaventure, but there was still room for the full team to assemble, talk, argue, agree, and plan. And that's exactly what we did. I invited the captain to sit in on the meeting because none of us would be more involved in the coming hours than he would.

Skipper brought up a chart of our position and plotted the ship that had been chasing us all over the ocean.

I began. "Ladies and gentlemen, I believe the man who killed Tony and nearly killed Hunter is aboard that ship. I intend to drag him by his hair to Skipper's feet so he can beg for mercy."

Warriors often communicate in sounds that don't qualify as words.

Those sounds are universal, regardless of the language the fighters speak, and the sounds that rose from my team were undeniable.

I continued. "Here's the plan. We're going to lure them in with a distress call and a little ruse. I'll let Captain Sprayberry lay out the details for you."

The captain stood and wasted no time. "We're going to set our ship on fire and beg for help."

The sounds my men made were punctuated with question marks, and the captain said, "Okay, that's not exactly what we're going to do, but it's close. I'm going to set vats of marine-grade diesel and kerosene on fire on the weather deck and put our bow in the wind. From astern, our ship will appear to be consumed by fire and billowing black smoke. With our bow in the wind, all of the smoke and fire will blow downwind and cause no damage to the ship."

"Why are we going to do that?" Kodiak asked.

The captain said, "I'm glad you asked. As soon as we have the fire roaring, I'll put out a distress call on the weakest radio we have aboard. It's a line-of-sight radio, meaning a ship would have to see us to hear us. The only ship in sight is our adversary over there."

"I like it," Kodiak said. "You're gonna put 'em right where we want 'em."

The captain looked at me, and I reclaimed the floor. "You're exactly right, Kodiak. When they move in to provide assistance to the crew of a burning ship, we're going to put ourselves aboard while they're looking the other way."

The warrior noises returned, and I felt like a Viking jarl in front of a bloodthirsty horde of Norse swordsmen.

I said, "We're looking for this man."

Skipper brought up Courtney Kellum's picture, and every eye studied the monitor intently.

"We're bringing him back alive, but not necessarily unharmed. If he gets rough, feel free to return the favor. He's no joke. He's older than you guys, but he's a fighter. Don't expect him to roll over and surrender. He'll put up a fight, but any two of us should be able to take him hand to hand. If he comes up shooting, that's another issue. The rules of engagement for this one are simple. Don't get dead."

Nothing says more about the mind than the eyes, and I knew the eyes of my team as if they were my own. The one wildcard in the room was the SEAL. His eyes had questions, so I said, "What is it, Charlene?"

A little nervous laughter rose before everyone in the room realized I was looking directly at Shawn.

He ignored the name and said, "Are you sending me?"

"No, I don't send people. I take people with me, and yes, you're on the list. What's on your mind?"

He looked away for a brief moment and back at me. "What if we get over there and it's just a merchant ship and your shooter isn't on board?"

"The chances of that happening are extremely slim. That ship has tailed us for two days, and there's no innocent explanation that could justify behavior like that. Something sinister is going on, and every indicator puts the shooter on that boat."

The look on his face said he wasn't satisfied, and my first reaction was a tinge of anger that he'd question my reasoning, but it only took an instant for me to put myself in his boots. He didn't know us. He didn't know me. He'd likely boarded more ships than all of us combined, and he'd probably seen everything that can go wrong on those hostile boardings.

I said, "If we get over there, and it's a non-hostile crew, we'll walk away, get back in our boat, and come home."

"Where's the ship flagged?" Shawn asked.

The captain took that one. "We don't know. She changes her AIS identification every ten to twelve hours."

"What language does the crew speak?"

The captain shrugged. "We don't know."

"Do we have enough men to stand up a QRF in case we get the crap kicked out of us over there?"

The captain turned to me, and I said, "Yes, we've got a quick reaction force. Her name is Ronda No-H, and she's the baddest door gunner you've ever seen."

Shawn nodded and said, "I've got one more question, if you don't mind."

"Go ahead."

"How many hostile boardings have you done?"

"I don't know, but probably not as many as you. If we do it wrong, I expect you to tell us. You're the SEAL." He chewed his bottom lip and watched as I pulled up my pants leg, revealing the state-of-the-art prosthetic that filled the space below my knee. "I got this after a boarding in Western Africa."

"Did you win?" he asked.

"I didn't get dead."

We moved the party to the stern deck that would soon be ablaze with a beautiful piece of nautical tomfoolery, and Shawn taught his abbreviated hostile ship boarding class to a team of warfighters who never missed an opportunity to learn from the voice of experience.

While we were talking through the scenarios, a pair of deckhands drove two forklifts onto the deck, with vats of filthy-looking gunk inside.

Clark said, "I guess those are our firepits, huh?"

"Looks like it," I said. "Do you want to come with us?"

"Everything inside me wants to come with you, College Boy, but I'd only be in the way. I'm old, broke down, and slow."

"You're none of those things," I said. "Well, maybe the old part . . . and the broke down part . . . and yeah, I guess now that you mention it, the slow part is true, too. Why don't you find a nice soft spot to sit this one out?"

He gave me a shove hard enough to remind me he was still a formidable force, even with his back full of metal and his body covered in scars from blades and bullets from all over the world.

My radio crackled, and the captain asked, "Are you ready?"

"Let's do it."

The deckhands lit the vats with torches, and the fire caught immediately. A rancid smell and pillars of black smoke filled the air in seconds.

The crewmen moved their forklifts away from the flames and assumed their positions beside the tender crane.

Armed to the teeth, we climbed aboard the RHIB in four pairs. Singer and Kodiak took the bow, Disco and Mongo took the helm, Shawn and I nestled onto the tubes at the waist, and finally, Anya and Gator took their position at the transom covering our stern.

The crane operator deposited us into the ocean, and I watched Shawn as the sea welcomed him home. He reached a hand beneath the surface and splashed a handful of salt water onto his face. I couldn't help imagining what must've been going through his mind. With a team of commandos he'd never met until a few days before, he was about to board a hostile ship with a mass murderer on board. He'd never watched us fight, and he'd never seen us brave the tide of battle, yet he volunteered to pick up a rifle and wade into the fray with brothers he never knew existed.

Everything about my team was changing before my eyes, and justice for James, Charlie, Tony, and Hunter lay just across the waves. I'd never wanted an enemy's throat in my grasp more than I wanted to look into Courtney Kellum's eyes and drive him into the deck. Valhalla thundered as Disco opened the throttles, and my Vikings— unafraid, driven, and unstoppable—gripped their swords.

For me, what lay ahead would hang me in the balance between revenge and justice. I would be weighed, and I would be measured. Did I possess the restraint to let Courtney Kellum live to draw another breath, or would I be ushered forward by an unstoppable wind at my back, driving me through the animal who'd taken a coward's stand against defenseless men who neither saw their murderer nor had the chance to stand toe to toe with him and fight like the men of honor they were?

Chapter 34
Dance Partner

Keeping the ever-expanding plumes of billowing smoke between our rigid hull inflatable boat and our adversary's ship, we maneuvered toward the bow of the *Lori Danielle*, waiting for the starter's pistol to launch us out of the blocks and into the heart of the race. We didn't have to wait long. Captain Sprayberry's seamanship would soon be on full display.

The radio call was weak by any standard. We loitered only a few hundred feet away from the ship, and the distress call was barely more than a crackling hiss.

"Mayday . . . Mayday . . . Mayday. This is the Research Vessel *Lori Danielle* lying one hundred fifty miles west of Bermuda at thirty-two degrees, seven point eight minutes north by sixty-seven degrees, fifty-one point two degrees west. We are ablaze and adrift."

The call sent cold chills through my body, even though I knew it was only a ploy. The thought of our ship burning and foundering at sea felt almost like the murder of another beloved member of the family.

The radio remained silent for another minute, and I thought the transmission may have been too weak to be heard by our chaser. A call from the CIC changed my mind.

"Sierra One, CIC."

"Go for Sierra One."

Skipper said, "There was no radio response, but the bogie is motoring inbound at twenty-one knots. Get out of our shadow. You'll be able to see her on radar."

I said, "Roger, maneuvering. Report her range until I get visual."

"Roger. She's five point two miles and closing."

Disco pressed the throttles forward and moved us abeam the *Lori Danielle* for a direct line of sight for our radar antenna mounted high on the RHIB's overhead.

Singer shot a finger toward the screen. "Contact. Four point seven miles and closing."

I reported radar contact with the CIC, and Disco expertly maneuvered the RHIB, keeping us behind the wall of smoke. Our mission relied on the element of surprise, and Disco was doing everything in his power to prolong our position out of sight.

Singer continued making range calls. "Four miles and closing."

The water around the stern quarter of the *Lori Danielle* swirled and churned, and Shawn noticed at the same instant I did.

He said, "Captain's coming astern to screw up their timing."

Weps, the weapons systems officer, told us Captain Sprayberry was a master at the helm, and I had the feeling we were about to have ringside seats for the nautical boxing match of the century.

The wind blew at twelve knots out of the northeast, and the captain brought his ship astern at four knots. It was a masterful piece of naval footwork. By the time the captain of the bogie figured out we were closing faster than his speed, it would be too late for him to escape Captain Sprayberry's trap.

Disco held us perfectly astern our ship as the miles between us turned to yards, and Shawn called, "Visual contact!"

Everyone aboard the RHIB ducked to peer beneath the massive wall of black smoke to see the bow of the bogie cutting through the wind and waves.

Suddenly, Captain Sprayberry's voice filled my ears. "Sierra One, Bridge. We're coming ahead to starboard at fifteen knots. Stay on our hip, and I'll take you to the dance floor."

Disco brought us within inches of the port stern quarter of the ship, and we hid in her shadow as the captain pounced. At our position nestled under the ship's mothering wing, we had one enormous advantage. The crew of the bogie ship couldn't see us with their eyes or their radar. They likely had access to the satellite feed, but with the clouds of black smoke filling the sky, I doubted they noticed the thirty-foot RHIB full of commandos locked and loaded for war.

We continued on the hip of the *Lori Danielle* as the captain brought her from dead adrift to fifteen knots in a continual right turn. I had no way to know the captain's ultimate plan, but I liked how it was coming together. Ninety seconds into the maneuver, it became crystal clear what the captain was doing. He rounded the stern of the bogie as she maneuvered to avoid the collision that appeared inevitable.

If the bogie were a conventional ship, she likely had twin screws and rudders with massive bow thrusters, but not Azipods like our ship. Our captain could make his ship dance the Virginia Reel if he wanted. As for me, I didn't care if he was about to clog or break dance. I was just proud to be his partner, and I was happy to let him lead.

Solidly astern the bogie, Captain Sprayberry said, "It's time for your solo, Sierra One."

Disco broke cover behind the L.D. and pinned the starboard tube of our RHIB to the hip of the bogie ship. Shawn launched the hook over the stern rail and deployed the rope ladder. I was first up the ladder and over the rail. Shawn bumped me at every stride, forcing me to pick up the pace. His operational tempo was a little stronger than mine.

When Shawn crossed the rail, he instinctively moved ahead and took cover behind a piece of machinery on deck to cover the rest of the team as they boarded. I broke right and lay prone in a position from which I could see the bulk of the deck and count each of my teammates as they came over the rail.

Singer stumbled when he caught a boot on the rail, but he fell to the deck and performed a roll that would've made a gymnast proud. Gator was on his heels and scooped the sniper back to his feet. They recovered and took up a position behind Shawn while Anya sidestepped toward me.

The way she moved was like watching water flow around stones in a mountain stream. Every step, every slide, every advance and retreat was fluid and perfect. The rest of the team moved in staccato motions with strong, deliberate advances, but her tactics were melodic, like those of the prima ballerina she should've been.

Kodiak leapt the stern rail like an Olympic hurdler and stayed on his feet with his rifle pulled tightly against his shoulder to cover the giant's entrance.

Mongo lumbered across the rail, tapped Kodiak's shoulder, and said, "Last man."

We advanced across the deck and stayed low beneath the wall of black smoke encompassing the ship from Captain Sprayberry's masterful orbit of the bogie. Anyone in the superstructure would be blind, but the deck cameras were still a potential problem for us, so I gave the order. "Kill the cameras."

Shawn put two rounds of .300 Blackout into two lenses while Singer did the same to a pair of cameras on the starboard side. As I scanned the superstructure of the vessel for prying eyes, an explosion of fire, smoke, and chaos echoed from the bow.

The only reasonable explanation was a collision, but the ship didn't shudder or rock. A collision at fifteen knots should've knocked us from our feet, but it didn't happen. Every member of the team hustled to the rails to port and starboard to get eyes on what happened at the bow. Everybody except Shawn the SEAL. He continued forward on his track with his rifle at the ready. He was unshakable, and I liked that about him. I wondered if he knew that day, on that ship, in that environment, that he was right in the middle of a job interview.

Our open-channel comms gave us immediate and uninterrupted access to every team member simultaneously, and from my vantage point, I definitely needed some help. "I'm on the starboard rail, and it's bedlam up there. I can't make out anything. Anyone have a clear line of sight?"

Singer said, "Me and Gator are going up. We'll have eyes on it in sixty seconds."

They scampered up the towering superstructure and disappeared into the dense black smoke choking the ship.

With still no contact with anyone aboard, we continued forward and prepared to step into the interior of the ship, where everything would change. We'd be trapped in steel corridors acting as fatal funnels should anyone open fire on us. No gunfighter liked that environment, but if we were going to clear the ship and find Courtney Kellum, we had no choice but to take the risk and dispense more firepower than our enemy.

Singer said, "It looks like the captain dumped the fire from the L.D. onto the foredeck of this ship. It's a mess, and everything's on fire."

How he'd done it, I didn't know, but pouring vats of flaming fuel onto the bow was a masterful piece of strategy. As long as the fuel burned, the bridge crew and captain would be blind in a blanket of roiling black smoke.

Through the mayhem, I heard automatic-weapons fire, and I wasn't the only one.

Shawn yelled into his comms, "Fire from the bridge wings!"

I peered around the superstructure to the portside and saw a man with a rifle pressed to his shoulder. He was pouring lead into the air ahead, blindly throwing bullets toward the *Lori Danielle*.

Shawn said, "Call it, boss. I've got the angle on the portside shooter."

I trained my rifle on the starboard-side gunman. "Put him down."

I pressed my trigger twice and watched the gunman in my sights fall from the wing and onto the burning deck below.

Shawn's calm tone came. "Splash one."

I responded with, "Splash two. Keep moving."

The roar of the fire, wind, and ships filled the air with utter confusion. My implanted hearing aids hated everything about sound, and I instantly wished I could turn them off.

Skipper said, "Sierra Five, get off the stern. We're coming around to kill their rudder."

Disco said, "Roger. I'm rolling off to port. I'll fall in astern when you come around."

I tried to picture the maneuver in my head while still focusing on my sector of fire. Captain Sprayberry was whipping all six hundred feet of the *Lori Danielle* around like a speedboat and making it look easy.

Mongo said, "Their tender cradle is empty."

I said, "Roger. Their tender is fiberglass scraps. Disco and I shot it to bits a hundred miles off St. Marys."

Mongo said, "Roger."

I called our snipers. "Sierra Six, can you and Eight take the bridge from your position?"

Singer said, "Negative, but we can move forward for a direct assault."

"Do it," I ordered as I turned to see the rest of the team poised to penetrate the superstructure.

The instant before we threw open the hatches to make our way inside the ship, the massive shadow of our ship in Captain Sprayberry's hands loomed over us, and I turned to watch what happened next.

The water roiled as a pair of torpedoes left the ship and powered straight toward us. The L.D. was shooting at us from fifty yards away, but there was no way the torpedoes could arm themselves in that distance.

Weps's voice rang. "Snapshot. Fox One . . . Fox Two . . . Fish in the water and running true. Sierra Team, brace for impact."

I placed a hand on the hatch in front of me and readied myself for the rattle of a pair of torpedoes, but the explosion didn't come. I was right. The fish couldn't arm themselves in fifty yards, but what did come was the jolt reverberating through the ship when the two torpedoes collided with the rudders or spinning propellers beneath the stern. Weps had just turned his torpedoes into rifle shots, and he scored a pair of bullseyes.

The ship lurched to port, and the mechanical sound of metal failing echoed through the air.

No matter how badly Weps had damaged the ship, we still had to clear the interior, so I gave the order. "Go! Go! Go!"

As we breached the hatches, we sprinted for any cover we could find while scanning the corridor.

I said, "Report contact, and remember, don't get dead."

We continued sweeping the interior, but the vessel looked and felt like a ghost ship.

Singer reported, "Bridge secure. Two hostages and one enemy casualty."

I said, "Roger. Weps shot away their rudders, so if the screws are still turning, we're making way and not under command."

He said, "Yeah, there's a Christmas tree of lights and alarms going off up here. The pumps are pouring water on the bow, but the fire's still burning."

I said, "That's as good as napalm. Pouring water on it will only make it spread out and keep burning."

We continued our careful probing of the vessel, but the deeper we moved, the more it looked like we were the only ones on board.

Mongo said, "We're descending into engineering. Somebody's got to be down there."

"Roger," I said. "Report contact."

Anya and I pressed our way into the galley, and there was food scattered about, but not a living soul in sight.

"Where did they go, Chase?"

"I don't know. It's the weirdest thing I've ever seen."

Gator said, "Contact! Yellow lifeboat in the water to starboard."

I said, "Sierra Five, get on that lifeboat, and don't let her out of your sight. Return fire if they engage."

Disco said, "I'm on 'em."

I said, "Good eyes, Sierra Eight. That explains where everybody went."

Mongo said, "Two prisoners from engineering. No casualties. The engine room is flooding."

"Flooding?" I asked. "Why?"

He said, "Weps must've breached the hull when he shot away the rudders."

That didn't make any sense, and I didn't know enough about ships that size to get a mental picture of how the lower decks were constructed.

I picked out the man who knew more about ships than anybody on my team. "Shawn, are you in the engine room?"

"Affirmative, and I already know what you're thinking. I'm on it."

I ordered, "Kodiak, stay with Shawn. Everybody else, rendezvous on the stern deck."

Thirty seconds later, we were reassembled on the deck with two prisoners from the bridge and two from engineering, a burning, flooding ship, and the only lifeboat was in the water. Things were falling apart, and I didn't understand why until Skipper's voice exploded in my ear.

"Chase! We've been boarded! At least ten men, maybe more, and we're taking heavy fire."

Chapter 35
Captain America

Skipper's words felt like a spear driven through the top of my head and straight out the bottom of my one remaining foot. The ability to prioritize and make rational decisions quickly while under fire is the mark of a great tactical leader. I would never define myself as such, but in that moment, everything clicked, and all the pieces fell into place.

I gave the order. "Shawn, Kodiak, move to the stern deck ASAP." My next move was responding to Skipper. "Roger. Make sure the security team keeps them off the bridge and out of the CIC. Can you launch the helo?"

"It's already airborne and moving to your position, but expect heavy resistance when you return. These guys aren't Boy Scouts, Chase."

Shawn and Kodiak showed up, and the SEAL said, "They scuttled the ship. They're sinking her on purpose. The pumps are pouring thousands of gallons of seawater on board."

"We walked right into their trap," I said. "I can't believe we didn't see it coming."

I called Disco. "Stay with the lifeboat. The captain and most of the crew are probably aboard. We don't want anybody picking them up. Kill any antennae you see sticking up, and disable the boat if you can, but don't sink her."

"I'll do what I can," he said, "but I've got two rifles and a pistol. It's not like I'm loaded for bear."

The whop of the Huey's rotors parted the smoke and thundered through the air as Gun Bunny descended toward the stern rail of the sinking ship.

Gator asked, "What are we going to do with the prisoners?"

"I don't know yet, but we'll come up with something," I said.

Gun Bunny came to a hover with the right skid of the chopper resting on the stern rail of the ship. There wasn't enough deck space for her to touch down, so we'd have to load over the rail. Holding the chopper still against the rail of a pitching, rolling deck would push her skills to their limit. Half of our team and all four prisoners made it aboard before a gust of wind and rolling waves forced Gun Bunny off the rail. She hovered away and waited for the ship to settle down before flying back into position. Anya, Shawn, and Kodiak were next, and I followed them aboard.

I had to crawl across the four prisoners to find a place to kneel. The cabin of the chopper was full to overflowing, and that gave me an idea. I leaned toward the prisoners. "Can all of you swim?"

Their eyes turned to saucers, and I said, "If you can't, I recommend learning in the next thirty seconds."

I stuck my head into the cockpit, gave instructions to Gun Bunny, and she banked away from the burning ship and toward the east. In seconds, we were hovering alongside the lifeboat with Disco trailing in the RHIB.

Shawn and Gator cut the flex-cuffs from the prisoners' wrists, and I ordered them to jump. They hesitated, and my team took that as an order to help our guests out the door. All four hit the water feetfirst and resurfaced. If the lifeboat crew didn't pick them up, Disco would, but either way, the rest of their day promised to be far less than pleasant.

We banked away from the lifeboat and lowered the nose toward the *Lori Danielle* less than a mile to the west. Ronda No-H untethered her favorite toy, the M134 Minigun. It swung free on its mount, and Ronda buckled the harness and safety strap to the pad eye overhead.

Skipper's voice crackled in my head, but hearing her above the noise of the rotors was challenging. "They're attempting to penetrate the bridge from the wings."

Twenty seconds later, we flew across the bow from port to starboard, and Ronda leaned out the door with the Minigun gripped in both hands. Gun Bunny raised the nose to slow our forward motion, and Ronda let off a one-second burst of fire, cutting the two men on the portside bridge wing in half. The two gunmen on the starboard wing turned to flee for cover, but Ronda was too fast. Another one-second burst laced the two men with more bullet holes than anybody could ever count.

Ronda swung herself and the gun back into the fuselage and held up four fingers.

I gave her the thumbs-up and called Skipper. "Four down."

She said, "Roger. We're now counting fourteen boarders, so that means there are ten left. There's a gunfight in engineering, and it's getting bad down there."

I yelled into the cockpit. "Put us on the helipad!"

She banked for the pad, and a line of automatic-weapons fire tacked across the windscreen.

I grabbed Gun Bunny's shoulder. "Are you hit?"

Without looking up, she shook her head. "Not yet!" She continued for the pad and yelled, "We're going to bounce, so get as many off as you can on the first run. I'm not leaving this bird on deck."

I echoed her instruction, and everyone moved toward the doors. We made our first pass toward the pad, and more automatic fire thundered through the cabin.

We banked away, and Singer yelled, "Gator, get on your belly and pin those guys down. We're staying with the chopper for the first pass."

Gator obeyed and opened fire on the two men shooting into the sky. It was impossible to tell if he'd hit them or if they'd taken cover in time to save their lives.

Singer lay face-down on the deck with his head and shoulders hanging from the chopper, his rifle poised in front of him as if it were an extension of his own body. With every sight of anyone offering to fire upward at us, he poured lead down on them like fire raining down from Heaven.

Gun Bunny yelled over her shoulder, "We're going in again. Get ready to bail out. I don't plan to touch down."

We moved back to the doors on either side of the Huey and poised to spring from the bird and into the cauldron of gunfire below. Bunny dived at the helipad with the nose low and the airspeed high. Thirty feet above the deck, she hauled back on the cyclic and yanked the collective to its limit. She'd been wrong about not touching down, but the skids only spent part of a second on the pad before she had the Huey flying again and climbing away from the ship.

I hit the helipad hard and rolled to absorb the blow. When I came to rest on my knees, I counted heads. Shawn was at the aft edge of the pad, on his belly, with his rifle trained on the deck below. Mongo was on a catwalk to port, but I had no idea how he got there. Kodiak was headed for the ladder, and Anya was on her feet beside me with her rifle swinging left and right through her sector of fire.

"Is anybody hurt?" I asked. No one responded, so I handed out assignments. "Shawn, you're with me and Anya. Mongo and Kodiak, you two get down to engineering. There's a serious gunfight down there."

Everyone joined their team, and we headed down the ladders.

I called the CIC. "Skipper, we're five on board. Two are moving to engineering. The rest of us are headed inside."

Bullets bounced off the rail to my left, and I leapt from the ladder and onto a narrow catwalk below. As I scanned the area in search of the gunman, I came up empty, but our SEAL didn't. He pulled his trigger twice and sent two precisely placed rounds through the shooter's face. His head exploded beneath his helmet, and his corpse collapsed across the starboard rail.

"Are you hit?" Shawn yelled.

"Negative. I'm good. Keep moving."

When we reached the deck below, Shawn led the way. I trailed him slightly to his left, and Anya patrolled back-to-back with me, making sure no one got a shot at us from the rear.

We moved quickly but cautiously as we cleared every nook. Sporadic gunfire sounded from all directions as we stepped across the bodies of the four men who'd tried to assault the bridge.

Singer called out, "Anya! Eleven o'clock low!"

She immediately knelt, and I spun to see what our sniper had noticed from above. A gunman, lying prone beneath an equipment locker, twisted his body to open fire on us, but Anya sent three rounds through his neck and into his torso. She immediately dived to the deck in search of a partner for the shooter. An instant later, she looked up and said, "He is solo."

I reported to CIC. "Skipper, two more down. Say status."

She said, "Roger. That makes six down and eight still working. We're secure for now, but there's action in the corridor."

"Roger. We're on our way. If you've got any way to let the security team know, tell them we'll be three friendlies on-site in thirty seconds."

I grabbed Shawn's shoulder. "Move to the CIC, now!"

He turned in a run just as the Minigun came alive overhead. I glanced up to see Ronda hanging from the chopper with the gun belching smoke, fire, and lead toward the bow.

As they climbed away from the ship, Singer said, "Two more down on the bow."

That's six, I thought. *Our odds are improving.*

As we stepped through the hatch and into the interior of the ship, Mongo said, "Two down in engineering. Area secure. Three friendlies wounded and one casualty. Irina was down here fighting alongside the security team when we got here. She's safe."

I felt my heart sink in my chest. "Roger. We're moving to CIC."

He said, "Roger. Where do you want us?"

Where would I go if I were assaulting the ship?

I said, "Double-check the engine room for explosives, then head for the bridge."

Captain Sprayberry said, "Bridge is secure. Only minor injuries."

I closed my eyes for a second to gather my thoughts. "Check the armory on your way to sick bay."

Mongo said, "Roger. Moving."

A layer of white smoke hung in the corridor leading to the CIC. We hit the deck and took cover around a corner and inside a hatch. The scene was gruesome, and bullets were still flying. The report of the rifles echoed through the space like thunder. Two of the ship's security personnel lay on their backs ten feet down the corridor. The closer of the two bodies appeared to be breathing, and Shawn said, "I'm getting that guy out of there. Cover me."

I raised to a knee and laid suppressing fire down the corridor. The SEAL moved without any apparent fear to drag a fellow shooter from the fight. He didn't know the guy, but he was a teammate, and Shawn obviously felt the warrior's cry for help calling through the hail of gunfire. Nothing was going to stop him from pulling his teammate from the battlefield.

He dragged the man around the corner and assessed him quickly before yanking his med-pack from his belt and pouring QuikClot into a wound high on the man's shoulder. He shoved the wound full of gauze and quickly taped it in place. I met his gaze, and he heard my unspoken question.

His answer was, "Maybe."

I reached above my head and pulled a massive fire extinguisher from a hook. I threw the red tank down the corridor, and Shawn put a round in it before it stopped rolling. The air was suddenly full of white powder, and the three of us advanced, staying as low to the deck as possible. Rounds ricocheted off hatches and bulkheads above us, and we answered with a wall of fire that should've annihilated anything in front of us.

Slowly, the snapping of gunfire fell until only the report of our weapons echoed through the space. We continued our advance and found two bodies riddled with bullet holes.

I called Skipper. "Corridor outside CIC is secure. Stay in there and don't come out."

She said, "We're not going anywhere, but sick bay was just breached. Dr. Shadrack reports three gunmen."

I ran the mental count I'd been keeping. "If he's right about three shooters, our count was off."

"That's what he said, but I can't reach him now. He's not answering."

I felt like I'd been mule-kicked in the gut. I called Mongo. "Did you copy that sick bay has been breached and the doc is down?"

He answered, and the sound of his voice made it clear he was in a sprint. "Armory is secure, and we're moving to sick bay."

We ran as fast as our bodies would move and beat Mongo and Kodiak to the main hatch into sick bay. It was closed, so we took a knee beside the hatch. Shawn looked up at me as if awaiting an order, so I said, "We're breaching and clearing. You go left, I'll go right, and Anya will cover the centerline. You good?"

He nodded and reached for the handle of the hatch. It moved freely beneath his grip, and he turned it ninety degrees and waited for my call.

I said, "Execute!"

He threw open the hatch and burst through the opening like lightning. The instant his boot hit the deck inside the bay, a spray of red mist filled the air in front of me, and the sound of metal striking flesh and bone echoed. I raised an elbow to block the hatch from closing on us, and Shawn's body collapsed backward toward me. In that instant, it became clear what I'd just witnessed. Someone from inside sent at least one round high on the SEAL's body and butt-stroked him in the face.

I forced myself against the hinge side of the opening, allowing room for him to fall backward into the corridor. The surprise of the attack caught me off guard. I'd expected to move through the doorway and send three gunmen to the promised land with a handful of well-placed rounds, but everything I expected exploded in my face.

An unseen hand struck my rifle, driving it to the right and twisting me from the opening. A hand grabbed the back of my neck and forced me forward. I spun with all my strength to avoid contacting the deck with my face, taking the blow on my right shoulder and then rolling onto my back.

Someone kicked the hatch closed behind me, forcing Anya backward and locking her back in the corridor with Shawn, and apparently, the same booted foot landed solidly between my legs. Wincing beneath the pain, I forced my vision to clear, and the muzzle of a rifle came into sharp focus an inch in front of my right eye.

I gripped my rifle, still in my right hand, and twisted to bring my muzzle on line before the gunman could get off a round, but another heavy boot pinned my arm to the deck.

The shooter with his muzzle in my eye said, "Well, look who finally showed up. If it isn't Captain America himself."

Chapter 36
Clear

As long as you're still breathing, the fight isn't over.

Those words kept ringing in my ears, and it was the voice of Clark Johnson spitting them into the air in front of me every time I wanted to quit. No matter how hard I willed him to be there, Clark wasn't on the deck beside me for this fight. I was in it alone . . . or so I thought.

The same adage I'd beaten into Gator's head pounded in mine with every thump of my heart.

Admit nothing, deny everything, make counteraccusations.

"Who are you?" I demanded as my breath came hard and my heart thundered like a bass drum inside my chest.

The man standing over me pressed the muzzle into my cheekbone, just below my eye, and hissed, "Able was I ere I saw Elba."

For an instant, I believed I'd gone entirely mad, or was, perhaps, already dead, until the phrase leapt from the pages of a history book I'd long forgotten.

The phrase, "Able was I ere I saw Elba," was rumored to have been carved into a wooden writing desk by Napoleon Bonaparte while he was in exile on the island of Elba. It was one of the world's most well-known palindromes—phrases spelled the same backward and forward —just like each of the phrases micro-engraved on the bullets from each of the four shootings.

"Dennis sinned" on Charlie Bevins's bullet.

"Drab as a fool, aloof as a bard" on James Fairmont's.

"We panic in a pew" on Tony's.

And "Ah, Satan sees Natasha" on Hunter's.

Why would anyone do that? What's the connection?

The skin beneath my right eye split under the pressure of the muzzle, and a warm stream of blood ran down my face and into my ear. That feeling, along with every breath, reminded me that I was still alive and still in the fight.

"Napoleon?" The name escaped my lips before I meant to speak, and the man smiled.

"Ah, I see that all those years of formal education weren't wasted after all. Very good. I'm impressed, at least on one level. I have to admit, though, I thought you would be much harder to take down once we finally met face-to-face."

"And you thought you'd show off your intellect by using palindromes? Let me up, and I'll show you how hard I am to put down."

"Oh, come on now, Captain America. Surely you already know I'm not that foolish."

As my heart pounded in my ears, I heard Skipper's calm, smooth voice. "Chase, we're with you, and I can hear everything you're saying. How many are there?"

I settled my mind enough to say, "Let me up, Napoleon. Surely you and your two squires can handle one man. What pleasure will you get from putting a single bullet through my head while I'm lying on the deck? I expected you to be a man of action, not a coward who kills his enemies on their backs."

"Napoleon?" Skipper said. "I'm working it. Keep him talking, Chase. You've got to stay alive long enough for us to get through that door."

I squirmed beneath his boot and muzzle. "Look, Napoleon. You've won, but there's no way off the ship for you. All of my men are still alive, and they'll never let you get to the topside. They'll cut you down the instant you open that hatch."

He applied more pressure to the boot and spun his rifle, striking my left temple with the butt. The blow sent stars circling my head, but I didn't go out. It took several beats, but I finally summoned the strength to shake off the staggering shot.

When I could finally see clearly again, I said, "I can order my men to stand down and let you leave the ship."

He dropped to one knee on the center of my chest and held his face only inches from mine. "What have you learned about me that makes you think I'm an imbecile? You and I are fighters, Captain America. Lying to each other is so unbecoming."

I struggled to fill my lungs as his weight bore down on my chest. "Who was next on your list, Napoleon?"

He roared with laughter. "The consummate leader right to the end, you are. I hadn't decided if it would be your giant or your priest— Marvin Malloy or Jimmy Grossmann. I was leaning toward the warrior monk so you would have to endure my torture without your spirit guide, but Mongo was such a tempting target. I liked the symbolism of bringing down the behemoth, but alas, you jumped right into my hands and all the way to the front of the firing line."

I fought to fill my lungs again. "Why those two?"

"You're stalling, Captain. You believe your little boys' club will come bursting through that hatch any minute, just in time to save their fearless leader, but oh, how wrong you are."

"Why am I wrong? What makes you think they won't come through the hatch?"

Skipper said, "Keep talking, Chase. We're working the problem. Tell me what's happening with the hatch if you can."

Napoleon stood again, relieving the pressure from my chest, but he planted his boot back in my crotch, just as before. "You see, Captain America, the hatch is rigged to fill the corridor with shrapnel next time it opens."

"Why would you rig the hatch?"

"What a foolish question. It's exactly what you would've done if the roles were reversed. For me, though, it's part of the fun. Imagine the joy in which I'll bask when I wade through the remains of the boys in whom you had so much faith. Don't you find it humbling to know that it will be impossible to tell the difference between the entrails of your merry band of bumbling fools and the blood of cowards?"

Why does this guy sound like an English professor? Who is he? Why hasn't he killed me yet?

His weight shifted ever so slightly as if he were growing tired of standing on my crotch, and I took full advantage of his tactical error— the first one I'd seen him make.

I pulled against the boot on my right wrist until I slid my hips far enough to roll onto my side. When Napoleon flinched, I yanked with every ounce of strength my body could create, freeing my hand from beneath the booted foot. I caught Napoleon's ankle and brought him down on top of me, and I was an instant away from learning if he could wrestle as well as he could speak the King's English.

He was strong and flexible, but I was stronger. In seconds, I had an arm laced around his neck, and I was planting my feet to gain the leverage I needed to separate his spine from his brain. As I arched my back to bring the pressure to bear, a flash of a rifle stock raced through my vision, and the butt of the weapon collided with my forehead an instant before I could end Napoleon's life.

The contact felt like the Earth falling on my head, and the world turned black.

When I opened my eyes again, nothing made sense. I was on my back, but not on the deck. I was lying on something soft and warm. Everything in front of me blurred into a single melting pot of color and streaks of light. I tried to raise my hand against the light, but it wouldn't move. Neither hand would answer my mind's command to shade my face, and slowly, I gained enough consciousness to recognize my dire position. I was on one of Dr. Shadrack's beds with my arms and legs lashed in the same restraints that had held Gabrielle Kellum and Maria Dean only hours before.

Sounds were muffled and far away, but Skipper's voice cut

through the fog. "Chase! If you're there, say something. Make a noise. Anything."

I let out a long moan, and she said, "Oh, thank God. We thought they'd killed you. If you can understand me, make that sound again."

I repeated the moan, partially because Skipper asked for it, but mostly because everything hurt.

"Look who's back," Napoleon said. "How was your slumber, sweet prince?"

I begged my eyes to focus, and they answered my plea, but not completely. My left eye was useless, but I could form shapes with my right.

A face slowly came into partial focus beside Napoleon's, and I blinked, desperately trying to make out who it was. When the face spoke, I instantly knew it was Maria Dean.

She smiled down at me with a sadistic glow. "You thought you could trust me, didn't you? You believed I was in your camp. What was it you said? We seem to have a common enemy? What we have is a gullible fool masquerading as a world-class covert operative."

She came into sharper focus and ran her hands over Napoleon's face, pulling his lips to hers. When they parted, she whispered, "Enjoy the gift I've given you, but please don't kill him quickly. You deserve to savor my gift. Make it last, my love."

Maria's face was replaced by Gabrielle Kellum's, and she wore the same satisfied mask as Maria. She ran her fingertips through Napoleon's hair and kissed his cheek. "I'm so proud of you, son. Your father has never been the man you are. He let this pitiful, filthy vermin embarrass him in Bulgaria and did nothing to make him pay. Only you preserved our family's honor. Only you, my son."

It can't be real. It can't. I'm only dreaming. It's only the musings of my mind. It's not real.

Skipper's voice cut its way into my skull. "Oh my God, Chase. Napoleon is Gabrielle Kellum's son, but . . ." She either stopped talking or I was unconscious again. When her voice returned, she said, "Chase, make a noise. I need to know you're awake." I cleared my throat, and she said, "He's Gabrielle's son, but her husband, Courtney, isn't his father."

Subconsciously, I said, "Huh?"

"He's Roger Dean's son, and Gabrielle Kellum is his mother. He's some kind of freaky genius. Double PhDs in English literature and philosophy, and he was a legionnaire, too. A sniper."

I tried to make her words come together, but none of it made sense. I had to be imagining her voice.

I believed it was all a psychotic dream brought on by the trauma to my skull from the butt-strike, but the next several seconds shattered that errant belief.

Skipper said, "Cover your face, Chase. We're coming in."

I yelled out, "No! The hatch is rigged to explode!"

The explosion came before I could finish the warning, and debris flew in every direction. Dust, smoke, and an echoing roar filled the air.

Rifle fire cracked from somewhere near the demolished hatch. First, one rifle, then two, and maybe a third.

Clark Johnson's North Alabama twang was the first voice I heard through the chaotic roar. "Clear!"

The second was Singer's soul-stirring baritone. "I'm clear here."

And finally, the third could be none other than my favorite Russian. "Is clear also here."

The concussion of the blast left me dazed even further, but knowing my team was only feet away and fully in command of the situation granted me the freedom to close my eyes and breathe freely for the first time since my failed attempt to clear the sick bay.

Clark planted a hand on the center of my chest and gave me a shake. "I should've known you'd be in here taking a nap while the rest of us were busting our butts out there."

"Did you kill them all?" I asked.

"Nope. Just the two goons who thought it'd be a good idea to point guns at us. I don't love it when people do that. How you feeling?"

"I took a couple nasty blows to the head, but I'll be fine. Get me out of these restraints, would you?"

He unbuckled the cuffs and shackles, and I threw my feet over the edge of the bed. The world in front of me swirled for several seconds before finally settling upright. Napoleon lay face-down on the deck, trussed up like a hog with his hands flex-cuffed behind his back and his ankles tied to his wrists with a short piece of rope.

Gabrielle Kellum and Maria Dean lay on the floor several feet away in similar confinement.

"Did you figure it out?" I asked.

He gave Napoleon's boot a solid kick. "Skipper did. This guy's wanted on several international warrants for a whole list of misdeeds like numerous war crimes, murder, and generally being a jerk. They call him 'the Scorpion' because he's said to make his sting and vanish before his victims hit the ground. I guess we lopped off his stinger."

I glared at the two women. "What about those two?"

He shrugged. "Yeah, they're a whole twisted mess. Apparently, they weren't happy with what we did to hurt their little feelings when we kicked the crap out of their guys in Bulgaria last year."

As I tried to make the crazy puzzle make sense, I glanced up to see Anya approaching as if she were seconds away from taking my face in her hands, but Penny ran into the room and brushed past her.

Her hands, and not those of the Russian, held my face, and horror overtook her beautiful features. "My God, Chase. Are you all right?"

I saw my reflection in her glasses. My forehead didn't withstand the butt-stroke very well, and I was covered in my own blood. "Yeah, I'm okay. I think I might've cut myself shaving."

She hugged me, and I never wanted her to let go.

I stood from the bed and grabbed one of Napoleon's ankles. "I made a promise, and I intend to keep it."

I dragged the Scorpion out of sick bay and down the corridor on his face. When we reached the ladder, Mongo assumed control of the animal. He dragged him up two ladders and down another long corridor until we reached the hatch outside the CIC. Skipper buzzed us in, and I dragged her husband's murderer across the deck and dropped him at her feet.

Without a word, I drew my Glock and laid it on the console beside my baby sister.

Mongo said, "We'll be right outside if you need us."

Epilogue

We took the lifeboat in tow and left it and the crew of the sunken ship in the capable hands of the Royal Bermuda Regiment Coast Guard. Gun Bunny choppered a pair of dark-eyed Mossad interrogators aboard the *Lori Danielle* from Bermuda, where they'd landed only an hour before.

The two Israelis said little when they came aboard, but one of them pulled me aside and whispered, "We have Roger Dean, and his version of the truth seems to bear few similarities to reality."

I didn't want to know what the Mossad officers dragged out of the minds of our detainees, so we gave them the privacy and space they needed to conduct their investigation as we cruised toward the Strait of Gibraltar and the Mediterranean. We rendezvoused with an Israeli ship off the coast of the tiny Italian island of Pantelleria in the Med. That was the last time I saw Gabrielle Kellum, Maria Dean, or the man they called the Scorpion. What the Israelis did with them is none of my concern, but I slept easily that night knowing I'd never have to deal with any of them again.

* * *

Back at Bonaventure, the team and I spent the requisite time licking our wounds and transitioning from warriors back into civilians capable of participating in polite society, if such a thing exists. Calvin Lynard, the homeless man who witnessed the arson of Singer's church, was still living in the roadside hotel when we got home, but our Southern Baptist sniper brought an end to that arrangement. Singer bought an apartment building in St. Marys that had been vacant and neglected for several years and put Calvin to work renovating the building.

Warfighters without a mission quickly become bored and dangerous creatures. Their morbid sense of humor tends to drive them to play terrible pranks on each other, and occasionally, those pranks overflow onto innocent bystanders. In an effort to head off any such mayhem, Singer and Calvin recruited the team to trade in their Glocks for carpenter's hammers long enough to turn what had been a ramshackle community eyesore into a transition facility and outreach for others like Calvin. Singer believed the societal outcasts of our community—and the world, for that matter—deserved the opportunity to reclaim their dignity and rejoin the society that turned its back on them.

The other major construction project in our tiny town occurred concurrently with the renovation of the apartment building. Singer's church rose from the ashes in grand fashion thanks to donations from my team. The massive stained-glass window that had adorned the northern wall of the church was recovered after the fire as random broken pieces of colored glass strewn throughout the post-fire debris.

A worldwide search ensued for a suitable replacement for the century-old work of art until Calvin Lynard said, "I loved that window, and I looked at it every day, sometimes for hours at a time. Ain't nobody on Earth who knows that window no better than me. If you'll give me them broke pieces of glass, I'll put them back together just like they was 'for the fire. I gots a picture in my mind of 'zactly where every piece goes."

Ten days later, a construction crew installed Calvin's rebuilt stained-glass window precisely in the center of the northern wall of the new church, and it had never looked more beautiful.

* * *

I sat in the gazebo, on the banks of the North River, in my favorite Adirondack. The bullet holes in the roof that I made while desperately trying to summon help for Hunter and the wound on the cannon's carriage from the Scorpion's second bullet would remain and forever remind me how delicate and precious life truly is.

I was surrounded by the people I love and trust the most, and regardless of the color of our skin, the first language we spoke, or any of our last names, we were a family by choice, and nothing would ever change that.

I lifted my tumbler in the air. "I talked with the doctor this morning, and she told me that Hunter is no longer considered to be in critical condition. He won't be joining us in the gazebo for a while, but it looks like he's going to make it. So, here's to the only guy I know who's too stubborn to die from getting shot in the neck."

Glasses joined mine in the air, and we drank to our friend and brother.

Shawn the SEAL lifted his guitar from beside his chair. "I'm taking requests. If Jimmy Buffett or George Strait ever sang it, I can play it."

A long, jagged scar ran from the inside of his left elbow, across his upper arm, and beneath the sleeve of his T-shirt stretched tightly across his skin. I replayed the scene in the hatchway of the sick bay when he took the bullet that left the scar behind.

I raised my glass again. "And here's to the only guy I know with bulletproof biceps."

Cheers went up, and Kodiak asked, "Can you play 'The Fireman'? After Captain Sprayberry's pyromania on the high seas, I think it's appropriate."

Shawn licked one side of a guitar pick, stuck it to his forehead, and fingerpicked the opening riff.

We joined in on the chorus, and when it was over, I said, "Welcome to Team Twenty-one, brother. We're proud to have you."

Author's Note

I hope you enjoyed *The Scorpion's Chase*. You're probably getting tired of hearing me thank you for making my dream of becoming a professional novelist come true, but don't expect me to stop anytime soon. I'll never take that enormous gift you've given me for granted, and I'll never stop working as hard as I can to make every story a little better than the last one. So, without further ado, let's talk about the lies I told in this story, with a few droplets of truth sprinkled in for good measure.

Killing Tony broke my heart. I didn't want to do it. In fact, I rewrote that passage several times before finally settling on the original version. The horrific tragedy gave me an opportunity to explore Skipper's psyche and demonstrate the bond she and Chase will always share. Getting my characters hurt is always painful for me, but the blow to Skipper was one of the most excruciating storylines I've ever created. I love them all, but Skipper will always be dear to me. Seeing her so deeply wounded brought tears to my eyes more than once while creating this story. Chase's promise to deliver Tony's murderer to Skipper's feet was a vow I couldn't overlook. The scene had to happen, but no matter how many times I wrote what happened between Skipper and the Scorpion, the passage always felt stronger when I left them alone in the CIC. We'll probably never know what she said to him or how it made her feel. Part of me wanted to see her pull the trigger with Tony's murderer on his knees, begging for his life, but having her choose the more devastating punishment of turning him over to

Mossad seemed more in line with her morality, personality, and true heart.

Let's talk about a happier scene now. When Chase and Disco flew the *Grey Ghost* into Knoxville, Tennessee's McGhee Tyson Airport, and Disco relived his days of learning to fly in Sevierville under the tutelage of Jack Shipe, I got to share a little personal history with all of you. That is where I learned to fly nearly forty years ago, and Jack Shipe was the instructor who taught me a skill I will treasure for the remainder of my life. It sometimes feels as if I've lived so many lives in my nearly six decades on the planet, but the one constant, no matter where I went or what happened around me, was my love of flying. I'll always be indebted to Jack and his old Piper Cherokee. They taught me that I was never meant to spend my life with my boots on the ground. Some of my best days have been in the cockpit, and I pray I can continue to soar among the clouds for another forty years.

Although the flying was true, Ontrack Global Resources is purely fictional. I made it all up back in *The Shepherd's Chase*. No such company exists or ever has existed, as far as I know. The characters of Roger and Maria Dean, and Courtney and Gabrielle Kellum, are purely fictional and figments of my overactive imagination. Most series writers are smart enough to write each installment in their series as books that can stand alone and be enjoyed without having read the previous books in the series. I'm not that smart, so every book I write is built upon the history created in previous books. To me, Chase's series is one long and winding story, told over multiple books and multiple years. I have no way of knowing how many books I'll write for Chase, but just like the endless blue Atlantic that Chase loves so much, I see the story extending beyond the horizon and into undiscovered territory. I look forward to taking the journey together as we brave the storms and roll with the punches for years to come.

I spent a few lines of this story talking about circumventing the National Airspace System. Although that system exists just as I described it, it's extremely unlikely that any pilot of a Gulfstream IV would work around the system as Chase and Disco did. It is possible, but not plausible, so I suppose that portion of the story qualifies as semi-true, which is, by definition, a lie.

I get a lot of emails from readers about Chase and Anya. Since book #5 in this series, *The Distant Chase*, there have been two distinct camps among my wonderful readers: Team Penny and Team Anya. Some people believe Penny is the greatest thing that could ever happen to Chase, while others seem to think Anya and Chase are a love story written in the stars. I love both Penny and Anya for very different reasons, and I didn't intentionally create conflict between them. It just happened. I won't deny enjoying that conflict. Every writer dreams of pitting two dynamic characters against each other, and for me, that's a lot of fun. I don't know what will happen in the remainder of the series, but having Anya flirt with Chase is something I love to write. Those scenes make me laugh, and they give the other characters a chance to pick on their fearless leader. I hope you'll stick around, and we'll find out what happens in the Bonaventure love triangle together.

Now, we have to talk about Hunter. I truly love his character. I have no idea why he had to get shot. I don't think I'll ever know, and it physically pained me when I wrote that horrific scene in the gazebo. I have no idea how well he'll recuperate, but I think it's safe to say his days of operating with the team are in the past. That brings us to Shawn the SEAL. Shawn is quite real. My physical and psychological descriptions of him are accurate. He's a dear friend of mine and probably the strongest human being I know. I don't know if his biceps are really bulletproof, but I wouldn't be surprised if they were. He's often accused of looking a lot like Channing Tatum, and that makes the rest of us guys around him feel like trolls. He's both physically powerful and undeniably handsome, but his character is his true strength. He's one of the most honest, hardworking, sincere people I've ever met. I'm proud to call him a friend, and I'm excited to have him on the team.

Finally, I'd like to talk a little about the action sequences in this story. As most of you know, I'm an enormous fan of Clive Cussler's body of work. In my opinion, he is the patriarch of the Sea Adventure Fiction genre. If you've not read his work, please put my books aside and read everything Mr. Cussler ever wrote. He was a genius, and he is sorely missed. Having read every word he ever published, I've wanted to create a story with a similar arc to his typical style for a long time. Once the action begins in a Cussler novel, it never ends until the bad guys are either dead or behind bars. I tried to accomplish that feat with this story, and I believe it worked out well. I won't deny that I was physically exhausted after writing many of the scenes in this book, but I loved every minute of it. I don't know if the next book will follow that same pattern, but I won't be mad if it does. If you liked or didn't like the nonstop-action style of this story, I'd love to hear from you. I can't promise I'll take your advice, but you're always welcome to email me at Cap@CapDaniels.com.

Cheers,

Cap

About the Author

Cap Daniels

Cap Daniels is a former sailing charter captain, scuba and sailing instructor, pilot, Air Force combat veteran, and civil servant of the U.S. Department of Defense. Raised far from the ocean in rural East Tennessee, his early infatuation with salt water was sparked by the fascinating, and sometimes true, sea stories told by his father, a retired Navy Chief Petty Officer. Those stories of adventure on the high seas sent Cap in search of adventure of his own, which eventually landed him on Florida's Gulf Coast where he spends as much time as possible on, in, and under the waters of the Emerald Coast.

With a headful of larger-than-life characters and their thrilling exploits, Cap pours his love of adventure and passion for the ocean onto the pages of the Chase Fulton Novels and the Avenging Angel - Seven Deadly Sins series.

Visit www.CapDaniels.com to join the mailing list to receive newsletter and release updates.

Connect with Cap Daniels:

Facebook: www.Facebook.com/WriterCapDaniels
Instagram: https://www.instagram.com/authorcapdaniels/
BookBub: https://www.bookbub.com/profile/cap-daniels

Also by Cap Daniels

The Avenging Angel – Seven Deadly Sins Series
Book One: *The Russian's Pride*
Book Two: *The Russian's Greed*
Book Three: *The Russian's Gluttony*
Book Four: *The Russian's Lust*
Book Five: *The Russian's Sloth*
Book Six: *The Russian's Envy*
Book Seven: *The Russian's Wrath* (2025)

Stand-Alone Novels
We Were Brave
Singer – Memoir of a Christian Sniper

Novellas
The Chase is On
I Am Gypsy

Made in United States
North Haven, CT
04 February 2025